The Summer of Our Foreclosure

Sean Boling

Published by Sean Boling, 2012.

THE SUMMER OF OUR FORECLOSURE

First edition. November 26, 2012.

ISBN: 979-8224884308

Written by Sean Boling.

Chapter One

Nobody will ever tear down our housing development, no matter how long it ends up abandoned. Nobody will find any use for the land besides farming, and there is plenty of space around it that can be farmed without having to demolish a bunch of houses first. Instead I imagine our neighborhood as an archaeological curiosity in a distant future: each roof missing, reduced to a spread of splintered wood and gobs of buckled shingles scattered about what remains of the upstairs floors, the rest of the wreckage having tumbled through jagged holes onto the cement foundation and the crumbling countertops; tattered loose ends of drywall quiver in the wind as they cling to the exposed studs that still stand and mark the cage-like frame of each house; the doors and windows have held nothing for hundreds of years. People poke their heads through the openings, squinting in contemplation and in defense against the wind-blown, sun-baked climate, wondering why anyone would build such a large colony in such an arid and remote location. They extract themselves from the frames and stand up straight, turning to face the fence posts that have but a few slats still between them, looking through the gaps at the dusty plains that stretch for miles towards the doughy hills on the horizon, the same expanse that I used to have to peek over the fence to see, and they wonder not only why anyone would build here, but why anyone would buy.

All of us kids thought the same thing, too, when we first arrived; when it was new, when the signs still bragged rather than begged.

"It's not here," I recall saying to my father before we moved. "I'm looking right at the map where the roads you said meet and there's no Rancho Hacienda."

"It's not a town, son. It's a housing development. A brand new one."

I enhanced the map on screen, zooming in as close to the point in question as possible, this time looking for a town somewhere near the intersection of the rural junction and county highway that Dad identified as our new home. Still nothing. Just the cross formed by the intersection. I widened the perspective again and in a couple of different directions I found a couple of very small dots with unfamiliar names I could tell had very few people or buildings. I found a larger, bolder dot with a familiar name that seemed rather far away from where Rancho Hacienda was rumored to be. I held my thumb and index finger on each end of the mileage scale at the bottom of the map and held them in the same position as I jumped from the intersection to the big bold dot. It took me several jumps of the space formed by my two fingers. I multiplied the number of jumps by the miles indicated on the bottom of the map and started to groan but was too bewildered to finish the sound. And that was a straight line between the two points, not even accounting for roads that would have to be taken.

"What does Rancho Hacienda mean, anyway, Dad?"

"Hmmm. I know Rancho is ranch. And Hacienda is I think like a large home with lots of land."

"Like a ranch?"

"Yes." Dad was trying to read between the lines of the Homeowners' Association contract.

"So it means Ranch Ranch."

"The development is only several months' old. The site you're using just hasn't been updated. Try a different one."

I did so, in fact tried several different map sites, and found only some railroad tracks passing by the intersection, indicated by a faint gray line with small horizontal lines along its length, looking like stitches keeping a wound from opening.

The drive created even more questions as the landscape grew more sparse, the valley widening and its floor flattening. I looked out from window to window, craning my neck to see around luggage and boxes that impeded my gaze. A sign of civilization would pass by and I would become intrigued.

"Who do you think put that there?" I asked as a red, white, and blue sign touting the name of a local political candidate stood staked into the dirt off the side of the interstate.

"Anyone could have," Dad answered. "It may seem pretty deserted out here, but there's people around. You get used to driving longer distances when you're out in the country."

"Are they going to have to take it down someday?"

Dad filled his cheeks with air and blew slowly out. "There was a town not fifteen minutes ago. The one with the McDonalds in the gas station. And there's all these little roads we've passed by."

"What do people do out here?"

"For a living?"

"For anything."

Dad ignored the question. "Don't worry, champ. It's just different. I've taken this drive several times now, and it gets shorter each time. And more beautiful."

Mom spoke for the first time during the trip: "We wanted it to be a surprise."

I saw a holding tank standing a couple dozen feet tall pass by on my side of the car. I wondered aloud what might be inside it, if it was still of use to anyone, and who would repair it if it broke down. But everyone was finished answering my questions, so we drove along in silence.

In between the freeway exits with their half dozen gas, food, and lodging stations clustered together with signs rising above them like a small group of protesters, the signs of civilization grew even more sparse. The ground was mostly fallow and sprinkled with tattered shrubs. Occasionally columns of leafy green crops hugging the ground would emerge, their lines passing by creating the effect of an enormous wheel of fortune spinning from a myopic perspective, as though I was just focusing on my section of the board as the wheel spun, hoping that I would hit the jackpot, that my luck would change. The spokes of the wheel would disappear and give way to more of the bleak high desert, then reappear again a few minutes later. The spin to nowhere started to hypnotize me. Spokes. Nothing. Spokes. Nothing. And then more nothing. And no jackpot.

Dad broke the silence with a "Here we are," as the car merged into an exit lane leading towards the latest huddle of fast food and gasoline. I snapped to attention and looked for houses, but there didn't seem to be any beyond the two fast food restaurants whose names I had heard of before but hadn't seen around our city, and the gas station with the mini mart attached to it. As we sank below the freeway and stopped at the base of the overpass, I peeked under the bridge and saw on the other side a vast parking lot with some big rigs parked in it, and a couple of gas pumps in front of a beige building made of cinder blocks that had "All Day Buffet" painted on the tinted windows. Still no houses.

"Good thing we have a gas station here. Mom and I have a long commute each day."

"Where are the houses?"

"Down this road a ways."

We turned right and gained speed, leaving the freeway exit business district behind and once again flying by sun-baked land interrupted by an occasional field in use. After a few minutes I was about to say "Not again," when I saw through the front windshield some illustrations of life that were not related to agriculture. An intersection loomed ahead, with a long, husky line of trees swaying in the wind on the left side, obscuring a large factory of some sort that I only assumed was there due to the three columns of smoke steaming up into the dusk. The road we were on disappeared into the treeless hills that rose like bread baking in the setting sun straight ahead of us on the horizon, while on the right side were houses. As we drew nearer, it was clear that the houses were very old and perpetually under construction, some appearing as though they may not be able to withstand the wind that blew up the dust along the dirt paths that separated them.

"That's not the development," Dad said with a slight chuckle. "We're up here." We turned right at the intersection, but I turned to look for proof of life in the old houses we passed. I saw a child with big brown eyes staring at us through a hazy window, and a frazzled grey dog with dirty fur springing from each side of his snout trotted out from between two structures to watch us pass. I turned to look out the rear window, and the glimpses of life I had caught somehow made the rickety dwellings seem all the more abandoned, as though they were being haunted rather than lived in. I turned to face forward again and wonder if I had really seen those eyes, that dog, when out the corner of my eye on the left side of the car I noticed that in the clearing past the splintery neighborhood stood an old wooden loading dock that was falling apart practically right before your eyes. It had a platform that was bowed in various places and a ramp on each end. It was surrounded by discarded rusting equipment, including a couple of old railroad cars, which led me to notice the railroad tracks running behind the derelict station.

"Ta da!" chirped Dad, just as I saw the clearing with the old train station give way to a brand new concrete wall with fresh, clean rooftops rising above it.

The concrete wall scrolled onward for several seconds as though a film had just finished being projected and a blank white screen flickered hypnotically in the aftermath. An eye-level sign staked to a couple of wooden posts blemished the clean canvas: "Final Phase" it proclaimed in red. "Now Selling". Then came the wrought iron words bolted to the wall, "Rancho Hacienda". Then came the gate. We turned left to position ourselves in front of it, Dad using his turn signal in spite of no cars being in sight for miles ahead or behind us on the flat two-lane road. As we faced the black metal bars that sloped from smallest on the ends to tallest in the center, Dad reached out to enter a code on the keypad sticking out towards the driver's window. The gate then slowly swung open with an occasional brief squeal, and we obliged it by slowly driving through.

Again I found myself looking back rather than forward. I watched the gate start to close behind us. Beyond the opening, across the road, a vacant field spread in all directions for acres. Dried remnants of some sort of leafy crop were plastered to the ground in random clusters, trembling in the wind. Several hundred yards in the distance, a bit off to the right, it appeared as though a portion of the field was being used to grow a new crop. The two sides of the gate finished coming together. My view was obstructed by the bars, but I kept on looking, looking at the metal bars themselves now. Mom and Dad started to point at some of the new homes and announce their enthusiasm. I settled back into my seat and looked at nothing in particular.

Chapter Two

All of the parents were more excited than their children about the move. They were so proud of themselves for becoming homeowners. They would stand arms akimbo in the center of each room and slowly survey what was now theirs, breathing deeply the smell of new carpet and fresh paint; they would stand arms folded in the front yard and face their possession with both reverence and smugness; they would greet each other with arms open and couldn't make it through a sentence without using the term "American Dream"; they would put an arm around us and introduce us to their new neighbors and tell us to "say hi" to them and their kid, and then ask their new neighbor's kid what their name was and then tell that kid what our name was, and it was assumed us kids would all become fast friends as well, but us kids kept our distance at first. Looking back, now that I'm older, it reminds me of when adults who work together or are in some club together keep saying they need to get their kids together, and so they have a party and assume the kids are getting together, and even if they are, eventually it's time to go, and the kids hardly ever see each other after that, only at the occasional next party, and it's kind of hard to pick up where they left off, so the kids pretty much give up and watch TV or play with their phones while the adults howl in the next room.

But we were stuck there, trapped at "Ranch Ranch", so we did start to bond, and ours was a bond much stronger than our parents, because they disappeared into the distance of their commutes, and the exhaustion that accrued during the week that caused them to hibernate on the weekends. They were the ones who hardly saw each other; they were gauzy faces in the drivers' seats of cars, shoes visible just before the garage door closed, vague silhouettes as indistinguishable from each other as the houses they had bought; meanwhile we took charge of the development and ran our own lives. The translation of Rancho Hacienda may as well have been "City of Children".

And I truly mean children, as for the most part there were no teenagers either. The nearest high school was a 60-minute bus ride (in parroting the brochures for the development, the adults always referred to it as 60 minutes, never as an hour), and for those old enough to drive, maybe about 50 minutes in a car. So within a few months of our first school year on Ranch Ranch, all socially fluent teens attending the high school had made friends there and subsequently made arrangements with those friends to stay at their homes during the week in what we referred to as High School Town. They eventually pretty much stayed there on weekends too, for what was there for them to return to in our neighborhood? Napping parents on the inside, cocky disrespectful kids on the outside.

The teenagers who did linger, who couldn't procure the connections to get out and instead made their peace with the commute, or the bus ride (which was of course even lower on the totem pole of lameness), were about what you would expect. We didn't see much more of them than we did the ones who vanished. The teenaged leftovers would leave about an hour after the parents launched their pre-dawn drive, and return at dusk, a few hours before the parents returned in time to go to bed. And while at home, they stayed in their rooms, on their computers, in front of their TVs. To come outside was to risk facing us and the insults we would hurl at them, in addition to the dirt clods and fruit we would also hurl at them.

Occasionally one of them would try to play the role of a cool older kid and offer to buy us beer at the gas station mini-mart off the freeway ramp since the cashier was willing to sell it just to make his job more exciting, or one of them would offer to get us stoned, chief among them a boy named Chris, who tried to repel the humiliation of being left behind and riding the bus by growing his hair long and dressing in black. But we always declined because we therefore associated such things with such losers. If someone who actually was cool had offered us drugs and alcohol, then we may have accepted. But that person didn't exist in Ranch Ranch. And certainly our parents would have noticed if any of their liquor was missing, as dependent on it as they were to help them dream up more reasons for why they were doing this to themselves and to their families, so we came up with all sorts of other ways to spend our days in our stucco corner of the valley.

School never posed much of a threat to our ample leisure time. It was essentially a one-room schoolhouse, with what amounted to three grades: K-2, 3-5, and 6-8. The teacher and her aides were accustomed to having a student population made up entirely of Spanish-speakers, the sons and daughters of the farm labor that lived in the blighted little anonymous town next to our gleaming eyesore. So in addition to trying to enhance the kids' English proficiency on top of all the other subjects required, the instructional team was used to assuming that there would be little to no assistance available at home, thus inspiring them to design lesson plans heavy on in-class work with minimal homework, a plan that proved applicable to our situation as well, we the influx of English speakers whose parents were even more absent than those working the fields. The newly-created split between native and non-native speakers was bridged by utilizing us as de facto instructional aides. This further enhanced our sense of self, as we not only saw ourselves as the head of each household, but the head of our school as well.

The campus, if that's the right word for it, was just down the road from the truck stop buffet on the other side of the freeway overpass, and looked like it was made by the same people in a couple of hours after they discovered they had some cinder blocks and rebar left over.

I don't wanna haul all this crap back into town; let's build something else over here.

Okay...there. Done. What do you think it can be used for?
I don't know. A rest stop?
A little too far off the freeway; nobody will see it. A school maybe?
Hmm. A school. What the hell, why not?

We would all wait for the bus together in the space between Rancho Hacienda and the labor town. At first some of us were determined to ride our bikes, but vehicles reached highway speeds on the road between the two points, and though there were not that many of them and they tended to veer into the oncoming lane and give you a wide berth, it was difficult to keep your balance and keep away the visions of carnage. The bus turned out to be a great way to ally with the kids from over the wall, anyway, before we would get to school and have to adopt the dynamic of tutors and pupils. Their English wasn't even all that bad. They could speak okay, they just weren't very literate and it was hard for them to understand some of the stuff in the textbooks. (Plus some of them admitted they had played up their second language problems in order to coast before we got there and blew their cover, including my good friend Miggy. We let them keep up the ruse, however, as it made life easier for us, too.)

Chris, the only high school castaway who continued to perceive value in campaigning to be king of the teenaged leftovers, suggested we should ditch more often, as there were no parents around to supervise us. We told him that ditching would lead to letters home, which would draw attention to our situation and remind our parents how little control they were maintaining over us.

"And why would we want to do that? We don't want your weed and we don't want your beer, so why would we want your advice?"

We got off the bus laughing at him and calling him an idiot as he sat there with another hour's worth of riding ahead of him, along with a few other teen stragglers strewn into their respective corners, while we cruised in to go through the motions of the hour-long tutoring session that was held before the opening bell rang.

Our showmanship in school bound us together and inspired one of our earliest covert operations: the border tunnel. We scoured the backyards that abutted the concrete wall dividing Ranch Ranch from the shanty town, looking for a depression or weak spot along its base. True, it was easy enough for us to come and go through my yard or any of the others whose property lines backed up to the two sides of the development that were not enclosed by the wall, and instead were sectioned off by a wooden fence that we could hop over. But aside from providing a more direct route between our neighborhoods, the wall posed a more tempting challenge, a sense of the subversive in burrowing under it. The front gate, of course, was out of the question, as it had a security camera embedded in the key pad and some distant property management company would monitor it remotely and notify the adult in charge of the homeowners' association that barbarians were storming the palace. Almost without fail as we exited the gate in the morning to wait for the bus and later entered the gate after school, at least one of us would stick our face inches away from the camera lens and scream "Get us out of here! Please! You're our only link to civilization! Help us!" or something along those lines.

We found our ideal spot for the great dig in the backyard of my friend Blaine, who was my best friend when we first moved in. There appeared to be an area where nothing grew; the groundcover and shrubs planted along the wall as part of the complimentary landscaping remained small and withered, while the rest of the foliage relatively flourished. We surmised that the dead zone must have been created by one of the construction crews dumping some toxic material into the plot, perhaps the cement contractors who had won the bid for the wall. Having the site in Blaine's backyard made it all the more appealing to our crew, as he was the most popular boy on either side, with a painfully beautiful older sister who was one of the expatriates spending almost all of her time in High School Town, living with a boyfriend and his family, so the prospect of improving our chances of glimpsing her provided additional inspiration. We had the tunnel completed within an afternoon.

We still had to find a way to camouflage the entrance on each end, however, and we knew where to shop for ideas: there was a section of the development that was unfinished, construction halted on a half-dozen homes in the farthest corner of the rectangle, away from our border and the front gate, where the wooden fences converged. The sales representative and head contractor had told our families it was under construction, but nobody ever came to work on it after we moved in. Perhaps none of our parents saw this as portending anything ominous because they were never home during the days when crews would have been completing that final phase. But our heads of household had developed such a keen ability to willfully ignore warning signs that they refused to acknowledge the houses stood frozen at the same point of incompletion the entire time we took up residence in plain sight of them.

But us kids, we noticed them. And once it became clear that no one was coming to claim any of the materials, much less use them to finish building the homes, we pounced.

In addition to being our own personal home improvement store with perpetual free shopping, the site served as a makeshift playground. There actually was an official playground in the development, squeezed onto a parcel that was smaller than any of the house lots, but we reckoned it was just leftover space that had been turned into a miniature park to help market Ranch Ranch as a great place to raise a family to prospective buyers, rather than to provide their kids a legitimately fun place to play. It had no swings, no merry-go-rounds, no moving parts that could result in a lawsuit; just a short slide drooping down from one side of a stepped platform and some monkey bars jutting out from the other, with a tic-tac-toe game between them that had the X's and O's on plastic rollers that spun like toilet paper. We never played on the structure as intended: the slide served as a bike and skateboard ramp, the monkey bars were for games of chicken in which we would hang facing each other while trying to kick one another in the groin, and we wrote dirty words on the tic-tac-toe rollers to create our own game called shit-fuck-piss.

As cat and dog turds started to accumulate in the rubber mulch that was supposed to provide a soft landing beneath the promotional tool disguised as a playground, we gravitated more towards the construction site. The houses were skeletal and yet to be fleshed out; they were all two-by-fours and plywood. The frames and roofs were in place, but stacks of drywall and faux southwest adobe shingles were stacked on both the ground floor and second story of each home, left under the assumption they would someday be installed. We decided that a section of drywall covering each end of our tunnel would keep it dry and prevent it from being filled in, but we had no tools to cut out a fitting size, and were too lazy to head back to our garages and root through our fathers' toolboxes. Besides, it was so much more fun to drop sheets of drywall from the second floor through the gaps of the wall frame and watch them splash onto the pavement with a cloud of white dust rising as fragments shot in random directions. Then we would take a section that seemed close to what we needed and trim it down by virtue of either beating the edges with a stray section of two-by-four that had been cut and tossed aside by the framers, or by grabbing the promising piece and slapping it against an edge of the cement foundation or a corner of the frame.

At first the Mexican kids were wary of participating, as construction site raids had been a source of conflict in the early days of Rancho Hacienda's development when some of their fathers had sent them on nighttime missions to swipe as many tools and materials as they could, while the development group responded by hiring a security guard armed with a paintball gun and a Taser. But our disregard for their past was brazen enough to help them get over any post-traumatic stress they felt, and soon they were wielding, launching, and slamming alongside us with just as much gusto.

Much of our reign was marked by destruction. We didn't ride a bike to get from one place to another: we rode a bike to go full speed and slam the brakes hard to see how long of a skid mark we could leave; we rode to bowl headfirst into a bush and see if we could launch ourselves into a summersault over the handlebars and shrubbery and land on the other side feet first; we rode them to throw them over my fence into the arid open spaces and race each other in our own private Baja 500, no protective gear, injuries a badge of honor, the marks they would leave on our bodies eliciting satisfied grins of having been somewhere and done something, as would the discreet marks we left around The Ranch: the jagged nub remaining on the tree trunk from which we had torn off a branch, the number "3" missing from the keypad at the gated entrance, the slowly depleting stock of landscaping rocks that we used for war games, the drain pipe twisted askew beside the entryway of various houses at various times that served as our signal that a parent was home. We were always in the neighborhood, and we didn't need to go so far as to write it on any walls, as graffiti would merely draw the ever-dreaded attention of the adults.

Our parents on the other hand constantly left written messages to remind us of their presence: on the dry erase board by the door reminding us to take out the garbage on Wednesday night, on the magnetic notepad stuck to the refrigerator door informing us of the dinner options that were in the freezer, on the yard sign planted in the front lawn broadcasting the family's name with the help of some cartoonish roosters and hens that were drawn in orbit around the letters.

But those were just letters, just a name. Our real family during those days was each other, the latchkey kids of RanchSquared.

Which sounds a bit like the kind of thing a gang member says to justify their decision to join, but our gang involved no initiation, no one sought to be a part of it; it was a purely natural process, a testament to the old trope that "it takes a village" to raise a child; though I imagine adults were included in the original expression of that village. But we were nurtured in the ways of the world nonetheless.

Anything gained from sibling rivalry, for instance, was gained tenfold in our village, as that rivalry was unchained and unmitigated and not limited to actual siblings. During games of chicken at the abandoned train station located a stone's throw from the neutral zone between the walled city and the exposed one, each of us stood our ground far longer than I suppose we would have had we played in civilization, had there been a sense of something else to do other than prove our mettle. Our initial foray into the ghost station had involved throwing any piece of rusted scrap metal we could hoist at the passing train, but that had resulted in a call from the shipping company to the development company, who then contacted the security firm that monitored the gate, who then contacted the homeowners' association, and eventually all of our parents. Apparently throwing objects at a train is a felony.

Going big on our first screw-up helped us come to our senses early, however, and appreciate what we had. It stirred our insight into how necessary it was to keep our kingdom under wraps if we wanted to keep it at all, and that would involve avoiding the kind of parental concern we had fomented due to our felony act. There was some discussion amongst the parents that weekend regarding the possibility of a select number of them quitting their jobs or cutting their hours to spend more time at home. Our child tribe endured a tense couple of days while the adults deliberated, as we were suddenly jolted into realizing what an enviable situation we actually possessed, having been unable to grasp it while clinging to our resentment of being dragged there. Almost losing it so soon helped us turn a corner. We went from not wanting to see our parents ever again for transplanting us to the middle of nowhere, to not wanting to see them ever again so we could enjoy our dominion over the middle of nowhere. Any talk of any of the commuters staying home faded quickly thanks to us assuring them that such a thing would never happen again, because that's what they wanted to hear, because their financial pickle would not allow them to hear anything else. The commute lived on, and we got smart about acting stupid.

We merely stood on the train tracks as long as we could before diving off, as risking your life to impress your buddies is not against the law. We studied the trains and gauged which ones at what times would stop at the factory on the other side of the tree line. Since all the trains that passed through were freight trains, which tended to be rather long, when they did stop at the factory, the last cars were near enough to our deserted station for the driver to contact the conductor, who would jog over and lecture us about what we were doing. When that happened for the first and only time, we made a snap decision to stay and let him talk to us, since running would guarantee another call, whereas standing our ground gave us a chance to charm our way out of it.

We listened to his stern warnings and noted that conductors don't dress like they do in children's books, at least not the ones working on freight trains, and then asked him what our old station had been used for. He was impressed that we had any interest in the past at our age and was glad to tell us.

"Never for passengers," he said, warming up as though telling us a campfire story. "After all, you need people to have passengers, and with all due respect to your neighborhood here..." He surveyed the area with a skeptical gaze and we dutifully laughed.

"It was an agriculture pick up," he continued. "These fields used to be a lot more prosperous, and trucks weren't as much of an option back then."

"What do you guys pick up from that factory?" Miggy asked.

"Who says we're picking up?" winked the conductor.

"So what are you dropping off?"

"I'm not at liberty to say," he said, having some fun with us. But before he could give us a straight answer, his phone flagged him and he took the call, which apparently involved someone telling him it was time to go. He waved to us while he walked back to the train as the engine blew its horn several lengthy times.

We never did find out what goes on inside that factory behind the trees, but did learn which trains would keep barreling past it so we could utilize them for our tests of courage. It was important to pass those tests, because the reason you were forced to stand out there in the first place was due to losing the slap contest or the arm punching contest. And while our dads and older brothers weren't there to throw the ball around, we were there to throw the ball at each other, and not just for dodge ball. Any game, whether it was pickup basketball at Blaine's hoop in the driveway or Strikeout against the other side of the cement wall facing the labor town, they all resulted in the losers having to stand and absorb a pelting with whatever ball was used. Rivalry, competition, hard knocks...none of this was lost on us.

But we also learned to nurture tact and chivalry, too, as our village was not exclusively comprised of boys. There were girls as well; girls growing as tough and uncompromising as we were, but girls nonetheless, so acting stupid could only get you so far. There was a point at which some degree of social skills had to kick in, even when exhibiting cruelty. Thanks to our sisters-in-arms, we learned how a well-chosen back-handed compliment can be more effective than an outright insult, how silence can speak louder than a shouting match, and how if you do it right, a certain look can hurt worse than a basketball to the crotch. They taught us that they would prefer not to ask for things directly, and instead offer hints: a remark about the heat meant we were supposed to ask if they wanted us to turn on the fan if we were inside or offer them a cold drink if we were outside; wondering aloud if they had forgotten something meant that we were supposed to look for it; and the correct answer to a question ("which shorts look better on me?") was often implied through tone of voice and inflection.

Nurturing those latter skills devoted to articulation and enunciation were more instinctual and required more experience, which we were happy to engage. Sometimes it was group experience, our two tides merging and swirling together, winding up in a game of tag that provided small opportunities for physical contact, or in flirty pods characterized by bad jokes that were supposed to show how wise beyond our years we were but mostly tested the limits of what was acceptable in mixed company. We were unified by immaturity and divided by glimpses into adulthood as this gender or that. We were more prone to extend the boundaries of our empire when we found ourselves co-ed, venturing forth by worming under the wall through our tunnel one at a time like a prison break, passing through the rural ghetto as if making our way through a bazaar in a third world city, until we reached the tree line, leaves crunching beneath our feet before emerging on the other side of our miniature dark forest to linger at the chain link fence surrounding the factory, barbed wire running along the top of the barrier and warning signs across the middle that proclaimed the electricity pulsating through it. All of the signs on the property that we could make out were warning signs: toxic materials in the tanks, extreme heat emanating from the silos, prosecution awaiting those who trespassed. The boys would dare each other to touch the fence and speculate on the best way to break in; the girls would speculate on what was happening inside, why there were so few cars in the parking lot, what was being produced, and where it was headed.

One day one of our fellow males, a little guy named Carl, tried to impress us all by peeing on the fence. The last discernable sounds that came out of his mouth were "Hey, check this out" before he was nearly turned into a eunuch by a bolt of voltage that flew through the liquid conductor he had created between himself and the source of electricity. His forced laugh turned instantly to primal screams and grotesque spasms. Miggy was smart enough to body check him like a hockey player and break up the current as Carl skidded across the dried leaves on his back. A weak fountain of urine sprinkled his pants and shirt as he slid, and the dribble continued during the tense pause after he stopped. Once we were certain it wasn't the last pee he would ever take, the rest of us joined him on the ground as we collapsed in laughter and vowed to call him "Nub" from that day forward.

Those of us who grew comfortable enough with some of the girls to hang solo with them at times would voyage even farther, risking a bike ride together out to the fast food cluster that bordered the freeway ramp for a "date". I liked going there with a girl named Shay who lived on the same block as me. Her mom worked at one of the restaurants and would float us some free food now and then. Not that it was entirely free. We had to listen to her complain quite a bit. She had sacrificed a job that she liked back in civilization in order to be a stay-at-home mom at Rancho Ranch, but the family had quickly realized that they needed the additional income to cover the father's commuting expenses. Shay's mom was not happy about this. Almost every conversation we had to endure when she stopped by our table had to do with how much better her old job was: how she wouldn't have to do *this* at her old job, or *that* at her old job, and how much money she earned at her old job, and how respected her old job was. I forget what exactly her old job was; it had one of those blurry titles that according to Shay, was a fancy way of saying she answered the phone.

Shay and I wouldn't talk so much as we would eavesdrop. We would listen to the motorists who were on their way from Point A to Point B and were stopping for rest and refreshment somewhere in between those two points on the part of the line that is just a line. We always got a sorry kick out of it when someone would be talking on their phone and say something along the lines of "I should be there in a few more hours; I just stopped for a bite to eat in...in...I don't know where I am." And when we would get wind of where they were coming from or where they were going, and why, either via their phone if by themselves or the conversation they were having with their traveling companion, Shay and I would share what we knew about that place or that task, and if we didn't know much about it, we would wonder about it. We would wonder what it was like to live there and have your own place and do that thing and make your own money, and go on road trips and have your own phone. We wondered when that would happen for us, and some days it seemed like it never would. It seemed like staring at each day was like staring into the distance beyond our fences, the space between us and whatever was over those hills too far and too murky to recognize.

When we did talk about our lives as currently constructed, that was when we got around to relationships, and attempt to understand what our imagined futures may hold when it came to the opposite sex. Confusion was the dominant theme of these discussions. Many refills of self-serve soda were spent with Shay expressing her frustration as to why every boy worshipped a girl like Blaine's older sister, a girl none of us even knew and had only seen, or a girl like Lana Torres, a girl our own age whose struggles with English made her excruciatingly shy (although Shay attributed Lana's quietness to aloofness). I had to pretend that I worshipped neither of them so as not to come across as being like every other guy. Shay never quite bought it, and she teased me often about my performance, but at least I was able to present myself as being in control of my admiration of them enough to offer some sort of perspective other than "she's hot." Meanwhile I had some questions of my own. It was easy to spend time with Shay, and I figured if I could find that kind of peacefulness with someone who made my heart race like Blaine's sister or to a smaller degree Lana, then I will have found love. But those two features seemed to be so opposed that I doubted love was possible.

Lana's mom worked at one of the other food stops in the exit complex, as did some of the other mothers from Miggy's side of the wall, but their English was thin so they worked in the back mostly, and tended to avoid eye contact when they were out on the floor sweeping or wiping tables. They were much more comfortable when you met them at home; different people practically. The communication was still dicey, but they were willing to try out some English without becoming flush or tongue-tied, and they loved to teach us words and phrases in Spanish. Whenever we felt like we needed some mothering, we would tunnel our way over to The Barrio. The adult presence was still sparse, especially when it came to the fathers, who had to spend twelve-hour days in whatever field needed them within a hundred square miles; but there were at least a few mothers and some grandparents lingering about the households on any given day.

Their homes were also the source of any lessons we managed to learn about compassion and empathy during the course of our boundless machismo tournaments and our sloppy attempts at courtship. It was a chance for us whiny ex-suburbanites to see legitimate hardship firsthand. And we ended up putting in a little work now and then because of it, as we would help tend their vegetable gardens that served as the landscaping in their raggedy but functional backyards. They would use our fantasies of masculinity to con us into shoveling chicken shit into the compost heap, and spread the compost around the garden, and even slaughter the occasional chicken, as having actually killed something boosted one's street cred, even if those streets were contained within the walls of Rancho Hacienda. Their homes smelled funny to us at first, like raw meat and chicken broth and cilantro, but eventually we got used to it, and realized that their homes smelled like life, while ours smelled like houses. Miggy's house even had a whiff of bird cage, since every so often his grandmother would bring in a couple of squabs from the large flock they raised in a shed out back and let them fly around the house, laughing hysterically as she watched her three chubby cats try to catch them with no chance of success. They would eat late, waiting up for the fathers to come home so they could all sit down together and pray before dinner. I can't speak for my fellow Ranchers, but I was also fascinated by the religious symbols that decorated most of their homes. Miggy's family had a particularly graphic crucifix above the toilet in their bathroom. Miggy said his folks put it there to try and keep his older brother from jerking off. I sometimes asked to use the bathroom just so I could stare at it. It never quite convinced me that it had the power to convert the skeptical, but it was definitely a potent reminder that things could always be worse.

And most of all, unlike our houses on the other side of the wall, with our identical floor plans sparsely furnished on the inside, and our identical facades in one of three earth-toned colors that alternated from house to house to house on the outside, not every household in The Barrio was exactly the same. If there was one characteristic which bound them together it was creativity; the ingenuity required to face the hardships they had no choice but to face. And creativity was likewise something fostered by our child tribe. Granted our spirit of innovation was in the interest of deceit rather than survival, in order to keep our antics confidential, but from our cordoned perspective, it seemed just as imperative as raising your own food or scavenging furniture left over from when the truck stop renovated their dining room.

Motivations aside, there was no denying the brilliance of the camouflage we designed to cover the crude drywall doors at each end of our tunnel we had dug. We at first assumed that covering them with dirt would suffice, but immediately realized how ineffective this was, as if there was nobody willing to stay behind and be the designated dirt replacer, the side into which you entered would remain exposed. So it was once more to the construction site to browse the discards. Shay came up with the idea to use the faux adobe shingles to build a fake birdbath that we could attach to the cover on Blaine's side, placing two of the curved southwestern style pieces together lengthwise at their edges to form a cylinder standing upright as the base, and breaking up three other shingles in half to give us six small concave pieces to place in a circle around the top of the base for the desired effect. Since we were definitely going to need tools this time, to fasten our mock birdbath to the piece of drywall, I ran and fetched my dad's toolbox from our garage, and we figured we may as well use the hammers to break up the shingles we would need for the top. This part was of course the most fun, taking turns battering one shingle after another from the stack to see who could smash out the most usable sections. And while what we came up with wasn't exactly precise, it didn't matter much in light of Blaine's backyard. His dad was originally from somewhere in the Caucasus; no one knew if he was Russian, Persian, Armenian, or Turkish, including Blaine. He always referred to himself strictly as American, and upon arrival to his new country had changed his last name to Ford, married a woman who looked like a prize awarded to the immigrant most willing to assimilate, and embraced conspicuous consumption as proof that he had earned The Dream. Apparently their house back in the suburbs had looked like a miniature Las Vegas casino, or at least the backyard did. They transported as much as they could reasonably fit into their current yard, so realistically we didn't have to construct something so involved; we could have thrown together some random materials and spray-painted it gold and it would have blended in. But we took pride in our work.

The concealment for Miggy's side of the tunnel required a different approach. The wall ran alongside the buffer zone between Ranch Ranch and The Barrio, which was in effect a very wide alley that served as our main route to the abandoned train station, so the tunnel opening was not located in anyone's yard. Aside from where we had trodden our path, the alley was choked with weeds year-round. The only other spot where the weeds had been flattened was the area around our drywall trap door, so we came to quick consensus that utilizing weeds to blend in made the most sense, but found that sticking actual weeds into some mud on top of the drywall didn't work because the dead weeds would bow soon after installation. A kid named Arturo from the weedy side of the wall suggested using long slivers of wood from the scrap heap at the construction site as decoy weeds, one set of slivers that kept its natural wood color to imitate the weeds in summer and fall, and one set that we would paint green to blend with the winter and spring weeds. We all thought it was not only a brilliant idea on his part, but a selfless one at that, since he was in eighth grade and wouldn't be around much longer to capitalize on it. He moved in with some family friends who lived near the high school soon after, but we continued to refer to the opening on that side of the wall as The Arturo Gate in his honor.

Chapter Three

And so when the first of the foreclosure signs went up, we weren't scared; we were angry. We were losing our independence. Our families' finances and our families' future meant nothing to us; what mattered was our families' intrusion back into our lives. By the time the red-lettered signs started to sprout, I was in the home stretch of eighth grade, so I had been planning for an even greater measure of autonomy with a move to High School Town, going so far as to request interviews with some of my friends' expatriate teenaged siblings when they happened to be at home so that I could gather some tips and form a strategy to ingratiate myself to my fellow freshmen and make my move away from Rancho Ranch as soon as possible. It was a rite of passage; and should one of those signs appear in front of my house, I would be denied it.

"Why does someone have to foreclose, anyway?" I asked Blaine one evening as we shuffled around the platform of the dilapidated train depot looking for things to throw.

He shrugged. "Can't afford the house, I guess."

"But if you still have your same job and you're in the same house, how does that suddenly happen?" I was barely searching anymore and instead trying to formulate answers to my own questions, thinking aloud in Blaine's presence.

"I guess the house must be worth less," he responded distractedly, as he was still pretty engrossed in finding chunks of cement and catapulting them onto the tracks.

"Okay, but you've still got the same amount you're paying, right? I mean, your payments are still your payments, and you could afford them when you moved in."

Blaine seemed to be getting a bit irritated now. "I don't know, Nick. Maybe the payments change. Maybe they don't stay the same."

I thought about that as he hit the far rail with a discus-sized piece of cement and we watched it explode into a half-dozen flakes. "Different payments," I pondered, "that's weird."

"Why do you think I would know anything about this, anyway?" he scoffed.

"I don't think that," I said. "I'm just worried. High school is coming. It's our turn."

He jumped off the platform onto the tracks and picked up the pieces of cement. "Relax," he grunted as he pivoted and started to throw them one at a time at the base of the platform. "My family has moved like a dozen times. There's always a way. That's what dad says."

At the risk of interrupting his game, I ventured to ask, "Maybe your dad could give my dad some tips."

"Maybe," he said, still focused on how hard he could hit the wall beneath me. "Hey," he stopped what he was doing. "Do you think Lana Torres likes me?"

"Um..." I recalibrated our conversation, "it's possible. Everybody else does."

"I'm not talking about everybody else. I'm talking about one very hot girl."

All of us would have liked to be liked by Lana, so surrendering that hope required definitive proof. "She's hard to read," I dodged. "She doesn't say much. She doesn't even look at people much."

"I think she does," said Blaine, going into his windup and throwing his last pitch.

"You think she looks at people? Or you think she likes you?"

"I think she looks at me because she likes me," he grinned as he surveyed the marks left on the wall below the platform.

"So why did you ask?"

He hopped back up onto the platform. "Just want to be sure, I guess. You really haven't noticed her checking me out?"

"No, Blaine, I haven't," I snipped. "I guess I've been too busy wanting to be sure that we weren't going to have to move."

"That again?" he slapped my upper arm and walked past, "Take it easy, Nick. We're good. It's just a few signs. Your parents aren't that stupid."

He continued to the far end of the platform and hopped down the collapsed staircase to the ground. I either thought to myself or said out loud, "Well, they moved us here, didn't they?" and followed him back toward the alley that split the neighborhoods.

When we reached The Arturo Gate, the trap door with the wooden decoy weeds stuck into it, I still felt anxious and needed some sense of comfort. Neither of my parents would be home for a few more hours, and Blaine's self-love was progressing at a discouraging rate, so I decided to veer off towards Miggy's house and see about hanging there for a while. I hesitated after altering my course to see if Blaine would notice. He was through the tunnel and on the other side of the wall before he did.

"Aren't you coming?" his voice called over.

"Later," I called back. "I'm heading over to Miggy's."

"Bullshit," he said. "You're going to Lana's. Backstabber!"

I heard him laugh and a few seconds later heard the sliding glass door into his house open and slam shut.

I drifted into The Barrio and noticed that the pummeled homes didn't look as bad in the sunset. I could imagine a professional photographer being intrigued by the way the shacks caught the setting light and cast shadows, inspiring the artist to create a series of prints lining the walls of a gallery or coffee house someplace far away, the collection perhaps called something like "The Twilight of the Working Poor".

Miggy's door was open, as always. I at first had marveled at the faith the denizens of the labor town had in each other, but Miggy set me straight by telling me nobody bothered locking their doors because if for whatever reason someone thought there was something worth stealing in any of the homes, they could simply push in one of the walls.

His grandmother was sitting in her plush dusty chair with one of the cats on her lap that jumped a foot in the air and fled when I entered. I apologized in Spanish and she responded with a stream of phrases I couldn't make out, but seemed to assure me it wasn't a problem; something about her "crazy cat". Miggy entered and didn't bother asking me if I wanted him to translate, as we had stopped doing that for the most part. He would instead just tell me how to react, and apparently my reaction in this instance was appropriate enough.

"You here for dinner?" he asked.

"Well..." I hedged.

"Just say yes, you fucking freeloader."

"Yes."

His grandmother chimed in with some sort of admonishment.

I started to backtrack. "If it's too much trouble..."

"It's not you," Miggy said. "She's on me for saying 'fuck.'"

Her voice rose again and Miggy went over and teasingly jabbed a forefinger up and down one of her arms while he said to me, "Why is it that people who can't speak a language still know the curse words?"

She tried to swat away Miggy's pokes, trying also not to laugh as she lobbed a couple of Spanish swear words at him. He let her be finally and gestured my way. "Let's go fetch some eggs. This filthy-mouthed old lady can make dessert tonight."

He translated what he said for her benefit and she waved him off as she got up and started to shuffle around and coo for her cats to come out.

We went into the backyard and raided the hen house for some eggs. Miggy left me with one and brought the rest inside. He came back out and we started our egg toss, stepping back a few paces with each successful completion.

"I'm going to miss this if we lose our house," I said after a few rounds and some light trash talk.

"You think your parents are in the same kind of trouble as those other people?" he replied, catching the egg and gently guiding its momentum to the side of his body before tossing it back my way.

"I don't know," I caught the egg and faked a hard overhand throw before tossing it underhanded. "It's just when I see a few of those signs go up at the same time, I wonder if it's a pattern; plus they're all in the first phase area, the first homes that were sold."

"Why don't you ask them if things are okay?"

"The people being foreclosed? That would be weird."

"Your parents, dumb ass." Miggy gave me a few pump fakes before lobbing it over. "Ask them what their deal is."

I caught the egg and quick-tossed it back. "I couldn't do that. That would be even more weird."

"What are you talking about?" he held onto the egg, pausing the game. "They're your parents."

"But I don't really know them anymore," I explained. "And I don't think they would be honest with me about that, anyway. I'm starting to think nobody was very honest with themselves when it came to buying these God-forsaken houses."

Miggy rolled the egg in the palm of his hand and, unlike Blaine, thought about what I said. For that alone I wanted to blurt out that he was now the best friend I ever had. But he responded as well: "Even if things are bad, hopefully they can hold out for a few more months, and you and I can find a place to stay in High School Town."

I considered the possibility. I lost myself in visions of us living on our own during the week and going to high school together. By the time I snapped back into the present and announced "That would be cool," the egg was already upon me.

We had a delicious dinner, a pungent tomato and chicken-based stew filled with almost every item from their backyard farm. Miggy's grandmother had started preparing it earlier by reducing the chicken and tomatoes on the stove, then later on when his mother got home from work she finished it off by adding the other ingredients. His father and older brother joined us well after sundown when they finally got home after their shift in a table grape vineyard fifty miles farther up the valley. I provided the entertainment with the dried egg on my shirt. Having a good sport to make fun of seems to be an easy avenue for different walks of life to get in stride with each other. Miggy had an older sister, too, but she was a student at the high school who stayed in town during the week, and even though it was Friday, she was active in student government and was staying back to work at a fundraiser over the weekend. It was her connections that Miggy and I were hoping to exploit in our plans for next school year. We talked about that future for quite a while in his room after dinner. When we heard the rest of his family start to retire to bed, I figured it was about time I left.

The Barrio was pitch dark, but the street lights of Rancho Hacienda leaked over the wall and cast just enough of a glow for me to find my way to the tunnel. Now that I had been crawling through it for a couple of years and grown a bit, the tunnel seemed more like a big hole. If I lied on my back in its middle, right underneath where the wall stood, I could touch one end with my feet and the other with my hands. I did that as I returned from dinner at Miggy's, to measure myself and gauge if each side was as far away as I seemed to remember them being when we had first constructed it. I decided that I hadn't grown all that much, that I had tailored my recollections to make my time at Ranch Ranch seem like a longer part of my childhood than it really was.

Honestly, I never really established much of a presence in my old neighborhood that we lived in before our move to The Ranch.

I read, played video games, and the few times I had friends over my parents seemed uncomfortable or irritated by them. I went over to a few other kids' houses, but all we did was play video games, and eventually we seemed to realize we didn't really need to be at each other's houses to do that. My sociability started to atrophy, and it didn't bother me. I was content with my books and games. It made no sense, really, that I had been the least bit concerned about moving to the middle of nowhere, as I was already there in a lot of ways. But it was a change, and I had become familiar with my own personal middle of nowhere. Thinking back on my arrival at The Ranch brought to mind those videos of animals who had been rescued as babies from some family tragedy in the wild and raised in captivity, and how when their wounds heal and they grow up and they're released back into the wild, they just sit in their cages with the door open and peer out cautiously for a while, not really sure what to make of it all. They don't recognize their own habitat at first. But it starts to dawn on them. Whether it's the smells, or the sounds of others just like them braying nearby, or simply some sort of feeling, they venture out. The seal gets his first dose of the open sea, the lion feels that tall grass brushing his flanks with every step, the child takes a baseball bat to the neighbor's garden gnome and hears no adult rebuke...and they're off. The cage may as well have never existed.

We became more untamed than the pets that were initially part of our families when we arrived. Sometimes someone's dog would escape from the backyard and sprint with no idea where it was going, just wanting to run somewhere, somewhere fast, tired of defending its small piece of territory through barking and rushing the fence, at last able to go on the offense, to chase something, chase down whatever it could find; one dog ran away, another was brought back to civilization for adoption by a parent's co-worker, another dog took up residence with an elderly member of The Barrio after escaping, preferring companionship to nicer lodgings. All of the animals brought to The Ranch eventually vanished; the cats turned feral, the birds sat neglected, as none of us could be trusted to take care of the pets we once clung to during the first weeks of our residence; we were too busy setting an example for them, showing our animals what it was like to be limitless.

Now here I was facing the specter of being led back into the cage. I kept lying there in our tunnel, in that which I helped build, enjoying the coolness and smell of the moist earth, letting the darkness thicken around me, listening to myself breathe, finding comfort in thinking that if this is where we all end up, then so be it. Nothingness seemed so relaxing. A heaven full of things to do sounded exhausting; full of leisure sounded dull. This was just fine. I may have even lightly fallen asleep for a few moments, as my body abruptly lit up with adrenalin and wanted out.

I pushed up slowly on the drywall above me, being careful not to jerk our homemade birdbath off of its foundation. Though my head was not facing Blaine's house, I could see that the wall and garden were illuminated, indicating that some lights were on in the house. I lowered the drywall back down and spun over onto my stomach before raising it again so I could assess the situation. The lights were on in their living room, but no one seemed to be there, at least from my vantage looking through the sliding glass doors. I decided to wait a few minutes just to be sure. Soon my caution was rewarded.

There, gliding into the frame, was Blaine's older sister, making a rare appearance in their house, and an even more rare appearance in my line of sight. She had practically become a myth, but now here she was, wearing a tank top and boxer shorts. I nearly choked on some soil from the deep breath I took upon seeing her. She was smiling at whatever she was reading on the screen of her cell phone as she paced aimlessly, absent-mindedly strumming her stomach and breasts with her free hand. She then stood still facing the glass door and used both hands to type a message. There was a quick reply to whatever she wrote, and she was delighted by what the other person had to say. She looked around the room furtively, then held the phone in front of her at arm's length and took a picture of herself giving a pouty smile. After checking to see that the picture met her standards, she sent it and within seconds was stifling a laugh at the reply received. She held the phone out in front of her again, but this time kept it closer and aimed it at her chest, lowering the collar of the tank top to a point where her breasts were almost completely exposed. She took the picture, and the exhilaration I felt was matched by the agony of knowing that it was not intended for me.

Whomever was the intended, her boyfriend I assumed, apparently increased his demands. She covered her mouth in manufactured shock and after looking around once more, seemed to realize that she needed to take this out of the living room. She dashed away and the lights went out. Within several seconds the lights turned on in an upstairs window. I hoisted myself out of the tunnel and replaced the drywall and its camouflage, then turned to focus on that window up above. I wandered towards its beam of light with my eyes looking skyward as though witnessing a UFO hovering just overhead. I saw her shadow moving on the ceiling. I saw her arms raise and the tank top slide over them. I quickly surveyed my surroundings to see if there was anything I could climb up to get a better view, but the trees were still too young, and the fence dividing their yard from the one next door too exposed. I looked back at the window helplessly. The shadow was no longer there. She was now below her lamp, either on the bed or the floor. I stared at the window hoping she would become visible again. My entire body throbbed, I felt indistinguishable from my erection. I barely maintained enough foresight into what might happen should I take off all my clothes right there and stroke myself in their yard to prevent myself from doing so. When the lights finally went out, I was afraid that a girl so beautiful would never love me.

Exiting Blaine's backyard silently had never been a problem; I knew just how to unlatch the gate without a sound, knew exactly where the pavers were as opposed to the gravel. But I had to get my breathing under control before I could follow my standard escape route this time. It took several minutes, but finally the dampness and the darkness and the feeling of loneliness settled me down, and I was off.

Once on the street and walking home, I noticed some smoke rising from the factory behind the trees in the distance, and it occurred to me that I still did not know what went on inside there. And before tonight I did not know what Blaine's sister looked like in underwear, and I never would have known had I not happened upon her, had I not eavesdropped on her. If I went up to the factory and shook the gate and asked someone what they were making in there, I doubt they would tell me. And if I had asked Blaine's sister to walk around in a tank top and boxer shorts, she certainly would not have done that for me. So it was with my parents. If I asked them what our deal was, if we were going to have to move, I could not imagine them telling me.

When I arrived home I couldn't really tell if they were there or not. I opened the door that connected the kitchen to the garage and saw both of their cars. I scanned the kitchen for a note or something written on the dry erase board and found nothing. I walked quietly past their room, pausing to press my ear against the door. I heard one of them snoring, the other breathing heavily just short of snoring. I decided I would go ahead and ask them if a sign with red letters would be staked to our lawn any time soon, let them reply however they wanted, and seek my answers through closed doors and open windows.

Chapter Four

We had been a rather tight-knit family before moving to The Ranch. We went on a lot of road trips together to aquariums and amusement parks and saw movies together. We ate dinner together while watching television shows that we could all agree on before we would go our own ways before bedtime with books, websites, or movies that appealed to our more specific tastes. But there was always a "good night" before turning in. There was an "I love you". There was a familiar sense of humor that we shared. It may not have been funny to anyone else, but certain phrases that made us laugh developed organically from situations we encountered. At a baseball game one day we overheard a mother and father explain to their children why vulgarities were being shouted all around by declaring, without a hint of irony, that "not everyone is as nice as us". We adopted the phrase as a family motto of our own, with plenty of irony attached.

But my parents started to believe the motto. The irony evaporated, and they really did seem to think that not everyone was as nice as us, and that our version of niceness defined the word "nice" for society. Maybe it was their jobs, which I had never really thought of much before; it was just a place they went for the day to make money so we could do all those things together. They were on staff at an insurance company and investigated claims; Dad was more of the type who was out in the field inspecting sites and interviewing people, while Mom was more of a forensic accounting type who looked for suspicious numbers buried in someone's paperwork. They had always shared the occasional anecdote of chiselers great and small, but it was usually intended for laughs or eye rolls: some dimwit trying to swindle his way into some money, because apparently he thought that having money would show the world he wasn't really a dimwit.

The anecdotes became more frequent, however, and became full-blown stories told with agitated hand gestures and raised voices by Dad, and sometimes Mom. They would preface and conclude each yarn with assertions of how much it made their "blood boil" or how "infuriating" it was, and how the world is "such a mess" and "going to the dogs" (or "downhill", or "to hell"). And they never understood it. "I don't understand it," they would say every time. But in spite of not understanding it, they knew who or what to blame. They would profess theories that blamed music or the web, politicians or schools, a turning away from the values they had grown up with.

And their vision became so filled with examples of the dregs of humanity that they felt like the best thing was to get as far away from humanity as possible. But since finding a new job was something that scared them just as much as the people they were exposed to by working at that job, they sublimated their inaction by moving us to Rancho Hacienda. So while I gathered that most of my friends' families moved here thanks to the seduction of home ownership, mine seemed to do so in the interest of protecting me. Though I imagine not having to rent anymore while protecting me at the same time had its appeal, too.

I also got the impression from talking to my Rancho friends that they were already accustomed to having a certain amount of distance from their families, and that moving out to Ranch Ranch merely extended that distance. Their parents were already working multiple jobs and leaving early and coming home late, and they wanted something to show for all that hard work; something like a house, something they assumed would be a safer investment than the kids they already had, which were so far producing disappointing returns.

I wasn't sure whose situation was preferable, mine or my friends': to have had family ties and lost them, or never had them at all. I thought perhaps my folks and I would still be able to maintain some sort of connection on the weekends. Even when it was apparent that on those weekends they would be too tired and everything would be too far away to plan many getaways, I assumed we would still have our in-home bond. But I started to feel like our bond had simply been a summer romance; we had met under ideal circumstances and kept in touch upon separating, but each visit seemed to douse what we once had. Unlike what I imagine often happens to a lover in a long distance relationship, however, I never much brooded over the situation. Aside from reveling in my newfound freedom at The Ranch, I also took solace in knowing that my parents were still close with each other. They continued to work together and regard themselves as some sort of crime fighting duo, a line of defense between us nice people and those others. I was the third wheel in the house. But I was grateful to them. They had wanted to protect me, and in the process of inadvertently setting me free helped me understand how little I wanted to be protected.

I initially figured it was this protective instinct that motivated their evasive answer when I asked them about our house. They didn't want to worry me. Then it dawned on me that I was probably overestimating my effect on them, and more than likely what really drove them was crushing embarrassment. Regardless, it was hardly necessary to eavesdrop on them in order to uncover the truth, so obvious was their attempt to cover it. But I wanted to hear them talk about it, see if they were being any more honest with themselves than they were with me. Besides, I wanted to start practicing and perfecting my reality checking, which sounded so much more palatable than "spying" or "snooping".

"...I just wasn't sure if Nick could handle it," I heard Mom say as I lied on the floor near the base of their door, just to the side of the frame, so as not to cast a shadow. In order to avoid stepping on any creaky floorboards, I had slid there on my stomach, pulling myself along by extending my arms in front of me, then dragging my body forward with a little help from my knees, as though doing pull-ups while lying face down on the ground.

"I know, I know. I wasn't sure, either," Dad agreed. "But then how could we know at this point how he would react to anything?"

I had been prone there for several minutes waiting for them to say something related to my pursuit, and now that they finally were, I had to regain my concentration, as their discussions of work and their minor physical ailments had nearly put me to sleep.

"What do you mean by that?" Mom said.

"We don't know him. That's what I mean. We don't know him anymore."

Dad's assertion led to a bit of a pause. Mom ended the brief silence. "I'm not sure I would go that far."

"We don't."

"We don't need to talk to him every day to know him."

"We haven't talked to him in two years."

"He's our son," Mom was getting more defensive. "We know him."

"Two years is like, twenty percent of his life."

"It's less than that."

"Okay, fifteen? What's one-sixth? You're the numbers person."

"We know him," she held her ground. "Kids are who they are when they come out of the womb."

Another hesitation, and this time it was Dad who broke it up. "He'll find out eventually," he steered away from the point about whether they knew me. "Everyone will find out soon enough."

"Everyone will be in foreclosure right along with us."

Dad let out a long sigh. "How could we have been so stupid?"

"It wasn't that stupid. I showed you those studies about home ownership and self-esteem, and how it builds communities."

"You got those from the Rancho Hacienda sales rep."

"I did some independent research."

"But the math, honey. The math."

"The math was fine," she snapped. "I just didn't think hard enough of what the payment would actually look like with the new rate in place. I mean, a few percent more doesn't seem that big of a deal from a distance..." She proceeded to get more worked up. "And I didn't think the value of the house would drop so low, and I was too loose in figuring out how much our commute would cost, and I just wanted it to work, because I wanted a house, so I made it work, because I deserved a house, god dammit! I worked hard, I'm a good person, I did nothing wrong..." She stopped and I could hear her catching her breath.

Dad tried to soothe her by saying "hey" and "shhh" several times each. "I'm not blaming you," he finally said. "I wanted it, too."

They were either lying in each other's arms or on opposite sides of the bed. The pause was so long I almost started crawling back to my room when I heard Mom say, "Well, like I said, we all wanted in. Nobody wanted to be left behind."

"I never thought I'd succumb to peer pressure as an adult," Dad seemed to say more to himself than to Mom. "That's supposed to be kids' stuff."

"From the womb," Mom reminded him of her earlier point. "From the womb to the playground to adulthood. You've been in the business long enough to know that. You've studied enough people."

"But I thought I was smarter than them."

Mom sounded like she appreciated the opportunity to laugh. "You just have stronger morals."

"Yeah, I only defraud myself."

I heard them kiss and Mom muttered something mischievous about putting those morals aside for a while, which immediately inspired my departure crawl. It was much faster than my arrival, with a lot more squirming.

Chapter Five

The sign didn't arrive as soon as I thought it would. It was childish of me to think that my questions and reality checking were part of an ordered chain of events that would naturally lead to the redness being raised the next day. It didn't even come the next week, or few weeks. The lax timeline made it more comfortable for my parents to lie. They had plenty of time for either me to forget I had asked, or for them to concoct an excuse.

Other signs arrived. Several of my friends' families had stakes driven into their fronts. A grizzled man in a pickup truck would come once a week, with the signs perched on white wooden crosses lined up in his bed. We would watch him like a roulette wheel, stalking him slowly on our bikes, some of us on foot, wondering where he would stop next, as he would perform his ritual a couple of times per visit: unfolding himself with a grunt from the driver's seat, already brandishing his rusty spade with the splintered handle; plunging the tool into the lawn a few times, turning a small patch of green into a dark hole rimmed with loose dirt; shouldering one of the white crosses from the back of his truck and dragging it over to the spot; planting it, tamping down the dirt around it, and ignoring our presence the whole time.

About half of the homes that had been marked were occupied by my friends and their families. Shay's house got hung with one during the second visit from the old man with the truck. She mentioned that we would not be visiting her mother at the fast food restaurant from now on, as the resentment her mother was barely able to conceal while working that job was uncontrollable now that they were resigned to foreclosure. She and I spent a lot more time together, though, because she wanted to avoid her mother when she was at home as well. We all spent more time together than ever before, which of course was already quite a bit. But those who had been marked with the red words proceeded to lose whatever feelings of obligation they had maintained toward their families when it came to making up some time with them on weekends or holidays, for if the walls of their houses weren't vibrating with anger, they were sagging with sadness. And no one really wanted to see their parents like that. So we commiserated and tried to make each other feel better without actually talking about anything specific. Instead we would understand why that rock was thrown a bit harder, or that bike wiped out from taking a turn too aggressively, and we were no longer surprised when we would see tears flow in the process, and we pretended not to notice when they would continue to trickle down long after the physical pain of the fall had subsided or the loss had been tallied.

Most families decided to keep living in the house until they were forced out. From what I was able to glean from my friends' tales of their home life, the reasons why they stayed were varied: some seemed to do so as a matter of convenience, others as a form of protest, while the rest had lost the will to do much of anything, much less plan a move. They all kept working. In fact, many of them worked longer hours than ever before, and worked weekends, apparently just as interested in avoiding their families as their children were.

Occasionally a family would leave in the dark, sometime past midnight and before dawn. Nobody's house was furnished very thoroughly, so it was easy enough for them to try to pack up and escape undetected. We had all moved from smaller homes or apartments, and getting into our Ranch houses stretched the budgets enough to render new or additional furniture unaffordable. A few of us would always be aware of when someone was trying to sneak out, however. We would hear the car doors slam, or see the headlights filter through the blinds in our windows, and if we hadn't caught sight of them in their driveway, we would wait and see in the morning who was missing, whose parents had whisked them away without letting them say good-bye.

Other houses that were paid a visit by the sign man were occupied by people without kids, so they had been empty most of the time, anyway. And then there were others that received a red mark that really took us by surprise, since we had never seen anyone in them, and assumed there was no owner. Blaine informed us that those houses must have therefore been investment properties, and he clearly took pride in having to explain to us what that meant. Once he did, I debated consoling my parents by telling them that as stupid as they may feel about buying at Ranch Ranch, at least they weren't stupid enough to see it solely as an investment opportunity, and kid themselves that anyone would want to rent here. But that would blow the lid off my surveillance, my reality checking, for even when the time inevitably came that my parents would have to acknowledge they were drowning, most likely after a sign had finally been raised in front of us, they certainly would not go so far as to admit any feelings of stupidity. Not to me, at least.

Meanwhile as most people were trying to avoid looking at the sign on the cross stuck in their front lawn, or looking constantly in the direction where it may appear someday to see if it had arrived, something of a very different sort arrived at Blaine's house one Saturday morning.

A huge pleasure boat, hovering somewhere between a yacht and a speedboat, was towed through the gate by a diesel flatbed truck, like a set piece being dragged onto the field for a Super Bowl halftime show. The procession slowly made its way along our streets, people coming out to stand on the curb and watch it pass. And while there was no Grand Marshall or beauty pageant winner seated on the bow waving at us, there was Blaine's father waving it proudly over to his driveway. The adults who had lined the streets for the sparsely-attended parade went back inside, many of them shaking their heads, while all of us kids followed it to its destination, peppering the delivery driver and Blaine's father with questions upon arrival. The driver answered us by handing out brochures for the boat dealership, while Blaine's father gently waved us off with avuncular assurances that we would all have a chance to explore it once he took care of some paperwork and inspected it.

As our boat fan club dispersed and the buyer and seller went inside to finalize the deal, Blaine pulled me aside.

"You get first crack, dude," he told me. "We're taking it to the lake tomorrow."

"What lake?"

"That one out past the high school."

"I didn't know that was 'the' lake."

"It is to people who have boats," he grinned.

"I didn't even know there was 'a' lake out there."

"Technically it's a reservoir. But they call it Lake...some Spanish name. You coming?"

"Sure. What about Miggy?"

Blaine hesitated. "Well...it's a family trip."

"Oh, so my parents are invited?"

"Yes."

"Okay," I said, not sure whether I liked the prospect of having them along. I looked over at the vessel. The driver had backed it in and it took up the whole driveway. Blaine's family had parked their cars on the street to make way. "It's a big boat. I'm sure Miggy's folks could fit on there, too."

"They'd be uncomfortable," Blaine quickly replied. "I'm not bringing Lana and her family."

I paused and tried to figure out how that was relevant, but could not. He and Lana had yet to spend any time together in school or in either of our neighborhoods.

"I wouldn't be *bringing* Miggy," I finally said. "He's your friend, too."

Blaine acted as though I still had not said anything. "Do you want to come or not?"

I shrugged. "I said yes already. It sounds fun."

"Cool," he put his grin back on. "Tomorrow morning, bright and early. Come on over when you hear us loading up. Tell your people." He drifted in to their open garage. "I'm going to see if Dad needs any help with anything. See ya."

"See ya," I replied in kind, though I wondered if he would have noticed had I not replied at all.

The kids from The Barrio tended not to come over to The Ranch on weekends since our parents were around, if not always visible, and I wanted to see if they had caught sight of the boat sailing past their neighborhood on its way to the Rancho gate. With all of the activity at Blaine's house, the tunnel was inaccessible, so I went back to my house to hop the fence.

As I reached our driveway I saw my parents peering out the window above the garage, pressing the sides of their faces against the glass to get as clear an angle as possible of the boat. They sheepishly acknowledged me with waves and I decided to tell them later about the invitation to ride on it.

I went through the side gate into our backyard, swung myself onto the top of the fence, and jumped to the ground on the other side. I looked straight ahead at the barren plains of beige, the train tracks hidden behind a lengthy embankment made of leftover dirt from the construction of our homes that had now settled into the same tone and consistency and hosted the same weeds as the earth around it. The wind whipped my eyes dry and I imagined, as I almost always did when I first landed on the other side of our fence, that there was nothing behind me and I was the lone visitor on a distant planet, or the sole survivor on ours.

The walk along the fence line was marked, as usual, by very little noise coming from the backyards, while the wind that kept people inside, particularly the parents, screamed across the valley floor and pelted the boards with pebbles and particles of dirt. Occasionally the muffled sound of music could be heard from inside a house, or the sound of someone yelling, or the squeals and commands of children playing in a yard, and in rare instances an adult could be heard puttering outside, watering some plants or scraping the rust off the grill of a barbeque on wheels.

I came to the corner where the fence met the wall, and turned into the alley that separated the two territories. At the other end of the passageway, lingering by the street, I saw Lana Torres and her former school bodyguard, Dulce Villanueva, who was now one of The Barrio's versions of a teen leftover who couldn't score any living arrangements with anyone in High School Town. She was only a year ahead of us, a freshman, so theoretically she still had a chance to swing a deal in the future, but she was big and loud and everything that Lana was not. Her dad did a lot of landscaping work in the high school town and gave her a ride whenever he had a job there, so she rarely rode the bus with us. She waved me over in a manner that suggested she would hunt me down if I didn't comply. So I did.

"Whose boat was that?" she said with her heavy accent that I was always convinced she clung to and made heavier than necessary, like this guy my dad worked with who was from Boston originally but hadn't lived there for thirty years and still insisted on speaking with an accent that sounded like a comedian imitating someone from Boston when he would call Dad at home.

"So you saw it?" I asked, which I knew was a stupid question, but it was my reason for coming over.

"Of course, dumb ass," Dulce didn't waste the opportunity to pounce.

"Blaine's family," I said.

Dulce and Lana looked at each other and smiled.

"So, you like Blaine?" I asked neither one in particular, but kept my eye on Lana. She looked down shyly and added a blush to her smile. Dulce did the talking.

"Are you just gonna ask us stupid questions all day?" she said.

"No," I said, and debated whether I should ask the more pointed follow-up question I was forming. I held off and changed the subject. "I'm riding on it tomorrow with him."

"So?" Dulce snorted. "You think that makes you all hot shit, too?"

"I'm just saying I'm going for a ride."

"Yeah, that's right," she laughed, "You're just along for the ride."

Lana started to look a little embarrassed. I wasn't sure if it was for Dulce's sake or mine. I decided to roll out my blunt question after all.

"Do you really like Blaine?" I asked, "Or do you just like the boat, and his clothes, and the car he's going to get on his sixteenth birthday?"

Dulce looked like she was about to hit me. I tried not to look as though I was bracing myself and braced myself. Lana took a step back and now looked worried.

"Fuck you, man!" was what Dulce finally blurted out. "Are you calling us whores?"

"What?" I said, sincerely dumbfounded. "No."

But then it did occur to me, as Dulce started pushing me, that one could certainly interpret my question that way. She kept shoving me in the chest and started to taunt me. "Why don't you move out of your rich-ass neighborhood if money don't mean nothing to you, bitch! Join the real world, bitch!"

Her shoves were getting more intense. Lana half-heartedly tried to step between us, but it just wasn't in her to do such a thing. Meanwhile I was caught between defending myself against a violent girl who was bigger and stronger than me, and the old adage about not hitting a girl.

"Look," I said while trying not to trip as I let the momentum of Dulce's blows carry me backwards. "I didn't mean it like that. I just get jealous of Blaine sometimes, okay?"

"Why, bitch?" she said, unrelenting. "You got money!"

I steadied myself and absorbed her next shove without moving, and yelled right in her face, "I ain't got shit, you fat fuck! Any money we had is gone now! A nice house doesn't mean shit, Dulce! It's a mirage! A fucking mirage! Do you even know what a mirage is, you stupid asshole?"

"Who you calling stupid?"

"I called you fat, too, Stupid!"

She took a swing at me, but I saw it coming since I figured what I said would instigate a punch, so I managed to dodge it. Missing her target raised her temperature even more, so she decided not to take any chances and just barrel into me, driving me into the ground. Lana screamed for help, and as Dulce pressed my profile into the dirt with my face aimed toward The Barrio, I saw a bunch of the guys who like to drink beer by the road on weekends come running towards us. I felt myself being lifted from the ground, and among the gallery of faces I saw Miggy's older sister, Lourdes, stepping forward to take custody of me. The excited chatter that filled the air was all in Spanish, so I asked her, "Am I in trouble?"

"No," she assured me. "They think it's funny."

"That a girl was beating up a boy?"

"It's Dulce. She's always good for a laugh. I'm surprised they stopped her."

Dulce was still hollering at me, in both English and Spanish, filling in the blanks between calling me a bitch and a puta and a motherfucker and a joto with whatever came to mind, as the men chuckled and held her at bay. Her dad arrived and whisked her away as the beer-breathed men cat-called them on their way back into the pile of homes. I naturally heard my share of animal noises and whistles, too, as Lourdes beckoned me to walk with her to their house.

"Why?" she asked me as we drew farther away from the din of verbal ignorance. "I mean, Dulce? Are you kidding? How can you take that poor girl seriously?"

"I know, I know," I agreed. "She just got to me this time."

"What did she say?"

"She was calling me out for being some rich punk just because I live over the wall."

"So?"

We turned onto the path that led to their house and were now hidden from view of the fight audience. I stopped to catch my breath as I suddenly felt like crying.

"We're losing our house, Lourdes."

I barely managed to keep from bawling, but my efforts were no doubt very obvious. Lourdes gave me a hug and said she was sorry. I could not hold it any longer. I let loose a prolonged sob into her shoulder.

I composed myself as quickly as I could and apologized for laying that on her. She was nice enough to barely acknowledge it happened and instead picked up on our conversation.

"Why would she even say that?" she asked.

I sighed at having to admit my part in the incident, though doing so sped up my recovery even more. "We were talking about Blaine's boat, me and Lana and Dulce, and they were acting all gaga over him, so I guess I accused them of only being interested in his money, and Dulce took that to mean I called them whores."

Lourdes smiled. "I wonder what Lana thinks."

"Thanks," I groaned. "Like I ever had a shot, anyway."

"C'mon," she got us to walking again. "Miggy must have had his headphones on when the shouting happened."

We arrived at their house and made our way to the backyard and sure enough, Miggy was haphazardly tossing seed into the bird cage that took up one corner of the lot while he bobbed his head up and down to the music coming through some headphones attached to the player hooked on his waistband. He saw us and slid the headphones down onto his neck with one hand while birdseed seeped between the fingers of his other.

"What's up?" he looked quizzically in our direction. It occurred to me that maybe I had some visible cuts or bruises. Lourdes saw me check my face and neck with my fingertips.

She said to me, "You're clear." She said to Miggy, "He got his ass kicked by Dulce."

"Right on," Miggy broke into a huge smile. "Now you're really part of the neighborhood."

He flung the remaining seed over his shoulder into the cage and we all sat on some old patio furniture teetering on top of the parched bumpy ground that was lightly strewn with flattened dry weeds. I recounted the episode for his benefit, while Lourdes teasingly cross-referenced the version I told Miggy against the one I told her. They told me their respective Dulce stories, and we came to the conclusion that if she had been born under more affluent circumstances and attended a leafier school, she would have a prescription for every psychiatric medication on the market.

Lourdes jumped up and retrieved her high school yearbook, which had just been distributed the previous week. Dulce's class photo betrayed none of her hardly-suppressed rage. We marveled at the ability of the photographer to coax such a pleasant smile out of her, and searched for any candid shots which may have captured the truth. None were listed, which in itself was somewhat revealing, but then again she was only a freshman.

Since Lourdes had the book out, she went through it with us practically page-by-page and provided biographies of the people featured most prominently and background information of the events that marked the key points in the year and locations that provided the backdrops in the pictures. We found out who was dating whom, who had been dating whom, who would like to date whom; we found out who was friendly with whom, who comprised which cliques, who had broken ties with whom, and most importantly, what we should learn from these maneuvers: how to maintain one's dignity in the pursuit of a relationship or friendship, for the duration of it, and at the end of it should it come to that; and how much more difficult it would be to apply those principles in practice than it would be to grasp them in the abstract while learning about them in the yard on a Saturday afternoon, as the emotions that would come into play would be powerful factors, and we needed to steel ourselves in preparation for them, to not fool ourselves into thinking we could completely avoid them, but not let them fool us into abandoning the rational doctrine we were being armed with. We got her take on who the up-and-comers were amongst the junior and sophomore ranks, who would be the biggest influences on the student body. She included herself on that list without the slightest bit of hesitation. She gave us tips on how to recognize whether someone of higher social rank was worth responding to should they approach us: if it was a legitimate outreach and an opportunity for elevation, or if it was the groundwork for a joke or an attempt to find a lesser light to hang around with and make themselves look better. She wanted us to understand which people, organizations, and clubs not considered cool were worth the risk in the interest of developing a persuasive college application. She prepared us for how kids from the countryside are perceived on campus, and how we could make sure to avoid falling into the stereotype. And she emphasized that all of the above was extremely important if we expected to find a place to live in town, as that would only happen if we attracted an invitation. Asking around was not an option. If you had to ask, you weren't welcome.

The last point she made before excusing herself to see what was available for us to eat and drink was that she would not be able to assist us in any way directly; she would help in subtle ways and be sure to casually praise either of us if by chance we were mentioned in conversation amongst the campus select, but that any overt attempts at being our spokesperson would only damage our prospects, and lower her status. The cult of self-determination ran strong on a campus where projections concerning life after graduation were weak, for even though the town it was in held sway over us, it was nowhere to be found in the consciousness of anyone in the world who mattered, and any connections made there were not getting anyone anywhere, anyway.

Her explicit reference to all of us being on campus together caved in on my mood. I had been so excited to gather so much valuable intelligence that I had practically forgotten there was a good chance I may not end up going to the school with them, or perhaps only go for a brief stint. I wasn't sure what my parents' plan was: if we were going to move once the foreclosure was officially pronounced, or if we were going to squat in the house as long as we could before being evicted. The squatter option would provide me with more leeway to earn a spot in town and enjoy a successful four years thanks to Lourdes' mentorship, regardless of where my parents wound up. What's fifty miles compared to one hundred or two hundred if I was only going to come home on weekends, anyway? But my parents would have to agree to it.

Lourdes called Miggy inside to help her in the kitchen. I grew a bit melancholy as I found myself alone pondering an uncertain future. They mercifully re-emerged and saved me from my thoughts. Their parents and grandmother were off for the day with their brother in a distant farm town down the valley, meeting the family of a girl their brother had been dating. Neither Miggy nor Lourdes had any opinion on the matter, as they had never met the young woman, but meanwhile we were free to clear out the fridge and the cupboards at will, and they were getting the party started with every bag of deep fried items they could cradle in their arms and a half-full case of soda in tow.

Miggy brought out a radio and tried to get something besides Mexican stations, but we were as always out of range, and the only pop station that occasionally reached us was barely audible over the static. Lourdes chided him for denying his heritage, but he claimed he just wanted to show us some dance moves and needed the right music. He decided to make the best of his circumstances and fused his hip-hop moves with the Banda music he was dealt, slowing his gyrations down to the pace of the tuba bass line that crept under the accordion and brass oom-pah oom-pah beat cackling through the tiny speaker, deciding to invent a whole new form of expression. We joined him and tried to name and market our new form of dance. I can't recall any of the names we came up with, as our actions became incidental to my mind, and were absorbed by the joy they inspired; things felt right, felt like what people our age should be doing. Lourdes felt younger, we felt more mature, and all of us ended up about where we should be.

When the dance-off and laughter had worn us down, we sprawled out into various positions in front of the television, the satellite dishes perched anachronistically atop the shaky sheds providing our link to the mainstream. We surfed through waves of uninspiring possibilities and settled on a movie channel showing The Texas Chainsaw Massacre. Perhaps we felt obligated to experience some fear after all that wistfulness. Lourdes asked us if we had seen the original, and we didn't know there was one. She had seen it in High School Town at the small movie theatre there, which usually functioned as a last resort for blockbuster movies that were on their way out of a theatrical run and trying to squeeze a few bucks out of the nether regions before heading for people's homes. But on occasion the old one-screen cinema hosted a midnight showing of a cult classic or a weekend festival if there was a sufficiently determined band of film geeks at the high school, which there had been for the last couple of years. Lourdes didn't say much more about it until we started eewing and oohing at the parts splattered with viscous; she then kicked in with her comparative analysis about how the original was more about suspense than gore, how it was more about someone being chased than being physically taken apart, how little was actually shown in the interest of allowing one's imagination to do the rest, all of which sounded suspiciously to us like the critique of one of the film nerds she had earlier confessed to sort-of dating but never quite committing to, so we called her on it and she drily denied everything with a suppressed smirk. She finally admitted that she may have borrowed some of his ideas, but quickly tried to turn it into an example of the preparatory education she was trying to impart for our benefit, maintaining it was an illustration of dabbling in that which may be uncool to our townie campus elite, but cool to the larger elite who read college applications.

I may very well have fallen in love with Lourdes that day; it's hard to know exactly. I certainly started to admire her a tremendous amount. Though if you think you're in love, I suppose you are, even just for that moment. She was a safe way to consider whether I had found that sweet spot between my feelings for Shay and for Lana. Granted, she was even sharper than Shay and not as beautiful as Lana, but she had a few years on each of them, and Shay could still come up to that level with age and Lana could come down. In the meantime Lourdes became my standard, and I had a funny feeling that the admiration was mutual, that she felt something similar for me; a funny feeling in part because I was probably kidding myself.

We started to get drowsy as the sun set, and hanging around trying to force any more great moments struck me as potentially undermining all the greatness that had sprung freely throughout the day. I excused myself and Miggy asked if I wanted to hang out tomorrow. I was about to accept the offer when I remembered the boating invitation with Blaine's family. I mentioned my prior engagement and they looked at me incredulously from their languid poses amongst the furniture.

"Will Kelsey be joining you?" Lourdes asked condescendingly.

"I hope for your sake she is," Miggy grinned at me, "in a bathing suit."

"Oh, please," Lourdes said. "If you guys want to know what Lana will be like in high school, there's your role model."

I enjoyed Lourdes' reaction to Blaine's older sister because I could interpret it as jealousy and further enhance my self-flattery when it came to Lourdes seeing something in me that no other girl had.

"Is that so bad?" I asked, rubbing it in just a bit.

"Kelsey's okay," Lourdes qualified her previous dismissiveness. "I feel kind of sorry for her, actually. It's like she's so convinced that because of how she looks, people will think she's a bitch no matter what she does or what she says, so she doesn't do or say anything."

Her attempt to understand someone she didn't think much of prompted me to raise the pedestal even higher on which I had placed Lourdes. I considered dropping the word "admire" from my thoughts on her and jumping right into usage of the word "love" from that point on, but it felt a little juvenile; as if that many boys who fell for their friend's older sister ever ended up with them.

I told them I would give them a full report and then wondered aloud, on the subject of full reports, if my incident with Dulce would make the rounds at school Monday.

"She doesn't ride the bus," Miggy reminded me. "And Lana never speaks, so unless someone saw something out their window or Dulce's dad let her out of the house again for the weekend, which I doubt, you're probably in the clear."

"See, Lourdes?" I called over to her on my way out. "That would be the best part about being with someone like Lana or Kelsey: they'd be really good at keeping a secret."

"Well, almost the best part," Miggy added.

Lourdes rolled her eyes at him. Though honestly, she probably rolled them at both of us. I kicked myself a tad for giving her the opportunity to see me as a goofy kid once more, and hoped I had not tarnished any maturity points I may have built up for the day. But I had a feeling that people who respected each other allowed for some idiocy in the relationship.

Of course all of these notions I was forming about relationships were not really applicable to someone my age. The realization that I was not yet capable of trying out any of the ideas that were forming made me ache a bit as I walked toward the wall. Adulthood seemed so far out of reach. Though it was not as if the frustration of understanding something while being unable to effectively carry it out was exclusive to young people, as the foreclosure parade was making clear to me. And it was not the least bit comforting to think that I may always be susceptible to such a disconnect.

I saw some illumination hovering above the wall behind Blaine's house, and my contemplation was instantly drowned in adrenalin and visions of his sister. Lourdes was supposedly my new touchstone, my ideal, and here I was trying to maintain a straight line to my fence and not stagger over to the tunnel. But I could see it as a test of my resolve, a chance to close that gap between ideas and actions that was so befuddling. I could sneak through the tunnel and take a peek just to prove to myself that I knew better now, that there was more to what makes a girl worth pursuing than looking good in a tank top and boxer shorts and a willingness to take erotic self-portraits and yes, what a great idea. I decided to look because it was the rational thing to do, I told myself. I assumed she was home thanks to the boat trip tomorrow, which would provide yet another opportunity to solidify Lourdes' place as my benchmark.

I jogged over to the Arturo Gate and wondered for a moment if I would even be able to recognize Arturo if I attended the high school next year. I quickly fidgeted through and gently lifted the decoy inside Blaine's yard to survey the situation. Kelsey's lights were out, and the living room was dark, too. The source of the illumination turned out to be their parents' bedroom. With equal parts disappointment and relief I started to lower the cover, figuring it would be best to reverse course and continue on over to my back fence, since the side gate in Blaine's house was right underneath his parents' bedroom.

But then I heard the shouting. Blaine's mother was re-launching into a full-throated diatribe after what I presume had been a pause to catch her breath while I had been scanning the back of the house. I slid the drywall cover to the side and set it on the ground so I could concentrate on what she was yelling. I assumed her husband was the target, as they never did anything to their kids other than fawn over them. My suspicions were confirmed when I distinctly heard her bray at one point, "Of course you did, what American bank would ever give you a loan at this point?" and he barked at her to lower her voice.

She somewhat complied, so it became difficult to hear them. I noticed that along the wood fence delineating their property from their neighbor's stood a young tree that had grown just big enough to quite possibly provide adequate cover should I risk getting closer. The allure of potentially solving the mystery of not only where the father came from, but where his money came from, was worth the risk as far as I was concerned.

I crawled out of the hole and sidled over to the corner where the wall met the fence, and used the wall to help me spring to the top of the fence. I then took slow single-file steps towards the tree that caught the light from the combatants' window and beckoned in the breeze. I didn't have to worry about anyone next door seeing me, as the house was one that had never been inhabited. I carefully ducked and weaved through the skinny branches to find a sufficiently cloaked position. The fence wasn't high enough for me to see directly in, and the tree wasn't big enough to climb safely, but I was still able to see the mom from the shoulders-up. She was still doing the talking, and the dad must have been on the bed, as she was looking slightly down as she spoke. I had missed most of what she was saying during my acrobatics, but was able to once again tune in as I achieved a sense of balance.

"...American Dream, American Dream...you say it so much it doesn't mean anything anymore. You're like a parrot who was taught how to say it. What does it even stand for at this point?"

This jab inspired the dad to get up off the bed. His head and shoulders were now in view, too. Seeing them both from the chest-up made it look like someone was putting on a puppet show.

"You never knew," the dad said, now ignoring his own request for low volume. "You don't know anything about the American Dream because you never had to worry about it; it was always there for you, it was handed to you, so you never had to think about it. How could you know what it means?"

"So tell me, Yuri..."

Blaine's dad's name was Yuri? He always told us to call him Steve.

"...tell me what the American Dream is."

"You're standing in it!" he bellowed.

The kids' rooms were on the other end of the second floor. But since their rooms appeared dark, I thought maybe Blaine, and perhaps Kelsey if she was home, were on the computer in the downstairs office in the front of the house, since it was too early for them to be in bed. Whatever the case may be, I hoped that they were not within earshot of this. I was taken aback at how upsetting it was to watch even someone else's parents fight, to know it was real and not a public service announcement or a couple of actors attempting to win praise for their work. Also upsetting was how titillating I found it to be.

"Oh, you mean debt?" she cracked back. "I'm standing in debt? That's just the cost of it, Yuri."

He exhaled deeply and calmed down, much to my relief. Blaine may have been acting like a bit of a prick lately, but I wouldn't wish dueling parents on him. The dad even appeared to smile, as though his wife had provided him with just what he needed to steer the conversation back toward a conversation.

"You know that's not a problem, my love."

She was not the least bit soothed, however.

"Yes it is," she said forcefully while trying to keep her voice down by channeling her intensity into karate chop hand gestures that chopped to the beat of her voice. "Yes...it...is. You may not pay your bills, but we still end up paying in other ways."

He kept trying the comforting approach.

"Why don't you take some time off," he said, "or quit. Relax a little. You don't need to work, you've always done it just to give you something to do."

It still wasn't working. She clutched her head and ran her hands down the sides of her face before adopting a more desperate and imploring posture.

"I work," she started to explain slowly, "because I'm scared shitless that you're going to run out of bridges to burn and we're going to need the income."

He straightened up and went with a more stoic stance.

"Have I always provided for you?" he quizzed her.

"Yes."

"Have you ever wanted for anything?"

"No."

"Then why don't you trust me?"

"Just because something has happened in the past doesn't mean it's going to keep happening in the future."

"You don't even know what I do," he said.

"Yes I do," she sprang right back. "I do know what you do. I just don't know how you do it. I know that you never pay anything off and move on to another loan from another bank in another part of the world for another fake business venture..."

"...They're not fake."

"...Okay. Doomed. Badly designed. Cockamamie. Whatever. I know these things. But how you get away with it? You're right. I have no fucking clue. You didn't come to America to pursue a dream, you came here to hide from the rest of the world."

He gave up. His upper body sank below the puppet stage. She watched him descend but took no pleasure in it.

"Are you coming on the boat tomorrow?" I barely heard him say.

"Sure," she shrugged. "Why not? If we're going to hide behind the damn thing, we might as well use it."

"We don't need to hide behind it," he verbally gathered himself for one last shot. "It's to have fun. By the time they find out in Azerbaijan what's going on here, we'll be long gone before the foreclosure sign ever goes up."

He didn't actually say "Azerbaijan"; he said the name of some ancient town or province I assumed was somewhere between Europe and Asia with a name I couldn't quite place or re-pronounce, and thus could not commit to memory.

Meanwhile, she said something along the lines of "Thank God. Wouldn't want anyone to think we were just like them."

Regardless of what she actually said, her tone was unmistakably sarcastic. That much was true as I found myself staring into the leaves and branches of the tree with the window blurring into the background like an accident victim or a mentally unstable person I was trying not to stare at.

I dropped myself into the vacant yard next door and stood for a while, unable to complete a thought. The lights went out on the upstairs stage I had been watching, though the flickering of a television screen remained. I headed back to the wall and vaulted the fence parallel to where the tunnel mouth opened. Before I went underground I glanced up at Kelsey's window, which was still dark, then took a few extra steps to peer around at the other side of the house and saw Blaine's window casting a small amount of light, about the wattage of a reading lamp. He must have heard his parents. I wondered how he handled it: if he tried to make out what they were saying, or put on head phones to drown them out, or wrapped a pillow around his face and screamed into it.

Upon landing in my backyard, I saw through the glass patio door that my parents were huddled around the island in the middle of the kitchen, talking over mugs of something steaming, and I was grateful that at least they were unified in their deception, that they managed to bond over discussions on how to live their lie. I went around the house to enter through the front door so as not to startle them or elicit any questions, but I still felt as though I was intruding when I greeted them and assured them I had eaten. They seemed eager to resume their conversation from where I had interrupted, so I stretched and said I was heading upstairs. But before I did, I remembered to extend the invitation for a boat ride. They went from stunned silence to stuttering acceptance within seconds, and may very well have forgotten what it was they had been talking about.

Chapter Six

The sun was low on the eastern horizon and the wind had yet to pick up when I went out the next morning to see if Blaine and his family were preparing to launch. The boat was hitched to the massive SUV that the mom drove. The garage was open, and from my vantage several front yards away, I could faintly hear some activity in the garage. Soon Blaine and his dad emerged on each end of a cooler they hustled starboard. They hoisted it up onto the edge of the boat, and Blaine hopped up on board to guide it in the rest of the way. He saw me and waved, as did his dad upon turning around to see what Blaine was waving at. They beckoned and I gestured "one minute".

I ducked back into the house to call upstairs for my parents, but they were already dressed and in the kitchen with coffee brewing. Twelve-packs of light beer and diet soda were on the counter ready to be brought over as gestures of gratitude. They saw my look of surprise and grinned.

"Wouldn't miss this for the world," Mom cracked.

They also saw the look of surprise on Blaine's dad's face as we approached, and Dad whispered to me before we were within earshot, "Are you sure we were invited?"

"That's what Blaine said," I muttered, and glared at Blaine as he came out of the garage to join his dad in continuing to prepare for the trip. His dad rebounded and acted like nothing was wrong by the time we reached their driveway, and I realized I should probably do the same, though I wanted so badly to call Blaine on his oversight and ask him why he was so determined not to invite Miggy that he would fabricate an invitation to my parents on the spot and not be interested enough in covering his tracks to follow through on it.

The best I could manage when it came to concealing my anger was to stare really hard at things out the window from our seats in the absolute rear of the hulking vehicle and pretend to be concentrating on them, and then imagine my ire was still stuck on those things when I had no choice but to look at Blaine and remain as straight-faced as possible. He did briefly seem to suspect that something was amiss, as he asked me at one point during the drive to the lake if everything was okay. But my reply that everything was fine was apparently all he needed to convince himself that everything indeed was okay, if he really cared to begin with, and he went back to talking about himself.

Thankfully, most of Blaine's attempts at conversation were drowned out by the talk between the two dads in the front seats, even though we seemed to be dozens of yards away from them. My dad's background as an investigator and the self-promotion that characterized Yuri/Steve worked in tandem to create a steady, shallow stream of words, the only depth coming from the baritone of their voices. Everything was bluster and deflection; Dad would ask him about the engine and Blaine's dad would say that it was the equivalent of a long haul truck, and then talk about the truck engine because that's apparently what he knew more about. Dad would ask him how he knew so much about trucks, and Blaine's dad would say that he had a business that required a lot of items to be shipped via truck, and proceed to talk about the shipping industry, and how wise other businesses would be to emulate their model. Dad would ask him what his business was that required all that shipping, and Blaine's dad would say that he no longer had the business and talk about how stifling the regulations and taxes were and how difficult it was to keep a business open, any business, and compare the business climate in the United States to that of Albania, and suggest ways that America could benefit from Albanian practices. Dad would ask him how he knew so much about Albania, and Blaine's dad would say that he once had a business partner from Albania, and proceed to talk about the time he and this business partner ordered really great steaks at this place in Fresno...and on it went as we sped across the crusty basin, the dads getting louder, my dad occasionally interjecting some arbitrary fact regarding the subject Blaine's dad was currently lecturing about, neither one really listening to what the other was saying, listening instead for a pause to fill with something they knew that would add to their word count.

The moms, meanwhile, occupied the seats immediately behind the dads and engaged in an interrogation and evasion of their own, but in shorter bursts at lower volume. My mom was a bit more blunt in her efforts to uncover the financial situation faced by Blaine's family, her background in mining paper for information rather than people revealing itself clearly as she would ask Blaine's mom about her handbag or her sunglasses, and dive right into a follow-up question about its price tag; if Blaine's mom actually quoted a price, Mom would marvel at how successful they must be to afford it; and if Blaine's mom remained cagey about the cost, Mom would praise her reticence, and observe that the people most comfortable with their success felt no need to flaunt it. Considering Blaine's mom had spent an intense portion of the previous night berating her husband for dishonesty, I was hoping she would crack and scream that it was all built on a foundation of sand, but her smile held tight.

There was still one more bank of seats between us and the adults, which remained vacant since we were going to stop in High School Town to pick up Kelsey and her boyfriend. The town became visible in the distance several miles before we reached it, like a holy city in a desert thousands of years ago. The closer we drew, the further the resemblance faded: no walls surrounding it, no bazaar, no prophets shouting out their visions; just a couple hundred homes, the newer ones looking as though they were built in a matter of days, the older ones looking as though they may be torn down in a matter of days, many of them with brand new pick-up trucks and SUVs parked in front like some sort of consolation prize everyone gave to themselves. There was a shopping center with a box store and grocery franchise anchoring it, the parking lot practically empty at this hour on a Sunday, and a couple blocks' worth of downtown store fronts, half of which were vacant with "For Lease" signs in the darkened windows.

We didn't drive past the high school, which was disappointing because I had never seen it before. But when we pulled in front of Kelsey's boyfriend's house, I noticed some light standards rising above the houses a few blocks away, and I assumed they surrounded the football field. I thought about asking if we could swing by the campus on our way out of town, but as Kelsey and her boyfriend slouched out of the house, I could imagine their eye rolls and condescending snorts and decided against it.

Everyone else seemed afraid to say anything, too, as the couple took their seat and Kelsey wrapped herself around her boyfriend, barely getting the words "hi" out of her mouth while her boyfriend gave a "what's up" nod to nobody in particular. After a few brief attempts by Blaine's mom at obtaining some information about what had been happening at school and what was to come, the vehicle became quiet the rest of the way to the lake, as if the verdict of a beautiful young woman matters most in judging one's self-worth.

Our traveling party finally spoke up to help guide the boat into the water, shouting directions to Blaine's dad as he backed it down the ramp, telling each other to watch our steps as we boarded the vessel, and making sure out loud that everything and everyone was "okay".

Everything was okay, it turned out, and we were all okay, and actually feeling pretty good about ourselves, since we all had a chance to give orders or follow them accurately, and ask questions or answer them correctly. Then we hit the open water and the engine noise and wind prevented any detailed conversation; the adults could shout accurate observations about what a beautiful day it was and how beautiful the water was, while Blaine and I could stick our heads into the spray and hands into the water, and Kelsey could hunch next to her boyfriend and they could take turns running their fingertips over each other's palms and forearms. Everyone could do something easy, that they couldn't screw up, at high speed on the water under a clear sky. It felt great.

We had to stop eventually. Since it was a manmade lake created by flooding a valley, there were no beaches or flat shorelines aside from the marina, just the steep grades of the hillsides that once stood even taller. So when it was deemed time to pause and snack, socialize, perhaps save some gas, Blaine's dad simply cut the engine upon arriving in a heavily-wooded cove and we drifted in silence for several moments, the lack of any noise at all leaving us a bit stunned. A slight breeze broke the spell, animating the lightest branches of the pine trees that climbed the banks rising above us, around us, and someone said "how pretty."

It was Blaine's mom. Her statement was true enough, but also served as an introduction to take drink orders from the cooler and open bags of snack foods to pass around. As we settled into eating and drinking and admiring the surroundings, every so often one of the adults would remind us all that it was great to be there, or that the day was so relaxing, or they would just take a deep breath and exhale in a long, contented sigh, until my mom decided it was time to converse rather than comment.

"So how did you two meet?" she said in the direction of Blaine's parents.

They looked at each other and seemed to agree that it was a wife question.

"In Las Vegas," she replied, which prompted a playful "ooh" from my mom, chuckles from the dads, and a trip to the platform on top of the bow for Kelsey and her boyfriend, who wanted nothing to do with anything that involved other people.

"It's not like that," Blaine's mom continued in sporting fashion. "It's quite dull, actually. I was at a training seminar for the bank I worked for, and he was at some New Business Expo. A friend of mine knew someone at the expo and said she could get us into one of their parties, and well...there he was."

She looked slyly over at her husband, who played along with a shrug of false modesty. I wondered if this was the moment in which they were making up after their fight from the previous night, or if they were that adept at acting like nothing was wrong.

I glanced at the bow and watched Kelsey strip down to a bikini. She was very good at undressing. I suspected that even when she was alone, she would arch her back melodramatically while pulling off her shirt and bend over with her legs straight while pulling down her shorts, because it was so rehearsed. I still wanted to have sex with her in the worst way, but now felt like I wanted to have sex with her and then tell her afterwards that she wasn't so hot. This was of course even more implausible than ever having sex with her in the first place. I had no doubt that if it somehow happened, I would be begging for more before we were even finished.

My parents, meanwhile, were contributing their own Las Vegas story.

"Was that convention at The Hilton?" Dad asked.

"The business expo was," Blaine's dad answered.

"That place is huge," Dad said.

"We got lost there," Mom added. "We walked around that big convention center area looking for our insurance retreat, asked for directions and everything. It was like trying to find an address. Half of it wasn't even being used."

"I took a nap on a bench in one of the empty ballrooms I was getting so tired," Dad said.

"You couldn't have been that tired," Mom quipped, and they shared an inside moment.

Blaine's dad picked up on it. "We did something like that at the Moscone Center in San Francisco," he said. "But we were behind a curtain in our booth with hundreds of people walking by."

The moms cackled, while Blaine and I shared an inside moment of our own, deciding it was time for a swim. We shed our clothes down to our bathing suits about fifty times faster than Kelsey had, and dove in practically in unison. As we resurfaced, our parents teased us about being prudes.

"Yeah right," Blaine muttered to me as we treaded water. "Who doesn't like to hear stories of their parents having sex?"

I laughed and swallowed some water, which made Blaine laugh. As soon as we caught our breath, we established a race course and some rules and started our competition. Even though I knew Kelsey wasn't watching, I fought extra hard to finish first, in case one of the parents asked us who won. However, as was usually the case when going up against Blaine in anything, I lost. But I consoled myself with a reminder that for Kelsey to care about the results, she would have to hear them in the first place, which would require her to listen to somebody other than her boyfriend. Which reminded me...

"Has Kelsey's boyfriend said anything today?" I asked Blaine as we leisurely swam towards the boat backwards, jellyfish-style.

He snickered. "Has that guy ever said anything?"

I felt even better about Kelsey not being attracted to me. I took some time to pay closer attention to the hills and the trees, and to feel the water flowing past my body, which was pulsing with a satisfying exhaustion after our race. I found it all so much more beautiful than before, now that no one was telling me how beautiful it was.

We reached the boat and rested our arms over the stern on opposite sides of the motor. Our parents' conversation had turned from sex to money. And assuming the tales of public quickies had been true, they were being far less honest with each other about money.

"We'll probably end up selling before too long" Blaine's mom was saying.

"Part of being an entrepreneur is never being satisfied," chimed in the dad.

"You'll be selling at quite a loss, though," said Dad.

"You win some, you lose some," the dad replied. "That's the other part of being an entrepreneur."

"We're going to stay and hope the value goes back up," Mom said, never glancing at Dad to see if the plan was to lie.

"We're not kidding ourselves," Dad picked right up on her story. "We know it's never going to get back to where it was."

Only then did they look at each other with brave, sad glances. "But we're happy where we are," Dad continued. "So I'm sure we'll be around long enough to get it close."

I couldn't see Blaine's expression since the motor separated us. That was my only chance to see if he understood what was going on as well as I did, at least when it came to his parents, for I couldn't imagine talking to him about it in the first place, much less getting an honest answer from him.

He was rather quiet on the way home. Of course, so was everybody. It had been a long day, people were tired. But the expressions I saw in the reflections in the windows and in the rear-view mirrors were not contemplative, but brooding. The eyes were not looking back at a fulfilling day, but looking forward, and what they saw worried them. Even Blaine was missing the smugness that usually marked his moments of silence.

When we dropped off Kelsey at her boyfriend's house and she leaned back into the car with a forced, brief smile to accompany her forced, brief "thank you" before they melted back into the house, Blaine murmured "It must be nice" as he watched them go.

"What must be nice?" I said, matching his low volume.

"Having such a clear head."

I breathed a short laugh through my nose, taking his joke at face value, but wondered as we drove toward the sunset if I should read it as a cue to discover more about what he knew as soon as the chance presented itself. We weren't going to be neighbors much longer. Maybe an honest discussion about our circumstances would deepen what was turning out to be a shallow friendship that, as it stood, was going to end once we were no longer down the street from one another.

We said good night and I looked for another signal from him. My mom reminded me to "say thank you to Blaine's parents" as though I was five years old again, and Blaine just smiled at me, trying not to laugh. I smiled back at him and dutifully did as I was told. I would have to conduct my search some other time.

Chapter Seven

"I was pleasantly surprised," I heard Mom say.

"Anyone can be charming for a day," Dad answered.

I had not even been to my room yet, merely hesitating on my end of the hallway after saying good night to them, and then sneaking back to their door with the stride of an enormous rooster in slow motion.

"I'm not talking about them," Mom clarified. "Though they weren't as bad as I thought they'd be. I mean the lake, the drive, going somewhere besides work."

"Yeah," Dad chuckled, "You know you need to get out more if a reservoir full of drunk people on jet skis starts looking good."

They were quiet for a while, though I could hear dresser drawers opening and closing, closet doors sliding back and forth, and water running in the bathroom, so I held my ground, figuring they may still have something to say after they were done getting ready for bed.

"So I was thinking," Mom said as her voice bounced in time to her lowering herself onto the mattress, "Maybe we should enjoy ourselves before they pull the plug on us."

"How so?" Dad asked before grunting in relief at finally crawling under the sheets.

"We're not making any payments on the house anymore, and we've got months' worth of vacation time built up from working our asses off trying to get into this time bomb. So what the hell? Might as well have something good come from it."

Dad did not respond quickly enough for Mom's comfort, so she pressed on. "You said yourself we've been losing touch with Nick, and now I see what you mean. We hardly spoke the whole day."

"It was one of those parents-in-one-group, kids-in-the-other kind of days," he said. "Teenaged kids, no less. So what do you expect?"

"Wait, so you've flip-flopped on the Nick issue?"

"No, I still think we need to spend more time together..." he hesitated. "I just, well, have you asked anyone at work about this?"

"I just thought of it today, on the way home."

Dad paused again. Finally he said, "Do you want to look into it tomorrow or should I?"

Mom let out a small squeal that would have been louder if she had not thought I was in bed. "I'll do it," she gushed. "I hang out with the people in payroll all the time, anyway."

"The people in payroll," Dad said, amused by the sound of it.

"Maybe we could get some of the others to follow our lead," Mom speculated. "Get a summer-long block party going on."

She started snapping her fingers, and I imagine sprung into some kind of middle-aged woman dance move that made Dad laugh.

I chicken-walked back to my room, glad they had an idea that made them happy, and hoping the idea would not become reality, that I could spend my remaining days on Ranch Ranch as I had spent them the last couple of years: amongst friends, roaming, wild, doing whatever we wanted so long as we could get away with it.

Chapter Eight

The bus stop the next morning was filled with the usual competitive conversations about being able to do something better than someone else, the hurling of insults at Chris and the rest of the high school leftovers standing as far off to the side as they could while still being able to catch the bus when it came, the throwing of rocks as far out into the fields across the street or as hard into the wall behind us as possible, and the whipping of each other with young branches pulled from trees on the way to the bus stop. I was a bystander for the most part, however, as I tried to work my way through my fears of my parents being around once more. I thought if I figured out why I was scared, then I could start to address the problem. But I couldn't get that far. I wasn't sure whether I was more scared of losing my independence, or scared that I would discover my parents and I had completely lost touch, had nothing to say to each other, and from here on would be unofficially estranged.

I decided it would help to engineer some peer feedback to see how my friends would feel if put in the same situation, with a follow up question concerning their views on what it would be like if all the parents were to reappear. Of course it actually was a possibility in the event my parents' movement should catch on; but I preferred to think of it as a remote possibility, an unlikely event, while wanting to conceal my parents' role as potential instigators, so I presented the situation as purely hypothetical, something I just happened to be thinking of, at opportune times individually whenever I could catch someone by themselves for a moment, or at least in small groups if there were some potential respondents whom I couldn't seem to corner one-on-one. For the kids from The Barrio, I kept the focus on Ranch Ranch, since their living situation was not in flux, and asked how they would feel about coming over and spending their usual amount of time on our side of the wall should the proposed scenario come to pass.

The results were reassuring in the sense that everyone seemed to feel the same way I did, and unsettling for the same reason. No one was able to offer even a modicum of hope. The consensus of the kids from The Ranch side of the wall was that having their parents back, and all the parents for that matter, would be a lot worse than the last time the parents had been around during normal parenting hours, back when we all first moved in. They were there to monitor us, yes, and we were bored, true, but the parents were happy, as their euphoria over being home owners was still waxing. If they were to return home now, it would be in defeat, under duress, and their monitoring of us would be branded by frustration and lashing out rather than a newfound sense of duty and over-protectiveness. The dread expressed by so many when it came to their parents' state of mind actually provided the one reassuring result from my study: for all of my parents' charades, at least they had not sunk into the same level of despair that it seemed many of the others had. I may have been afraid of not being able to talk to them, but I was not afraid of them.

The Barrio kids, meanwhile, expressed little interest in spending time within the walls of The Ranch should our parents come back in full force. They had never been comfortable using the front gate; being put on camera and having someone track the frequency with which they came and went was not appealing from their perspective. And they couldn't imagine that hopping fences or burrowing through tunnels was going to be looked upon kindly from our parents' perspective. So it was going to be one-way access for the most part should the return come to pass.

Some of those I interviewed dovetailed into ideas on how to make it work, ways to acclimate to having a family again. They imagined that if we all played outside as much as we had been, maybe even more so, then perhaps the parents would be so impressed that we weren't hunkered down over computers or in front of the television that they would leave us alone. We could convince them through our actions that we had this under control, that we were not the disappointed, churlish souls who had accused them of dragging us here against our will. The place had nourished us, taken us back to one of those simpler times that so many older people seem to think is so great. None of us could pinpoint when exactly those times were, but we assumed it involved playing outdoors and making up games and being in perpetual motion until nightfall. We would probably have to ease up on the level of violence and degree of difficulty when we knew some of them were watching, but so be it. They would love us for it. We would show them that their decision was not a total failure. We could help them spend their remaining days at The Ranch in relative happiness without having to actually spend any time with them ourselves. Our circumstances could go on as long as possible and make theirs as satisfying as possible.

Their contingency plans had me feeling a bit better about what was left of our future, as once again, much like that morning, I found myself pondering on the outskirts while my friends darted around the asphalt playground in waiting for the bus to pick us up on its way back from High School Town. I may have looked more glum than I felt, as Miggy came over and asked me if I was okay.

"Fine," I responded in an upbeat tone that may have been overcompensating.

"So your parents' plan is to hold out, then, eh?" he said.

I looked at him as if to ask how he knew.

"I wasn't the only one you asked all those questions," he answered my expression.

"I was trying to be sly about it. Did everyone else notice, too?"

"I don't think so," he assured me. "So we can start high school together, then, yeah?"

"It makes it more likely," I appreciated the light he was shining on the situation.

"Cool," he said.

"And," I added, "I think I'll want to spend a lot of time over at your place, if you don't mind."

"Mi casa, su casa," he laughed.

"What, you can't use 'tu' with me?" I kidded. "I thought we were friends."

"We must be if you honestly feel like you don't want to move out of this place," he said, mixing in some seriousness.

"Tell me about it," I agreed. "I was too busy hating it when we first moved here to ever imagine I'd hate to leave."

"As if it's about the place," he said. "I mean, look at it." He disdainfully scanned the horizon. "Dude, seriously. Look at it."

I wasn't sure if he was fully crossing over into sincerity or not, so I split the difference with a low hum that could be interpreted as either a knowing laugh or commiserating sigh. He continued to look out into the distance as he pursued his point.

"And High School Town ain't much better."

I knew the situation now and remained quiet as he proceeded.

"The only chance I ever had at moving out was if our neighborhood got condemned. I used to wish for that to happen until I realized how hard it would be for my family to find another place to live."

He turned his attention to me. "Just keep in touch, man," he said. "That's all that matters. Whatever happens, just keep in touch."

"I will," I said, feeling both grateful and guilty.

We said nothing more until the bus arrived.

Miggy and I were the first to board, and as I reached the top step to turn down the aisle, my chest heaved and body froze before I could fully process what I was seeing: sitting amongst the scattered high school leftovers was Dulce. She didn't see me, though. She didn't see anyone, because she was staring at Chris, who stared back at her with matching adoration. They shared a seat and doted on each other, looking like an awkward vampire with the only victim he could manage to seduce.

Just to be safe, I found a place to sit way outside of her potential sight lines.

"Do you think she told her father why she didn't need a ride today?" Miggy said as he slid into the seat behind me.

"I'm sure he approves," I replied, continuing to look at them and hate myself for doing so. "He can't possibly think she could do any better."

Blaine sat next to Miggy. "What the fuck," he said in wonder as he stared at them along with us. "This is suddenly a very awesome bus ride."

We held our gaze until they stopped staring into one another's eyes and started slurping the insides of one another's mouths.

"And...we're done," said Blaine as Miggy and I muffled our screams. The three of us spent the last few minutes of the bus ride suppressing our laughter with tears spilling down our cheeks. As we pulled to a stop between our two worlds, it occurred to me that I hadn't yet surveyed Blaine about a parental invasion, and that doing so could be an effective way to bring up what I had wanted to ask him yesterday on our ride home from the lake.

I suggested we let the overheated couple get off first and I instinctively obscured my face as casually as possible when they passed us. Their attention remained on each other, however, and neither of them would have seen me had I waved and called their names.

Miggy was the first to say what I got the impression we were all thinking now that they weren't making out and we could just watch them walk down the aisle:

"Good for them."

"Maybe it'll mellow her out," I added.

"For now. Does Chris have a sign in front of his house?" Miggy asked.

"No," said Blaine, who then appeared to have some sort of revelation that aroused him to leap out of his seat and dash for the exit.

Miggy and I looked at each other and shrugged without actually moving our shoulders.

We disembarked and spotted the reason Blaine had bolted: he had caught up to Lana and was walking beside her, finally making his move.

"Time's running out," I commented on the proceedings.

"Huh," Miggy thought aloud. "I didn't think Blaine's house would be foreclosed. But I guess maybe it is."

"Looks that way." I stopped short of confirming that I knew it was, deciding to keep my nighttime reality checking to myself. I didn't believe Miggy would think any less of me for my voyeurism; quite the contrary, I suspected he may want to join me or ask me to report on future findings. So I kept private my invasion of others' privacy for purely selfish reasons (though I decided to classify my reasons as "logistical" rather than "selfish").

These thoughts of facades and the pursuit of romance against the clock had me longing for our unadulterated phase on The Ranch. I asked Miggy and then some of the other boys if they'd be up for a dirt bike rally out on the prairie behind my fence in about ten minutes, and most agreed it was a fine idea.

I considered walking along with Miggy and the rest of the Barrio boys down the alley and taking the tunnel or hopping my fence, but saw Blaine steering Lana toward the Arturo Gate, away from Dulce and Chris, so I decided to walk through the main entrance instead with my fellow Rancho Ranchers.

I brought up the rear as we approached the front gate. Carl, whose nickname "Nub" had caught on and become permanent since the electric fence incident the previous year, was the first one to arrive at the keypad. He punched in his house code and we all filed through before the gates had swung completely open. Nobody screamed into the camera anymore. We just shuffled past like factory workers heading in for a late shift. I was glad we were going to release some frustrations out on the savanna on our bikes in a few minutes. I was also glad that Nub had not developed a fear of electronic fencing and laughed quietly to myself at the thought.

I didn't bother going inside my house. I went through the side gate, grabbed my bike that was leaning against the door that led into the garage, dropped my backpack by the sliding door in back, and swung around several times with my bike in hand like an Olympic hammer thrower before letting it fly over the fence.

Someone yelled "Fuck!" on the other side. I sprinted to the fence and propped myself up on the top beam to see what happened. My bike was several feet away from Miggy and a couple of the Barrio boys, JD and Chuy. They had one bike between the three of them.

"You almost hit us, dude!" Miggy hollered.

"Why are you standing so close to the fence?" I half-laughed and half-hollered back. "You know the routine."

And as if on cue, another bike flew over the fence two lots down from us. Then another from a few lots up from us. In the distance behind the most recent bike landing, Nub came riding around the corner from the far end of the development.

"It's like one of those fountains in Las Vegas, man," said Miggy. "We should set it to music."

"Maybe some more of that Banda you like to dance to," I said as I joined them on the other side.

The other kids laughed. "You dance to Banda?" said JD. "What are you, man, like forty years old?"

"Dude," added Chuy, "it's like one of those movies where an old person and a young person switch bodies. So who are you really, your dad?"

"Your grandma?" I piled on.

"Your mom," Miggy shot back. The Ranch boys were just pulling up on their bikes and were able to howl at the mother reference without having any idea what we were talking about.

"If I knew my mother at all I'm sure that would really hurt," I said, guiding us out of the trash talk and into the rally. We stuck with the usual course: out over the embankment toward the train tracks, hitting the plywood ramp we had set up on this side of the tracks to jump them, and then on the way back after the turn jumping the tracks without the aid of a ramp, just pulling up on the bike as hard as possible, before riding back over the embankment towards our houses and making the turn for the next lap.

We modified the usual lineups, though, since the only other boy from The Barrio who owned a bike had failed to show up. Each race was a two-on-two, with one of the Barrio boys sitting out, and two of us from The Ranch sitting out, while one of us Ranchers who was sitting out would lend our bike to Team Barrio. Not that it was a team event; each heat was individual, but each individual tended to be influenced by their neighborhood. Barrio riders tended to be more aggressive, as though they had nothing to lose, but then got flustered easily when events weren't going their way. Ranch riders tended to be less daring, but able to roll with setbacks more unflappably, as though they could absorb the occasional loss. There were always exceptions to the stereotype in any given heat, of course, as was the case when Miggy and I found ourselves in front of the other two riders during the final lap of a heat in which we were competing.

He was on his bike and I was on mine, so we were both familiar with our equipment. We had conquered the previous laps flawlessly, distancing ourselves from Nub and JD by practically working as a team: one letting the other take the lead during the turns to prevent any bumping and consequent wipeouts, then fanning out side-by-side as we would take on the tracks and the embankment, shifting our body weight in unison over the dirt mound and getting air simultaneously over the tracks.

But as the boys on the sidelines yelled to remind us that it was the final lap, our teamwork ceased and the manners we had been minding evaporated in the dust that rose from under our tires and twisted in the wind. Our bikes started swinging more dramatically side-to-side beneath us as we pedaled upright. We drew closer together, our arms bumping each time our handlebars would thrust toward each other. Rather than let our bodies go slack and allow our bikes to glide over the embankment, we took it as a jump, barely giving us enough time to recover and hit the ramp in front of the tracks. We tangled briefly as we landed on the other side, managing to right ourselves in time to take the next turn, which we skidded through, each of us putting our left foot down to keep from falling as we came out of it looking momentarily as though we were riding scooters. I doubted we could gather the speed necessary to hop over the tracks on the way back, so I decided to try a double hop: one to get over the first rail, followed immediately by another one to get over the second rail. It actually worked, while Miggy tried the standard jump over both, but as I suspected, didn't have the speed to make it. His back tire caught the second rail and he wobbled enough to give me an opening. I picked up speed and figured I could make the conservative play and roll over the mound. As I reached the other side, I was stunned by Miggy landing next to me, having taken the offbeat tactic of jumping it, somehow managing to gain the necessary speed after his troubles on the train tracks. So once again we were in a dead heat heading to the final turn, the three boys cheering us on. I had the inside track and leaned into it first, but only by a split second.

I could feel the bike sliding out from under me, but knew if I braced myself with my foot it would be over, so I tried to hold on, but to no avail. I lost control and slid into Miggy, who managed to steady his bike after I swiped his back tire as I skimmed past. He yawped for joy as he rode between the two faux adobe shingles stuck vertically into the ground that served as the finish line, while I screamed in frustration and pain. I picked up myself and then picked up my bike, tossing it aside in disgust as JD and Nub passed me and were greeted by Miggy doing a celebration dance that looked a lot like the one he choreographed to the radio in his backyard. This one was shorter, though, and ended with him flipping me off. I tried not to laugh, but couldn't hold out any longer once he added a crotch grab in my direction. I flipped him off in kind and limped my bike to the finish line, flattered that the guys thought it was the best race they'd seen in a long time, and proud that I was injured.

I even thought I heard the wind whispering my name for a moment as I reached the hyped-up little crowd, but looked in the direction my friends were looking and saw my dad approaching. If not for the row of tract homes behind him and his dress casual work clothes, he could have looked like some mythic character in a Western, or Lawrence of Arabia.

"So that's your dad?" Miggy asked, never having seen him.

"That's him," I said, figuring that if he was home this early, at least part of my parents' plan was already set in motion.

"So that's what those two shingles are doing there," he said as he reached us. "Always wondered when I saw them from the upstairs window. I never get a chance to see what goes on here in the daytime with my usual hours."

He looked back at our house and I could see my mom looking out that same window. He looked back at us and greeted me. "Hey, Nick."

"Hey, Dad."

So they were both home. This was not looking good.

"Guys..." he addressed my friends, who mumbled a variety of vague replies.

"Now, I'm supposed to be scolding you right now," Dad continued. "So bear with me here for a moment while I wave my arms and look pissed off, and don't laugh or smile. Play along. Look serious."

The guys got a real kick out of that, and were only able to play the part by looking down and hiding their giggles rather than performing. I was perfectly capable of appearing stoic, however, since it wasn't an act. If Dad was this jovial, he and Mom must have gotten close to everything they wanted, if not all of it. I had parents again, at just the age and under just the circumstances kids tend not to want them.

In my peripheral vision I saw movement in our second story window, and looking to it saw that Mom had disappeared. In the midst of his pantomiming Dad turned and saw the empty window as well.

"Okay," he stopped gesturing and started talking again, "The coast is clear. Now, I see you guys are having trouble with the turns. Well, at least Nick and...?" he looked in Miggy's direction.

"Miggy," said Miggy.

"Miggy, right. Nice to meet you. At least Nick and Miggy are, and they look like pretty darn good bikers." He grinned at the two of us before continuing. "...So I assume everyone could use some tips on the turns. I don't know if Nick's told you, but I work in the insurance industry..."

"Why the fuck would I tell them that?" I thought, feeling myself transforming into a typically hostile adolescent, as though my chemical ingredients turned volatile when parents were added to the mix.

"...and so I investigate a lot of accidents, and one thing I can tell you that I'm sure you'll be taught in Driver's Ed class someday, but will come in handy in the meantime on your bikes, is to steer into the skid, rather than correct it. Can I borrow your bike for a moment, Nick?"

He held out his hand and I nodded. It took a few seconds for him to realize I wasn't going to bring it over. He jogged a few paces to get it, giving no indication he was irritated with me, and straddled the bike to demonstrate his point.

"So you're coming around a turn, and you feel yourself start to lose control..." He tilted the bike and started to jiggle it underneath him, feet still on the ground. "...Your first instinct will be to steer away from trouble rather than face it. It's a natural reaction. But that's not what you want to do..." He continued to push the bike in the direction he had used to simulate the skid. "See? It just makes it worse. The problem gets more severe. You feed into it. What you want to do..." He righted the bike and started to imitate a skid again. "...is go with it. Face the problem. See?" He guided the bike in the same direction as the fake skid. "Even though you won't be heading in the direction you want right away, at least you're going straight again, and can get back on track once you've regained that control. Thanks, Nick..."

He rolled the bike out from under himself and spun to face us, holding the right handlebar with his left hand, waiting for me to come take it. I just nodded again. He smirked and maintained his grip as he addressed us:

"I know you've all heard the expression 'go with your first instinct', yes?"

The rest of the boys grunted various forms of "yeah."

"Well this is one case where that is not at all true. But there is another expression you may have heard that is very true in this case. You've heard the one that goes, 'face your fears'?"

A few of them made agreeing noises.

"That's the one you want to keep in mind on those turns. If you don't face your fears, if you steer away from trouble rather than face it, those problems are only going to get worse. Clear?"

The guys didn't exactly hoorah their approval, but definitely seemed to appreciate the lesson. They nodded and smiled and the sounds they made indicated satisfaction. Then as if to usurp any remaining power I had to convince my friends what a phony he was, Dad encouraged them all to practice for a while and then come over to our house for a barbeque in an hour. He punctuated the invitation with "Just hop the fence!" and finally got the exultation from them he had so badly wanted during other parts of his speech. I felt like the fan of a visiting team in a stadium where the home team was enjoying a blowout victory.

Dad turned to me and smiled, though I have to admit he did not seem to be gloating. "Let's check that leg out," he said. "Mom's orders."

I slumped over and told the guys I would see them later. They barely acknowledged me as they haggled over who would be in the next heat, and as I turned to join Dad for the walk home, he cracked "As long as I've got your bike, I'll go ahead and walk it for you."

I looked over to see if he was at last recognizing my role as the antagonist in his production, or maybe even preening, but any leak in his bearing had been plugged by the time I started studying him more closely. He just looked at me a couple of times as though he was auditioning for a commercial in which he would play a father, and asked me if my leg hurt. I told him it didn't, naturally, but had difficulty getting over the fence, and allowed myself to wince as much as possible as Dad handed the bike over to me and my face was hidden from both his view and Mom's, who stood in the sliding glass doorway.

Mom offered to help, but I didn't want to take off my pants in front of her and said I'd take care of it. She insisted that I at least put on a pair of shorts and allow her to inspect the wound after I had addressed it.

I put on the shorts first before I went into the bathroom to sit on the edge of the tub and clean my leg, as I assumed it would not take her long to barge in on me. The area to the outside of my left shin initially looked pretty grisly with all the dirt, pebbles, and blood obscuring the thinness and superficiality of the cuts, so I was glad my mom did not succumb to motherly nosiness until I had completed the initial scrub.

"How is it, tough guy?" she asked, lurking in the doorway.

"About what I expected," I told her. "We've been taking care of ourselves out here for years."

My intent was to sound rugged, but realized it sounded accusatory to her, based on what I noticed about the musculature of her jaw and her eyebrows as she insisted on taking a closer look at my wound without asking. I tried to think of another way to put it without having to apologize, to explain that all I meant was we appreciated the chance to grow up so quickly, or become so self-sufficient, or free, or whatever it was we were, but I couldn't come up with a phrase that would placate her while allowing me to feel as though I did not give in, so I just let her inspect my leg and needlessly run a washcloth over it a few more times.

"Dry it off and come on down," she said as she wrung the water out of the washcloth into the empty tub. "Your father and I would like to talk to you about something."

I knew what it was, of course, and wasn't looking forward to having my fears confirmed. But on the other hand I was curious as to how honest they were going to be concerning their motivation.

When I arrived downstairs, Mom was in the kitchen organizing buns on a tray and chips in a basket, while Dad was out on the patio trying to remember how to operate the gas grill. They each greeted me as though I had just arrived, Mom with a trilling "Hello" and Dad with a big edgy smile and wave through the glass door and a signal that he would be inside in one minute, or one second; one something.

I sat on the loveseat opposite the couch, figuring they would want it that way: the couch serving as a roomy pulpit that would allow them to proclaim without having to stand, to gesture freely, and leave plenty of space for them to take turns leaning in and out at me.

Dad let out a satisfied whoop from the patio. He had managed to get the grill fired up, which Mom took as a cue to take their places on the couch, she arriving a few seconds before he did.

"We've decided to make some changes," Dad started, looking at Mom to see if that was an adequate introduction. She encouraged him to go on using only her forehead.

"At least for a while," he qualified. "See, it finally dawned on us that we've been spending way too much time away from home. The commute, our jobs...it's not that we wanted to, but that's just the way it happened. We're sorry."

"That's okay," I shrugged. "You're not the only ones. Don't worry about it."

"But we do," Mom took her turn. "Just because everyone else does something doesn't make it right. So we looked into getting some time off, giving ourselves more time to be together as a family. How does that sound?"

"Great," I tried to say as convincingly as possible, since it was clear they weren't going to attribute their inspiration to foreclosure, and I had some questions I wanted to ask that needed to be presented rationally rather than petulantly if they were to be effective.

"The way it's going to work," said Dad, as relieved as Mom was about my response, "is that we're taking half days like today until the end of the school year next week, and then full days off once you're on vacation. Cool, eh?"

"Very," I played along.

"But we can get the party started this weekend," Mom kicked in. "Since we won't be so tired thanks to the half days, we're thinking we'll head to the city and over to the coast on Saturday for the day, sort of a pre-graduation party, yeah?"

"Yeah," I kept it up.

"Yeah, baby!" said Dad, clapping his hands and non-verbally asking Mom for a high-five as they started to get up. "We're back!"

"I was just wondering," I cut into their celebration, "Why did you decide to do this now?"

"What do you mean?" Dad said, hanging onto his smile.

"I mean why now? Did something happen?" I asked as innocently as possible while they sunk back into the couch cushions. "Something at work? Did one of you almost die?"

Each hoped the other would think of something to say. Dad gave it a shot.

"Nothing like that," he stalled. "We just thought it was about time."

"The reason is because we miss you," Mom trumped his effort. "We miss you and we love you."

We stared at one another for several seconds. They could not run from the red letters much longer. It was going to be hammered into our front yard eventually. And when it was, that's when I would strike; the moment that sign hit the ground, I would hit them with everything I had wanted to say for the past few weeks.

"Well okay, then," I said. "Let's do this."

They bounced back up out of the couch and resumed their self-regard as though the last forty five seconds never happened.

I stayed seated for a while and watched them prepare for the barbeque, wondering if they were putting it on merely to be "cool parents", just as the high school leftovers had tried to be cool in the early days of our reintroduction to the wild, or if Mom and Dad had accurately assessed how accustomed to the parental void we had become and were trying to defuse the blowback created by their filling of that space. I decided that the most likely conclusion could be reached by underestimating them, and that they were just trying to present an enticing front. If they did understand the potential for animosity, that was a conversation of theirs on which I had yet to eavesdrop.

I left them to their preparations and went upstairs to look out of their window at the race course and catch the last few heats before my friends came over. The dust and the distance made it difficult to see who was doing what, but the intensity was perfectly clear; the soundless fury coming through the glass as they dedicated themselves to winning a race nobody else would ever see or read about, a result that would be forgotten even by us, the most important thing being that we were there, completely there, without a thought as to why we were doing it. Occasionally a certain maneuver, a jump or a bold pass on a turn, would have me exclaiming out loud, "We do that?" and laughing in disbelief at how stupid it looked through my parents' window, compared to how natural it felt in the midst of it.

This made me wonder how viable our emergency plan was, to show off our love of playing outdoors, if the seat I had now was going to be the typical perspective of the adults we would be trying to impress. Even when we played basketball it bordered on looking more like rugby at times. I could easily see us being relegated to tempered versions of our favorite games, our beloved outdoors becoming anodyne by decree, and all of us surrendering to our rooms and our computer screens, still being aggressive dicks to each other, but via poorly-spelled comments instead of a plastic whiffle ball bat to the head.

And even if we ended up being nice from one screen to another, I wondered how legitimate it would be, how honest; if it would be another flaw that did not discriminate by age. I couldn't imagine Blaine's parents ever sharing anything other than pictures of themselves enjoying the fruits of their ability to take out a loan, or my parents ever seeking comfort or help regarding their mistakes, because according to what they and every other parent presented, there are no mistakes, only pictures of food and of places and of their loved ones enjoying those things. I had found more truth in a few hours' worth of sneaking down hallways and into backyards than I had in years' worth of social networking in any of its forms, live or electronic.

The dust was settling out on the fallow plain as the last race was run and the guys were heading for our fence line, looking like an invasion by a small army of unarmed child soldiers. I hollered down to my parents that they were coming, then before going downstairs stopped by my room to put on some pants and cover my scrapes. I preferred not to draw attention to my loss, as gratifying as it was to sustain an injury in the pursuit of victory.

I arrived in time to see the boys storm the yard, dropping over the fence one at a time. As Dad turned from the grill to wave at them, I half expected one of the gang to jump him while the rest seized control of the house as if it was an embassy in a hostile country.

But what really happened was that my friends devoured hot dogs, chips, and sodas and gave no indication that the prospect of parents colonizing our territory had ever bothered them, like guard dogs distracted by an intruder throwing them some raw meat. It was weird hanging out with them in my house as opposed to the train platform, or the woods by the factory, or the construction site, or the streets; the closest any of us got to each other's living room while traveling in packs was the garage.

Combined with my parents orbiting the perimeter and guarding against any of us running out of something to drink or eat or looking even slightly less than thrilled, I started to feel less of the volatility that characterized my reaction to Dad interrupting our dirt bike rally, and more of the self-consciousness that had characterized my life before we moved to Ranch Ranch, back when I read books and graphic novels and surfed the web and the satellite channels, back when I was withdrawn and usually in my room. I had never really thought of it in those terms back then, had never considered why I may have felt like being alone so often.

So that was it, then? Self-consciousness? Being watched? Had I grown up enough to make those kinds of self-evaluations?

I tried to smile more often than I felt like smiling, as I didn't want my friends to think me unwelcoming or angry with them for being in our house, but I was so bad at manufacturing a smile that when I really did feel like smiling, I imagined it was coming across as insincere, that my performance wasn't what it should be according to everyone around me who could see me and judge me. My parents would gesture at me to "smile" whenever our eyes met, pointing at their own baring of teeth and tracing the shape of their lips in the air in front of them. I couldn't believe how quickly this was happening, how I could go from feeling the way I did when I was flying over the train tracks, to feeling like I did when I felt safest in my room.

I managed to secure a position in various circles of conversation often enough and imitate how others were reacting convincingly enough to keep any of my friends from asking what was wrong. Mom suggested all the boys call their parents and invite them over to pick them up and join the fun when they arrived home from work, that we would watch movies and keep the grill lit until the parents came, and that we had wine and beer ready to break out on their behalf.

The Ranch boys lined up at our kitchen phone to take turns leaving messages for their moms and dads. The Barrio boys hung back.

"You can invite your parents, too, you know," Mom assured them. "We don't mind."

"That's okay," Miggy adopted the role of spokesperson. "Walking through the gate feels kind of weird. And it would be stupid to drive such a short distance."

"They can jump the fence," said JD, which made us all laugh.

"Yeah, they should be pretty good at that," said Nub, which made us all nervous.

"Why don't you at least call and let them know where you are, and when you'll be coming home," Mom suggested. She then continued to stomp on the fuse Nub had lit by offering everyone another round of whatever it was they were currently lacking, and rattling off some names of movies we had in the living room collection.

After Miggy, JD, and Chuy left messages in the kind of rapid Spanish that always killed any dreams I had of becoming bilingual, we languished on the couch and watched a movie I could remember being very excited about seeing when it was released a few years before in a movie theatre, back when we lived near one, and was now just another title on our shelf filled with superhuman feats of computer-generated skill. I was not only tired like the rest of my friends, but relieved that I could just sit with them all and stare at what passed for a historical milestone in our young lives while our food digested and our bodies recovered. I assumed everyone's parents would also be too tired to do much when they came over, but that was hardly the case.

Evidently none of them had received an invitation to do anything other than sit for the last two years: sit at work, sit in their cars, and sit and take it as the bad news came at them. After all that sitting, the tug of free wine and beer had them speaking too loudly and laughing too readily before they had even finished their first few sips. Miggy, JD, and Chuy excused themselves soon after the parents started wading in.

"Tell your folks 'thanks'," said Miggy, not wishing to interrupt the burgeoning party.

"Take me with you," I joked.

"You need to chaperone," he smiled. "These people are ready to get crazy."

I chuckled, but none of the other guys seemed to hear it. They were buried in the couch and focused on the screen, intent on ignoring what was happening with their parents on the other side of the room. The Barrio trio slunk past the glass door and over the fence.

The movie was not quite over by the time the half-dozen parents on the guest list had made it into the kitchen and started infiltrating the living room area, which didn't matter because all of us had started rubbernecking what was happening to the grownups and ignoring the screen, anyway. I imagined the expressions on my friends' faces were much like mine when I was first privy to what my parents were planning as I held my ear to their door.

"This is really happening," Nub said in a bewildered whisper.

We watched them bob and weave around each other, embrace and form pairs and trios, talk directly into each other's ears and listen a little too intently to what the other was saying, looking more like they were deciding whether they would want to have sex with that person rather than actually listening to them, every one of them with a drink in their hand. They opened the door that led to the garage, then opened the garage door, and flagged down the other commuters arriving home from work, holding up their drinks and waving them over and yelling "Party!" and "Yeah!" and "Whoo!"

And many of the passers-by complied, rushing from their house to ours in a matter of minutes, some bringing half-cases of beer they had left in the refrigerator or bottles of wine that had been standing on their countertops, the number of cliques growing, their memberships turning over, everyone getting to know each other once again, commiserating without sadness, too interested in the thrill of saying "fuck it all" to worry about the future or mourn the passing of their dream. And this was on a Monday.

"Besides mine and yours," I asked Nub. "Do you know whose parents are whose?"

"Nope," he said, gazing at the scene that now surrounded us. Every once in a while some adult would look at us and raise their glass or bottle in our direction and shout something inane.

"So which ones are your parents, anyway?" I asked him.

"That guy over there is my dad," Nub directed my attention to an otherwise-trim guy sprouting a belly who was talking to a woman while running his fingers up and down the front of his polo shirt as though he was wearing a tank top and hitting on a girl during Spring Break at a beach bar.

"And that woman over there is my mom." She was sitting on the counter at the other end of the kitchen, holding court with my Dad and some other dad, making queenly gestures that indicated a running joke involving her being on a throne while they were subservient to her. The other dad seemed to appreciate the chance to flirt, while my Dad appeared to roll with it out of necessity while seeing it as a chance to impart some information, as though he was running for Congress.

"I think I remember them from when we were all moving in," I said, believing I had to say something.

Mom, meanwhile, was working the room making sure everyone was happy, or at least sublimating their pain, which was easy enough, but at the same time taking a moment with everyone she encountered to grasp their shoulder or their forearm and say something intended to be meaningful. At one point when she was close enough, I heard her direct the phrase "recapture the sense of community we had when we first moved in" to a particularly amped-up father before he gave her a soused hug and asked her how her marriage was doing. She politely replied that it was fine and suggested he needed to start drinking water.

None of the kids came over with their parents to join the party, and those of us bearing witness on the couch started to feel like we were intruding, so the guys excused themselves and went home without bothering to tell their parents, and I went up to my room.

Later that night I awoke to the sounds of my parents having sex so loudly I could hear them, which is something I had always managed to avoid hearing up until then.

At least I assumed it was my parents.

Chapter Nine

The bus stop was very quiet the next morning. I thought perhaps someone would recall the questions I had posed the previous day and ask "How did you know?" but they either attributed it to coincidence or had forgotten thanks to the previous night's tumult. The Ranch kids were dazed, and The Barrio kids confused as to why.

JD, who lived in one of the houses perched directly on the side of the road that our neighborhoods shared, broke the silence:

"I didn't see no headlights this morning coming from Ranch Ranch," he said. "So that party must have gone pretty big and pretty late, eh?"

Those of us from behind the wall exchanged looks, wondering for a moment if we were all thinking the same thing.

"My parents were still in bed when I left," said Shay.

And with that the testimonies started to flow.

"My dad was up, but he was hunched over the kitchen sink just staring into it."

"Mine told me they were calling in sick."

"Mine, too. They told me through their bedroom door when I knocked on it."

"I didn't even see mine. I just saw their cars in the garage."

"What time did yours get home?"

"I don't know. I was asleep. Never heard them."

"Mine woke me up. They came in laughing and talking too loud."

"Mine woke me up with all their screaming and yelling," said Nub.

"They were fighting?"

"Nope," he grinned, and everyone laughed.

Blaine laughed loudest of all as he stood by Lana, trying to encourage her to see sex from a lighthearted perspective. But of course with Blaine, haughtiness was always a possible motive. His parents had never associated much with the others even during the early days of the development, unless they were the ones throwing the party, and last night they had reaffirmed that tradition by staying away. So Blaine could have also been relishing the fact his parents managed to avoid embarrassing themselves, unlike the rest of us plebeians.

I, however, remained stoic, and not because Nub beat me to a joke that I could have just as easily made about my parents. Miggy noted my expression and approached me.

"What's so not funny?" he asked.

"It's happening," I said. "Already happening."

"It's just one day."

"It's just the first day," I snapped back. "They got them. Pulled them right in to see how fun it is to stay home. They're taking advantage of people's sadness."

"Oh, come on," Miggy waved me off. "You make them sound like criminals. What's in it for them?"

"Same as everyone else, but they get to take credit for getting it started. They get to be the coolest losers."

"Damn, man," Miggy chuckled. "You're tough. So they want to have a good time, go out in a blaze of glory, what's wrong with that?"

"Because they think they deserve it."

"Don't they?"

"They think that way about everything," I said, my voice rising. "If they want it, they deserve it."

He seemed to see my point, or at least how passionate I was about it.

The bus turned at the intersection by the tree line that shrouded the factory and made its way toward us.

"Well," Miggy said, feeling it necessary to put a conclusion on our conversation. "You can still hope it's just one day. You don't know for sure if the other parents are gonna play along."

He was right, and I could have waited over the next few days to see whether the remaining parents were falling in line. But I was now insatiably curious, and not just about their willingness to stay home and dance away their anguish, but how they were going to wrangle the time to do so.

I imagined they would all be plotting their time off throughout the day and coming to some decisions by nightfall. I wondered how much information I could garner by visiting multiple homes for some reality checking, as I suspected they would all claim they were simply taking time off, but that many would actually be quitting their jobs or conjuring up an injury or illness.

Throughout the school day, I concocted my route and schedule. I thought initially I would have to limit my gathering to the houses with fences in back, but as I considered the homes lining the wall, I realized each of them had at least one empty unit next to it, which would provide me with access. The reliance not just on stealth but on coincidence also infused some doubt into my planning, but I convinced myself that even if I didn't happen upon a conversation at just the right time, I could collect clues about their finagling from what was being said in the course of the scene I did happen to view. With that in mind, I estimated I could obtain a decent amount of knowledge by merely spending fifteen minutes at each house. Some would be a wash, just people staring at a television or performing some chore, but with four houses per hour over a couple of nights, I could compile a solid sample size that would give me a legitimate sense of what was driving the reappearance at The Ranch.

I would tell my parents I was visiting Miggy, knowing that they would never call his house for fear of speaking Spanish, and would return just before the hour became unreasonable, with the excuse in hand that "it's a school night" carried no heft since we weren't doing anything during the last week of school, anyway.

I enjoyed my expanded reality checking even more than I had imagined I would. The two-day quest for truth was an exhilarating mix of reconnaissance and enlightenment, and had me thinking that the return of the adults may not be so bad after all. Now there was something to see through the glass other than spent, mute people too tired to ponder or debate their choices. They were still sad and frustrated, but they were chatty about their condition, ready to plot against it by any means possible.

I heard people calling doctors and insurance providers while I crouched in the abandoned yards next door, close enough to their bedroom windows to also catch sight of them squinting and pacing with guilt as they tried to stick to the script composed in their heads. I watched them through the small windows above their kitchen sinks as they sat around countertops with pads of paper and calculators and estimated how much vacation or sick leave they had banked. At times I didn't even have to scale a fence to know what was happening; I could hear the arguments clearly enough from outside the property lines, listen to them fight over quitting their jobs, sometimes one wanting to quit while the other thought it unwise, sometimes both wanting to quit and each making the case why the other should be the one to stay employed, sometimes both agreeing that they would join the send-off and by what method, but disagreeing on their next move: where they would live, what they would do, how they would start over, which credit cards they would keep, which they would cut up, if there was any way they could avoid paying their debts, any way to keep their name away from the impending bankruptcy, and what stories they would tell others in the future, what the re-write of their history would be.

And though occasionally I missed picking up on how they were going to find the time to spend in the home they were going to lose, I would instead creep up on their plans to contribute to the festivities. They tabulated how much they had to offer, if they could pitch in a barbeque, a DJ, a band, a bounce house for the kids and one for the adults, how much it would cost to fill a rubber wading pool with cheap vodka on ice, how much effort it would require to turn a patch of the land beyond the fences into something resembling a softball field for a parents vs. children series.

None of the other children knew about these plans. I never saw any of them in the same room as the parents as they looked ahead to what the summer would look like, and what the fall would bring. We were left out of the exit strategy just as we had been left out of the plans for our entrance. And once again the parents had the best intentions. They were trying to "recapture the sense of community we had in the beginning." I knew this was their rationale because I heard that same line coming from about every house I checked. And by the fourth house on the first night I remembered it was the line that Mom had propagated at the party, and that Dad must have done his fair share of disseminating it as well.

Just as the other parents were imitating my parents' words, most had to imitate their actions, too, in terms of procuring the time off. Only a handful were able to start their vacation immediately, specifically the ones who quit their jobs, while the rest needed a few days to lay the foundation for what was to come. But even their scant presence marked a dramatic change in the atmosphere at Ranch Ranch. Some of us tried to play on the construction site, but there were a couple of men drinking beer in a garage near enough to see us, so we couldn't raid the materials or throw any of them off the second floor or smack any of them against the wood frame. We headed for the lame little promotional playground with our bikes and skateboards, but there was a woman across the street puttering back and forth between her garage and her front yard, pulling weeds and trimming bushes, occasionally pausing to size up her house as though getting to know it again, or taking one last look, so we couldn't have our way with that structure, either. We rode around the neighborhood looking for a place that was not under any coincidental surveillance, but found none. Every block had a garage door open, with a waving parent inside it. Blaine's parents were home, and Blaine wasn't with us, so we had no access to the tunnel. When we headed for the gate, a voice from a nearby garage asked us where we were going, and we were so unaccustomed to answering that question that we froze and changed course. We went to Nub's house because his parents were still working until the end of the week, so we used their backyard fence for access to the open range. But a few minutes into our ride a grown-up head peered over a fence and asked us what we were doing. We ignored it but then another head popped up a minute later and also asked us what we were doing. We stopped and looked at each other, once again unable to find an answer. All we found was self-consciousness. The Children's Dynasty was over.

I retired to my room so as not to overstay my welcome at Miggy's house, and finally started to read *Lord of the Flies*, which I was supposed to read in school earlier that year, but had skimmed and faked my way through an essay that received an "A". Mom tapped on my door and came in to invite me to dinner, claiming to have read somewhere that families who sit down to eat dinner together produce more successful children. I accepted; not to insure my future, but because I was still determined to combat becoming a cliché of a surly pre-teen, to challenge biology and circumstances and become something surprising rather than typical. I wanted my words to hold sway once the red and white sign signaled my chance to spill them, so that Mom and Dad could not dismiss them as the ranting of an angry boy.

Not that I could actually resist those feelings. They were a given. My charge was to see how civilized a veneer I could construct, which I supposed was a valuable skill to possess in the adult world that I couldn't reach soon enough. So we sat together at the table off to the side of the kitchen and ate macaroni and cheese and cauliflower, and Mom said "Isn't this nice?"

Dad and I agreed, and she shared with us more specifics on the dinner table study: how it was conducted and how success was defined and how time together affected personal well-being.

"Is it that simple?" I asked.

"What do you mean?" Dad said, sounding prepared to defend Mom rather than listen to my point. I saw this as a chance to practice my restraint and continued.

"Does just sitting at a dinner table make all those things happen? Or do certain people sit at dinner tables?"

Following through on his implied posture, Dad remarked, "Are you saying we're not those kinds of people?"

"No. I'm just asking questions."

"And they're good ones," Mom chimed in.

"You think so?" Dad confirmed with her.

I realized that I could thrust my chin in his direction all I wanted, but when it came to Mom, he was going to be very protective.

"Yes," she assured him before addressing me. "And I would say even if we weren't, the act of sitting together would help us become those kinds of people."

"But only if we weren't," Dad grinned. "And that's a big 'if'."

I had found a weak spot in him and understood that winning the battle against my age depended on my ability to resist pounding that spot, but my understanding was losing the battle with my impulses.

"If we really were those kinds of people," I teed up my insult before swinging through it, "would we get so touchy about it so quickly?"

The satisfaction I felt was brief, as though my swing had produced a beautiful, soaring shot that seconds later splashed into a water hazard. They looked at each other to help themselves stay calm.

"Look," Mom said. "I know you're in that in-between stage now, and that's a difficult time. But could you at least try to be nice?"

"That's my plan," I pleaded, which was certainly true, but hard for them to believe.

"Implement it," Dad said, and we spent the rest of our time at the table eating and asking questions that could be answered with one word.

I heard them later on debate whether they still wanted to take me on that trip to the coast that weekend or if they would be better off taking it on their own, maybe get a hotel room for a night and make it something special rather than strenuous.

"It's not going to take away the strain," Mom offered. "It will still be here when we get back, and may be even worse."

"You really think he'd resent not coming?" Dad asked, but wasn't really asking. "He'd be relieved."

Which I agreed with at first. But then, much to my surprise, the possibility of being disinvited by my parents started to hurt, in a much different way from the kind of hurting I was used to. The ache of not being able to attract the girl you wanted, the pain of not being as good at a game as you thought you were, the separation from your old home and from things you liked to do...all of these hurt, but when I thought about those things, they were kind of supposed to happen. This, on the other hand, was not supposed to happen.

"I could see leaving him behind so I won't have to watch him eat," Mom said. "It's like watching a dog that climbed up onto the table."

Dad laughed. "You'd think he hadn't eaten for days. Did you hear him breathing while he was biting and chewing?"

"It was like an obscene phone caller trying to eat and do his thing at the same time."

Now they were both laughing. Dad then changed the tone.

"And would it kill him to offer to help?" he said. "He just left everything for us to clean. And he didn't thank you for making dinner."

"Or ask to be excused," Mom added.

I felt like bursting through the door and shouting "Excuse me, but I'm a little out of practice from eating by myself or with other kids all the time!"

But instead I retreated in the exaggerated tiptoe that always marked my in-home eavesdropping. And rather than back to my room, I went downstairs, quietly opened the door into the garage, then sat in Dad's car with the windows rolled up.

I didn't want them to hear me cry.

If they did, then they would know I was listening in on them.

Chapter Ten

I'll never know why they ultimately decided to stick with their plan to take me along. I suspected it was simply because they had already told me it was a graduation present, and turning it into something just for them would be pretty selfish even by their standards. That night in Dad's car I had vowed to keep my parents out of my reality checking, and focus on the other adults. I was still interested in the truth, but not about myself.

Admittedly, it was helpful to know how I could improve my act. I already knew what I faced in terms of attitude, so that was nothing new, but in light of the challenge my emotions presented and how beyond my control they seemed at times, the insight into the deeds I could be performing to enhance my manners came in very handy. If I could not corral the instincts to spite either of them in conversation, then I could at least fetch them a drink refill; if I could not keep my eyes from rolling, I could clear the table. Suddenly these tasks that would have most kids moping about fairness and a lost childhood revealed their value; not in building life skills, but in rerouting all the psychological snot that was so hard to expel into tangible diversions. I may not be as nice as I wished, but I would be helpful. "There's good in him," they would say. "I can see it in the way he holds the door open for us."

None of which made the drive to the coast any less interminable. Much of the slowing of time was due to Mom's incessant narration, as though she was taking video of the proceedings with a hand-held camera and voicing what we were all seeing, and how we should feel about it. Dad meanwhile remained relatively quiet most of the day. While we were driving I assumed it had to do with concentrating on the road, or sharing my silent prayer that Mom's play-by-play would cease. Though I could not help but wonder if he was wishing that it was just the two of them on their way to a romantic weekend, and that I was getting in his way of being able to agree with Mom's assessments on how beautiful and fun everything was.

The coast was indeed beautiful. Saying it a thousand times would not diminish the fact. The shoreline district was filled with plenty of tacky pomp, but it was cleverly disguised in most cases and made for an agreeable lookout onto the ocean, which I hadn't seen in years and found very humbling. The day ended up even being kind of fun in its own odd, lengthy way. I could tell when we finally arrived and he was out from behind the wheel of the car that Dad was not irritated by my presence. He was neither upset nor content, having cast aside strong feelings for deep thought. He would look at the ocean as though asking it questions, and study fellow families of tourists walking by as though evaluating them for pointers on how to be a happier bunch. I found myself relating to his pensiveness, wondering what it would be like to come to a place like this someday with a girl, on our own, in love; I imagined being there with Lana, only she was able to speak; I then imagined Shay, only she looked more like a whitish version of Lana; I imagined being with Lourdes when we were older, both in our twenties, our respective ages no longer an issue. I thought of the things we would say to one another as we leaned over the wharf and looked at the tide swirling below us, the funny things and interesting things as our voices competed with the sound of the gulls and the sea lions, the flirty things that would lead to us kissing, and I wondered what those kisses would feel like.

The hush from the two males in her life only increased the intensity of Mom's verbal chronicling of our day, which made it more funny than grating. I practiced my newfound leveraging of attitude with actions by suggesting we get an early dinner, and then jumped at every chance to act on wrappers, cups, trash cans, and doors.

My foray into etiquette went over well. We spoke pleasantly, and when I felt the urge to peck at them, I grabbed some used paper napkins to throw away or took a trip to the condiments station and asked if anyone needed anything while I was up. They were impressed enough to let me in on the fact that along with some of the other parents, they were planning a surprise for after our eighth grade graduation ceremony that week. They wouldn't tell me what it was, claiming light-heartedly that they didn't trust me with a secret, but were clearly proud of finally being involved in something related to school, even if it was on the last day. The references to keeping secrets made me laugh, loudly enough for Dad to ask, "What, you think you're good at keeping them?"

I took a deep breath then shook my cup, rattling the ice inside. "Anyone need a refill?"

Chapter Eleven

I wasn't even sure what we were graduating from: Eighth grade? Middle school? Elementary school? So I would have been ambivalent when it came to the ceremony, anyway. But with the foreclosure signs staked out around our neighborhood, with the distance between The Ranch and The Barrio seeming to lengthen with each parent that re-emerged, and with the guarantee of everyone having to flee within the next few months, our commencement turned out to be a sad little affair, even more sad than most people would assume about any attempt to celebrate inside a building that looked like our school.

As we sat in a row behind our teachers while they made up nice things to say about us, I glanced around at the faces of my classmates and saw their eyes either wide open rimmed with tears that occasionally broke free to run down a cheek, or their eyes being pressed down upon by their furrowed brows. A few just stared, such as Blaine, and none were content.

Most of the parents in attendance were those starting to re-populate The Ranch, and they either misinterpreted our expressions, thinking us overcome with happiness, or they characteristically ignored what was happening right in front of them. They beamed and gave us condescending pouty faces that were intended to be compassionate, accompanied by "aww" sounds. It served to me as something of a clue that while they could no longer pretend to afford a home, they were now pretending they could comfort a family. But what they were most interested in doing was comforting themselves.

For example, the big surprise they had planned for us was a banquet at the truck stop down the road by the freeway ramp. This would have been a paternal enough action, as it was the only restaurant space available to rent in light of everything else being a fast food franchise, but lining the rear of the buffet table were cases' worth of wine and beer, which I assumed were cheap. They drank immediately and heavily, despite the fact it was barely noon when the graduation had ended and we had taken the forty-five second drive from one cinder block bunker with the playground equipment in front of it to the other cinder block bunker with the diesel pumps and weigh station in front of it. After everyone had rummaged through the line of potato salads, cold pasta salads, and jello salads, the room gradually became partitioned with parents imbibing on one side, and children studying them on the other. We laughed at them at first, their slurred toasts to the future and teary paeans to their sons and daughters, which tended to include the phrase "I may not have always been there" (as opposed to the more apt "I may have never been there"), and which served more as confessions for them than tributes to us (though each tapping of a glass with a butter knife did help us connect yet another parent to their corresponding child). By mid-afternoon, however, we started to fret over them; not because we were concerned about getting home safely, as the road to The Ranch was wide open and sparsely traveled, but because we started to ponder the larger navigational problem we faced: who was steering our lives.

Some fathers were drifting through the vinyl curtain that hung from a track nailed to the ceiling that divided the rental space from the daily use area and inviting truckers to come and join them. Mothers posed for pictures with the drivers who did venture over, grabbing the hats off the truckers' heads and making funny faces and the horn-honking hand gesture while hugging them; some drivers took advantage of the situation to cop a feel while posing for the pictures, which induced braying laughter from all.

Some of the kids from The Barrio whose parents couldn't attend the graduation were there, and they would occasionally tear their gaze away from the spectacle in front of them and look at one of us, and that person would shrug.

"I wish I had gone home with Miggy's or Chuy's parents," Shay said to me at one point, and before I could answer, three other classmates said, "Me, too."

"Maybe we could give one of them a call," I offered. "Anyone have a phone?"

Nobody did, so we exhaled back into our chairs and looked into our glasses, at the ice melting into our flattened sodas.

"Let's just get out of here," Shay said. "I still know some of the ladies my Mom worked with over at the franchise. Let's walk there and tell them we're worried about being driven home by a bunch of drunks and maybe they'll take us home after their shift. Even if we have to wait a bunch of hours, we won't have to watch anymore of this crap."

Those of us sharing a table with Shay agreed that was a good idea, and we asked the others in the children's viewing area if they would like to join us in abandoning our view of the adults' staging area. The movement grew, and each of us with parents approached them and told them we were heading out under the overpass.

"You are?" Mom said, her physical teetering now paired with confusion.

"But we did this for you," Dad gestured around the room as though presenting me with a kingdom I would someday inherit. "For all of you. We all pitched in."

"I know," I said as agreeably as I could muster. "And it's great. But it's just getting a little long."

Mom and Dad looked at each other for a moment. "Well..." Dad started, seemingly testing out an idea telepathically with his wife before verbalizing it. "We'd like to stay a little longer. Do you need some money? We'll swing by and pick you up."

Mom gave no indication that she disagreed with his plan. "Sure," I said. "Some money would be good."

They seemed to like the idea even more now that I accepted their terms. Dad pulled out his wallet and handed me a ten dollar bill. "Buy a few rounds for your friends," he joked, and they grabbed one another and spun around a few times back toward the buffet table.

"See you in a little bit," Mom said, trying to regain her equilibrium while fending off being goosed by Dad.

I nodded and joined the procession gathering at the door.

Not all of us made it. A few parents took our action as a hint and decided it was time to go home. But most of our guardians stayed at the party. We trudged along the desolate road in our graduation outfits, more dressed up than we had ever seen each other as we marched dolefully underneath the freeway. Occasionally a car carrying some of the parents who left would pass by, and they would honk their horn and wave hysterically while their son or daughter sat in back and wished they wouldn't.

After we emerged from the other side of the overpass, the last car passed by, horn honking as usual, only this time instead of waving hands, a mom's bare ass was pressed against the backseat window. We weren't sure whose mom it was, as our classmate had buried himself or herself out of sight, presumably in the fetal position, and we were too fixated on the flattened cheeks to notice the driving dad. We also weren't sure how to react. We paused for several moments, a few snickered, a few simulated vomiting sounds, and then we pressed on, slowly storming the fast food restaurant and eliciting the same befuddled stares from the well-spaced patrons that we must have worn on our faces upon seeing our friend's mom's butt crack.

Shay found a familiar face behind the counter and explained the situation. That lady then translated for the rest of the employees behind the line operating the fryers and grills, and a disbelieving series of yelps filled the service area. We were treated to free drinks and a couple orders of large fries to share, then we filled a corner of the dining area and began to speculate on whose mom it was. The consensus deemed Nub's mom as the most likely candidate.

Within an hour some of the parents started to pick us up from our exodus. The stray Barrio kids asked for rides and were sporadically granted them. The ladies behind the registers and behind the line glared at each arrival, pitching especially dirty looks and even some verbal abuse at Shay's mom, since they were no longer co-workers and could jettison decorum and unbridle their feelings about having had to work with her, their disgust regarding today's action providing an excuse to vent.

Shay enjoyed the razzing, while her Mom was belligerent about it. She launched into a sloppy "fuck you bitches" routine characteristic of drunk girls at dances and parties.

"Don't worry, Mom," Shay assured her while guiding her toward the exit. "You won't remember any of this tomorrow. Let's not keep Dad waiting."

Shay flashed me an eye-roll after forcing her Mom through the door and said, "So much for the bare-assed mom being the most embarrassing."

I laughed. "It's going to be a long summer."

She switched to seriousness, and asked that I never tell anyone about this, as I was the last member of our wandering tribe left in our convenient portion of the desert.

"I wouldn't dream of it," I said.

"I love you," she blurted out, then took a few breaths to convince herself it was okay that she said it.

Meanwhile, I convinced myself that it was a friendly version of love, and said "I love you too."

Her Mom was pacing back and forth outside the front window, her curses and epithets muffled by the glass, looking like a furious talking fish in an aquarium. Shay looked very grateful that I had returned her declaration before she went outside to corral her mother into the car, where apparently her dad sat and waited.

It took another hour and a complimentary burger for my parents to finally arrive.

"We met the most interesting trucker," Mom said.

"This guy could have a PhD if he had grown up in a different environment," Dad added.

"Plus we helped clean up a little," Mom piled on.

I felt like a parent whose kids had broken their curfew.

"Can we just go home?"

"Sure", "Yeah" they said more or less in unison.

The employees stuck with visual darts as we left and withheld any verbal ones, allowing Mom and Dad to remain oblivious to any of it. I nodded in the direction of the front counter and thanked them en masse for everything as I walked behind my soused parents.

"You're welcome," Mom said. I briefly considered explaining that I was thanking everyone else in the restaurant other than her, but didn't want to expend the energy.

We drove home towards a setting sun and Dad managed to keep the car remarkably straight considering his condition. Nonetheless I was relieved that no other cars approached from the opposite direction. They joked about forgetting the code to the gate, and then as it swung open, Dad drove through too soon, the edge of the left gate swiping the driver's side of the car with a metallic screech, leaving the gate to bounce and quiver and my parents to laugh and rejoice that the damage wasn't any worse.

"Especially the gate," Dad said, wiping tears of laughter from his face. "How would we keep out the Mexicans?"

They both started laughing even harder. "Oh, God," Mom found the breath to gasp. "If the Mexicans ever get in, then we're really screwed."

Dad had to stop the car and compose himself before driving on. Just when their laughter was fading and he seemed ready to continue, Mom shrieked, "Eek! The Mexicans!" and they started laughing all over again.

We finally got the car moving. They were still giggling but Dad was able to maneuver the turns well enough. When we turned onto our street they fell silent. Their abrupt shift caught my attention. Were Blaine's parents throwing a party of their own that we weren't invited to? They had all disappeared after the ceremony, with Lana in tow. I leaned over to look between them through the windshield and didn't see it at first since I was focused on a few doors down from our house, but then it jumped out at me from our front lawn:

The sign with red letters hanging from a white cross had arrived. We were official. Our territory had been marked.

I leaned back and fought feeling too smug so that I could think of just the right thing to say. My satisfaction was so great that I found it difficult to decide which scathing one-liner was best to lead with, which self-righteous speech was best to fill the middle, and which devastating tag line would ring in their ears for the rest of their lives. I had practiced them all before, but now realized I had too much material and needed to whittle it down. Then again, if I had them sufficiently paralyzed with my opening remarks, I could very well let it all out, every bit of it: from their stupid decision, to their denial of it, to their covering of it; from leaving us on our own, to allowing us to grow attached to it, to taking it away; from being there, to being absent, to being there but absent.

They pulled the car into the driveway but didn't get out. We sat there and I decided it would work best to make the first move before they could say anything. I got out and strutted toward the sign, imagining that my diatribe would be enhanced by standing in front of it for dramatic effect. I could even use it as a prop when inspiration dictated.

I heard their car doors slam as I took my place in front of the cross and pivoted, ready to breathe fire. But what I saw froze me and wiped all rehearsed vitriol from my mind.

They looked as though the only thing they had left in the world was their vulnerability. They reminded me of cartoon field mice in a children's picture book, the daddy mouse wearing a felt vest held together with a big safety pin from the human world, the mommy mouse wearing a babushka made from the corner of a checkered tablecloth they had nibbled off together. Their eyes were sadder than any of my classmates' had been during graduation. I could no more verbally whip them as I could club a couple of baby seals to death.

We stared at one another a short while before Mom fell to the grass crying. Dad quietly said "We're sorry" to me and kneeled down to comfort his wife. I stood still for some time, unsure which way to go, and finally decided to walk over and join them on the ground. Dad started sobbing as soon as I touched him.

I managed to stave off any tears of my own. I was too stunned by what was happening to feel much about it.

Chapter Twelve

Mom and Dad were somewhat manic in their attempts to be nice to me after the incident at the sign. It was as if they wanted my vote. They pandered so thoroughly that they had a hard time noticing when their attempts at not offending became offensive. Mom's favorite term she used to describe me over the summer was that I was going through an "in-between stage". And as much as it drove me nuts to hear that phrase repeated with such frequency, I realized she was right. I was hovering between childhood and adulthood, destined to bypass being a teenager whenever one stage gave way to the other.

But the stages I was caught between were specific. The adults at Ranch Ranch weren't sure what they were caught between, and their attempts to escape from what flanked them illustrated their confusion.

Just like my parents, all of the parents tried too hard. They would start a game of two-on-two basketball in a driveway, or a video game tournament in a living room, or badminton in a backyard, or lawn darts, or ring toss, or just about anything that was supposed to be a fun distraction leading up to a barbeque later on, and the game would turn into a measure of self-worth. The kids would slowly bow out and leave it to the adults as their passion became ferocious. Nobody would throw a punch, but the ball would be slammed against the garage door, the clever trash talk would devolve into a hollering of Fuck Yous, and wives would herd husbands into corners and soothe them and assure them it was just a game, that they loved them no matter what happened. Then later at the barbeque after a couple of beers the husbands would embrace and slap each other on the back so that the hug would not be too intimate, and say that they were in this together, that they had each other's backs, that they loved each other, but the word "love" didn't seem to mean anything, it was just something to say.

At night the desperation was more naked. The horror of first stumbling upon a couple of parents having sex had long since sunk any fantasies I entertained about sexual voyeurism as part of my reality checking. But as the block parties and the feelings they were trying to mask started to intensify, catching some of the adults in compromising positions became even more disturbing for reasons beyond their deflated bodies; so much so that I actually found myself lingering by those windows in spite of my repulsion, unable to look away. I learned just how much sex depended upon feelings. The emotions they relied on to propel them through the act were so unmoored and damaged that they could not function sexually for very long, and their attempts would end badly.

Some men would start to weep as their penises would remain limp in their wives' hands or mouths, the slightest twinge of an erection merely reminding them of what used to be, what could have been. Others who managed to get hard would become too aggressive and their wives would have to ask them to stop, softly at first, politely, but eventually in a raised voice and a single command: Stop!

Some women seemed to be trying to convince themselves that their husbands were still worth the effort. Even those moments when they were obviously enjoying it were soon followed by a vacant expression unbeknownst to their husbands, as though something rudely reminded the women of better times, of an era when sex and alcohol enhanced their appreciation of life rather than offered an escape from it. They would then force themselves back into the moment, but may as well have been masturbating. I would wonder if the husband didn't notice or didn't care that their wife had clearly decided "Well, at least this loser still has a dick." Perhaps it's harder to notice such things when you're in the moment rather than observing it.

Nonetheless, this was the thought that would motivate me to stop peeking and move on: the threat of being so immune to your partner's feelings unless it inhibited your ability to have an orgasm. As I crept to the next backyard and the next grid of lighted windows after one of those disheartening sex scenes, I would brood over whether my reality checking was going to turn me off to sex, that maybe I was going to become phobic about intimacy. But then I would assure myself that I had seen plenty of accident sites by the side of the road and still wanted to learn how to drive, just as I still fantasized about Lourdes and Lana and even Blaine's sister on occasion in spite of seeing such depressing displays of sex through the portholes of our sinking neighborhood.

Many of the parents tried to make up for however emasculated or abandoned they felt in their relationships by formulating grand plans for their economic recovery. If they were going to cry and disassociate in the bedroom, well then by God they were going to make amends in what was destined, in their minds, to become the home office.

Some of the plans were laid in groups, some individually, depending on whether they needed to recruit neighbors and friends, and depending on the plot's degree of shadiness. So the insurance scams remained between husband and wife, hunkered over their office desk or in the corner of the kitchen close enough to the window so I could hear their concentrated whispers; and as far as I know, none of them ever followed through on a scam, since no homes burned down, and nobody took in a group of unrelated elderly people or orphaned children.

The sales pitches, on the other hand, started with individual couples, who would then strategize on how they could turn their home into a platform, their neighbors into customers, and our development into a market, with the neighbors-turned-customers either unaware of what was being done to them, or embracing it thanks to the brilliance of the pitch or value of the product. The various couples would role play, practicing how to guide a conversation toward a plug for the product or an invitation to a sales meeting.

"That was a great game the other night, wasn't it?"

"Sure was."

"I think if they can avoid any major injuries, they could go all the way."

"I hope so."

"Me, too. Want another beer?"

"No. I'm good."

"All right. Hey...how happy are you with your current line of household products?"

Then they would imagine out loud how they would spend the money, keeping their aspirations reasonable, as if lowering their expectations made success any more possible.

"Wow. That sunset sure is relaxing."

"Sure is."

"Do you often find yourself feeling pretty tense?"

"I don't know. Maybe."

"Are you interested in a stress reliever you can use when you can't see the sunset?"

They would pay cash for a modest house, invest in municipal bonds, buy conservative stocks that held their value and paid a dividend.

"I was thinking of not going back to my job once this vacation is over."

"Really?"

"Absolutely."

"Got something lined up?"

"How does five thousand dollars a month working from home sound?"

Only when they applied their rehearsals to an actual conversation, as with everything else in their adult life recently, it did not go as planned. The farthest they could push anyone was to a promotional party in their living room. These presentations were held at night, at a house where the kids were sleeping over at someone else's house, as though the ceremony had to be hidden from the children, like some primal hazing ritual or tribal initiation. What it most resembled, however, was a séance; because in terms of finances and morale, they were talking to the dead.

Some of the people being pitched had given essentially the same presentation in their own living room days earlier. Sandwich boards featuring diagrams of pyramids with ascending dollar amounts working their way to the top would be held up by the wife; bar graphs charting future growth would be hoisted by the husband; the signs in hand would mount to a degree that made the presenters look like someone standing on a street corner advertising a new tire store down the street, or that they were on strike, protesting unfair treatment. Only the products differed, which is perhaps why each thought their version would be more convincing than yesterday's. They touted kitchen knives, pots and pans, algae from a lake in Southern Oregon that had medicinal qualities and was now being domesticated in a cement reservoir in Southern California, earthworms that had been genetically modified with the ability to burrow into harder soil and withstand higher temperatures, hand-held computers, software applications, water softeners, even real estate.

Real estate.

And when the circular firing squad of network marketers had all shot each other, a new kind of meeting dominated the ground floors of Ranch Ranch after dark.

"You're upset that you've lost your house. We've all lost our homes. We're all upset. I know I am. Or at least I was. Then I realized it was never my house. It was God's house. It was always God's house."

Everything else would be God's, too.

Even before we ended up a hundred miles from the nearest church, we had never gone much; just a couple of times, and it was out of state, at my grandmother's church: once to see her sing in the choir, and then one more time to attend her funeral. I had also failed in several attempts to read a Bible that a very sweet lady had given me one afternoon as I sat in the fast food restaurant waiting for Shay to return from the back of the restaurant where she was needed in the manager's office to verify her mom's excuse for missing work the day before. I must have looked especially forlorn sitting in that booth by myself in what had to be the least lucrative franchise in the chain. The lady said if I needed companionship, I could open The Book and find it. I thanked her and was genuinely intent on reading it, but for a different reason: I wanted to be familiar with the stories that inspired so much great literature. But all of my efforts only solidified my love of the re-writes.

So all of this was new to me. Giving everything up to God, including the decision to take out a mortgage, at first struck me as directing blame rather than accepting responsibility, but I could certainly understand and relate to how comforting that is. It was always our first reaction when any of us kids got in trouble. And unlike the sales pitches, I wished I could participate. I often felt like tapping on the window to ask a question or for clarification on a point.

The props were also more interesting. Rather than items bought from an office supply store, they appeared to have been bought from a feed store: seeds, small shrubs, pruning scissors, a trowel, landscaping rocks, a watering can, wooden lattice, and tomato stakes; the seeds and small shrubs playing the role of the soul, the pruning scissors and trowel in place to demonstrate the slings and arrows of life on a dangerous planet, the rocks and water playing God and the things God does, the lattice and tomato stakes illustrating a world bound by God's love. Seeing all of the hardware reminded me of the accounts I had read of gold and silver rushes throughout history, how the ones who grew most wealthy were those who sold the dreamers all of the tools they would need to go out and not find what they were looking for.

Not that anyone seemed bent on making any money off the people in their living room (another difference between the prayer meetings and marketing presentations), but the chance to affect someone's life seemed to stimulate a kind of motivation just as powerful as the pursuit of money, a chance to still leave a mark when using wealth to do so was no longer an option; instead of commissioning a statue of themselves in a town square or lobby, they could erect themselves in someone's memory, preferably a whole bunch of people's memories. I had not grown so prematurely jaded to discount the idea that they may genuinely see it as God's work and not their own, but concluded that even if this was their perspective, successfully persuading someone to see God would arouse feelings that were powerful, satisfying, and all theirs.

The mood was usually optimistic, but every so often a parent, or a pair of them, would have a breakdown like the one my parents had in front of our house when the sign went up. It usually happened in the prayer circle at the end of a meeting, when everyone had their chance to pray out loud for a few moments. Most of them would stick with praising God, some would also invoke Jesus, and they would offer thanks for the chance to be alive, and promise to show their thanks by living a good life, and ask for the strength to do so. In asking for strength, some would say they need it because they're so weak, and the ones who would fall apart were the ones who couldn't stop saying that, who would get stuck on saying "I'm so weak, God; I'm a weak person; please give me strength; I'm too weak to do it without you; please rescue me from my weakness; I'm too weak; please God forgive me for being so weak…" until they would start to cry, and the person next to them would rub their back, and they would cry harder, so hard that they would become too weak to say anything more out loud.

I saw my parents at some of the meetings, one of which included such a breakdown. When it happened they didn't look at each other, and didn't make a move to comfort the woman who was crying. They had already had their front-lawn catharsis, and now it was supposed to be time to have fun, to send everyone off in a contented and hopeful haze. Seeing other people in tears was not part of the plan. They remained expressionless as others hugged the woman and convinced her that better times were ahead, to focus on the strength and not linger on the weakness, until she finally pulled out of her funk with an embarrassed giggle and an apology, which seemed to assure my parents that it was okay to unthaw their faces. They moved in for some last second back slaps, like football players jumping on the pile after several teammates had already made the tackle, and said something about it being darkest before the dawn, or about a silver lining, or a rainbow.

Occasionally I would see some of my friends sitting at the God meetings. They never seemed as moved as the adults. They were rather more concerned with the present, too young to think about leaving a legacy or what comes after their heart stops beating; what was to come after the move from Rancho Hacienda was more important to them. And if their body language wasn't enough evidence of their point of view, the kids' platform was summarized in a conversation I heard through the side gate of a hosting house one night between Nub and his parents as they exited down the driveway:

"You wouldn't need to go to these things if you hadn't bought a house you couldn't afford."

"Life isn't always easy, son. We go through some tough times, and that's where God can help."

"Then ask for help before you make a stupid decision, and save the healing kind of help for an accident."

Chapter Thirteen

When the party burden started, right around the time school and jobs ended, some of our dads thought it would be fun to have an event that was based on father-son teams, and decided the best game for it would be Strikeout, since it worked well with two-person squads. Our house ended up as the venue for it, so Dad made a strike zone out of painter's tape on our garage door, with the groove between the driveway and the sidewalk serving as the pitching area. Hitting the tennis ball across the street on a fly was a home run, making it across on the ground past the lone fielder was a triple, over the pitcher's head and in front of the fielder a double, and past the pitcher on the ground was a single. The loser of each game would throw a buck into the pot, we would keep track of the standings, have a regular season and a playoffs, and the championship team would win the money.

It was immediately clear, however, that our league had a problem with parity. There were a couple of dynasties and a bunch of doormats. None of us saw it coming because we kids had never played any form of baseball before that summer, and our fathers had just assumed baseball was one of the things we had been doing with all of that free time we had. We knew how to swing a bat, since we had swung them for destructive purposes many a time, and throw a ball, thanks to all the rocks we had thrown at each other, but making contact with a thrown ball and catching one with a glove only came naturally to a few of us. So the games featured a lot of frustrated coaching by the dads, and constant grumbling by the fathers stuck on the doormats about breaking up the teams, which was resisted by the fathers who had lucked into a dynasty with their sons. The doormat dads, which included mine, then suggested that the losers stop putting money into a pot, that we just play for fun, which was greeted with jeers and mockery by the dynasty dads. Then one of the dynasty teams left, since the dad's vacation was almost up and they needed to spend some of that time moving out of the house they no longer owned. That left us with one team that had no rival: Nub and his Dad, mostly because his dad was so good while Nub was just competent enough not to undermine his dad's performance. The rest of the dads threatened to boycott their remaining games against the clear favorite. So Nub's Dad claimed he could still take the title while batting left-handed the rest of the way, and the others agreed to that handicap. He did prove to be just as good from the other side, as though he had been waiting to play that trick on everyone the whole time, and he crowed and trash-talked all the more because of it, all the way to the championship game.

My Dad and I were the last doormat standing, so we were stuck providing the platform for Nub's Dad's moment of glory. The other teams and a few other friends, including Shay, came by to watch; not so much to see who would win, but how the dad dynamic would play out. The innings alternated between sons pitching to sons and fathers pitching to fathers, and after my Dad gave up a few runs in the top of the first, the expected blitz was on. When Nub took the ball for his side and I stepped up to the garage door, I noticed Nub giving me a slight grin and a weary gesture behind him, where his dad was launching into his rapid-fire chatter, loudly encouraging him to dominate me. Nub and I had decided to get this over with quickly, so I was planning on swinging at just about anything close to the strike zone. Nub had agreed to do the same when he was batting, but apparently had come up with a pitching strategy that he didn't share with me beforehand.

The first pitch came in so nice and easy that I was way out in front of it, hitting it almost directly to my left into the driveway next door. "Way to fool him, son!" yelled his Dad, not suspecting anything yet. "That'll keep him guessing!"

But the next pitch came in just as straight and true, not too slow, not too fast, and I hammered it over his dad's head for a home run. And every pitch after that was just as easy to hit. If I was a better hitter, I could have had a home run practically every time. But I was able to get enough hits to keep it close, and keep Nub's Dad on a path towards insanity.

"What are you doing!?" he would bellow.

"Sorry, Dad. My arm hurts."

"Well do you have to throw it right down the middle!?"

"You're just gonna have to be on your toes out there, Dad."

And he did chase hard after everything I hit, at one point even diving forward on the pavement to try to catch a ball before it landed in front of him for a double, skinning the length of his forearm in the process.

"Godammit!" he yelled. "This is NOT happening!"

But it was happening. My Dad seemed enthused enough by the events to retire Nub's Dad often enough so that we started to pull away. He wasn't striking him out, but was getting him to chase bad pitches as his frustration built, swinging at them too hard, hitting weak pop flies to me in the street and high bouncers to Dad on the driveway.

"Fuck this!" he finally screamed in the final inning. "I'm batting right-handed!"

"Oh, so who's wussing out and changing the rules now?" Dad taunted him.

"It was never a rule, I was just giving you limp dicks a chance."

All the kids laughed at that line, while the fellow parents winced, especially Nub's Mom.

"Go ahead," Dad said, enjoying the opportunity to come across as cool and collected. "It's too late now, anyway."

"Bullshit!" he barked. "Pitch!"

His wife told him to watch his language, but he didn't seem to hear her amongst the children's laughter and his fury.

Dad threw him a pretty neat breaking pitch, and got him to hit the ball into the ground and bounce high into the air. As soon as it happened, Nub's Dad slammed the bat into the ground and it careened into the garage door, leaving a small dent. Dad took a few steps back and let the ball land in front of him, and kept backing up, letting ball bounce lower and lower until it almost came to a stop, at which point Dad picked it up and showed it to him. "Game over. You owe me a garage door."

"What do you care? It's not even yours anymore."

That shook Dad out of his role as the calm one. "Oh, and yours is, asshole?"

"What did you call me?"

"You heard me."

They started walking toward each other and the surrounding adults stepped in. I walked over to Nub, who was near our side gate, the same place he had been standing to watch the last at-bat.

"Let's get out of here," I suggested to him.

"Good idea," he agreed.

I led the way into our backyard.

"Can I come?" said Shay, catching the gate before it closed.

"Sure," I said, walking through our yard to the back fence.

"Where we going?" asked Nub.

"I need to get off The Ranch for a while," I answered, grabbing the top of the fence and vaulting myself over. Shay and Nub followed, and we walked toward The Barrio.

"Thanks for the fat pitches," I said to Nub.

"No problem. It was my plan all along, no matter who we played. I like seeing my Dad rant and rave. It's funny."

"You're not embarrassed?" Shay asked.

"I got over being embarrassed about anything a long time ago."

"Around the time we started calling you 'Nub'?" I posited.

"Before that. Why would I pee on the fence in the first place?"

We laughed at the memory and decided to stop by Miggy's house. He answered the door and was glad to see us. I looked past him and saw his grandmother in her chair upholstered with cat hair, but no sign of Lourdes. She had taken a job in High School Town over the summer, catching a ride with her dad and brother in the mornings, so she wasn't home very often. It appeared today was no exception, so I had no mixed feelings at all when Miggy said he wanted to get out of the house and suggested we walk over to the factory.

"Funny, we were just talking about that place," Shay teased Nub, as if that was possible.

Nub laughed, always the good sport, and said, "We'd invite you over to Ranch Ranch, but it's a little bit crazy right now."

"Miggy doesn't come over anymore, anyway," I said as we started to make our way toward the tree line.

"I don't blame you," said Shay.

"Like you come over here," Miggy addressed me.

"I had to cut down," I defended myself. "I get all these questions about when I'm coming home, and what we're going to do, and they say I shouldn't bother your family so much."

"They put you through all that when you go over to someone's house in your neighborhood?"

"I know what you're getting at, and no. They don't. But it's because they can see me over there. And even if they can't, the place is crawling with parents. It's like a big daycare facility."

"Run by drunks," Shay chimed in.

"What Shay said," Miggy laughed. "I wouldn't go over there if everyone was named Rodriguez and Gomez, either. I was just messing with you, Nick."

"Sorry," I said. "I'm a bit jumpy."

"Relax, man," Nub patted me on the shoulder. "You're the Strikeout champion. We should be celebrating."

Miggy asked what the deal was, and we told him about the championship game and its aftermath. It was the first time any of us had a chance to tell the story, the event was only ten minutes old, and we were already embellishing it: making up new dialogue loosely based on the original, adding some rollovers by Nub's Dad and run-ins with parked cars as he tried to reach every single ball I hit into the street, exaggerating the moment between me and Nub before he threw the first pitch, touching up the sounds and visuals to a point where I was already wondering how much of what we shared was true.

"That was cool of you, Nub," said Miggy. "So cool I'm feeling bad about calling you 'Nub.'"

"Ah," Nub shrugged. "I did it for myself more than anything. My Dad was a hot shot jock when he was young, and he's always been disappointed that I got my mother's height and suck at sports. Not that he ever says it, but it's pretty obvious."

He may have been trying to be funny, but there was just enough sincerity in his assessment, whether he supplied it with his voice or we projected it with our minds, that we didn't laugh.

"Let's stop here," Shay suggested as we were about to pass through the tree line. "We've stared at that factory forever and still don't know what it is. I want to feel like we're out in the woods somewhere; someplace far away."

"Everybody's full of good ideas today," I said, and sat down with my back resting against the trunk of a tree. Miggy and Shay also found trees nearby to support their backs, while Nub lied on the ground staring up at the sky through the branches.

"This reminds me of Outdoor Ed in fifth grade," Nub said, keeping his gaze skyward. "Did any of you guys do that in your old schools?"

"I was always here at our crappy little school," Miggy said. "So no, I didn't."

"Yeah, we did that," Shay said.

"Us, too," I added.

"So what is it?" Miggy asked. "Who's Outdoor Ed?"

We cracked up.

"It's not a *who*," Shay explained. "It's a *what*. Outdoor Education. It's like going to camp during the school year. For a week, right?"

"That's how long ours was," I said.

"Mine, too," said Nub, who then continued. "And I never went to summer camp, so it was the only time I had been to one. But I remember that it seemed like I finally found the coolest people to hang out with at the end of the week."

"That's what happens at summer camp, too," Shay said. "Even if it's two weeks, or a month, you find your best friends toward the end."

"So is this the end?" Miggy asked no one in particular.

We all seemed to either be thinking about our answers or waiting for someone else to respond first. Nub went first.

"We're out of here in a couple days. We probably should have left earlier, but Dad wanted to win the Strikeout league."

Shay was next.

"I give us about a week, maybe longer. I doubt we'll make it to Fourth of July."

Which seemed to make it my turn, but I didn't want to say out loud what I had suddenly realized. Miggy prodded me.

"So what about you, Nick? We gonna make it to high school?"

All I could do was shake my head and avoid looking Miggy in the eye.

"Did they tell you that?" Miggy asked.

"There's just no way," I admitted to myself out loud.

"But they haven't said anything," Shay joined in, trying to be encouraging.

"Of course not. They never do. We don't talk any more now than when they were gone all the time. Well, we talk, but it's about nothing. And it's pretty obvious the plan is to trash this place and leave it, like they're rock stars in a hotel room or something."

I got a few chuckles out of my last line, but still didn't feel like looking at anyone. So I followed Nub's lead and slid onto my back and looked up at the branches getting tossed around by the wind. I was sad, but not in a way that made me feel like crying. It was a new kind of sadness, an empty kind, where the emotion was just out of reach, on the other side of the emptiness. Nobody said anything for a while. Shay and Miggy joined us on the ground, on their backs. We listened to the wind cast aside the leaves on its way through the trees, and to the hum of the factory. Eventually the sound of a car engine distinguished itself from whatever was throbbing inside the enigmatic building, a car coming from the hills, growing louder as it closed the distance, finally passing by our hidden spot in the trees on its way to the freeway, already driving at interstate speed. Its volume lowered for several seconds and then disappeared. The familiar sounds from before once again whispered in our ears, as though the car had never existed.

"Has anyone seen Blaine lately?" I asked, all of us still looking up.

"You haven't?" Shay asked back.

"Nope."

"Hmm. Weird."

"Lana's seen him," Miggy offered.

"Yeah?" I asked.

"Yeah. I see her walking over to the tunnel."

"So that's what he's doing with that empty house," I said.

"Are they staying, then?" Nub asked.

"There you go, Miggy," Shay said. "You can at least go to high school with Blaine."

"No sign on their front lawn?" Miggy asked.

"No sign of them at the block parties, either," said Nub.

"They're not staying," I said.

"How do you know?" Shay asked.

"I heard some things when we were still hanging out," I replied, not wanting to give away my nighttime hobby, no matter how close I felt to the three of them at that moment.

"Where do his parents go all day?" Nub asked.

"Beats me," I answered. "Work, maybe. But I know they're not going to be in that house much longer than anyone else."

"So I guess his sister is still living with that dude and his family in High School Town," Miggy said.

"Yeah," I sighed. "That dolt."

"You met him?" Shay asked.

"Yup. On the one day they took out the boat."

"Then they're perfect for each other," Shay said.

"Man, we could be having some great parties in that house," Nub speculated. "Separate from the adults."

"That's Blaine," I said. "Always looking out for himself."

"I don't blame him this time," Miggy said. "I never thought anyone would get to Lana."

"Lana..." Shay sighed. "Do we have to have that conversation again?"

"I didn't bring it up," I reminded her before turning my attention to Miggy. "Shay has some pretty strong opinions about girls like Lana and Kelsey."

"Oh, you mean hot girls?" Miggy piled on.

Shay sat up and glared at him.

"Who's Kelsey?" asked Nub.

"Blaine's sister," I answered.

"Oh. That fits."

"Anyway," I continued, "it's between me and Shay. Don't worry about it. And leave them alone, Shay."

"So how do you feel about Chris and Dulce, then?" Miggy asked Shay.

Nub laughed, and I tried unsuccessfully not join him. Shay remained focused.

"It's the same thing," she said.

The three of us sat upright and spluttered variations of "What?"

"Absolutely," she defended her point. "He obviously isn't dating her for her personality, either. Lana's a beautiful zero and Dulce's a bitch. Can't you guys come up with a longer list for what you're looking for in a girl? Longer than one thing?"

"*You guys...*" Miggy said. "Are you lumping us together with Chris?"

"I'm lumping all guys together."

"Maybe we should talk about girls' taste in guys," Miggy smiled.

"Okay," Shay parried. "Chris would jump at the chance to be with Lana, just like the rest of you. Do you think I would want to be with Blaine?"

"Yes," said Miggy and Nub.

She looked over at me.

"Probably not," I admitted.

She smiled at me. "And that's the difference between boys and girls," she said, holding her gaze long enough for Miggy and Nub to notice.

"Is there something else between you two?" Miggy asked. "You know, besides that conversation you keep having?"

"I've tried," Shay said. "Lord knows I've tried. But he's a guy; one of those typical guys."

There was a pause, and all I could do is look down at the ground, at the fallen leaves. Miggy then took mercy on me by making fun of me:

"So what you're saying is girls are more willing to go for dorks like Nick instead of popular guys."

Shay sighed, but I was grateful for any chance to squirm into a lighter tone, even if it meant having to acknowledge my lower social standing compared to Blaine.

Nub piled on. "I'd go for you too, Nick," he said. "Piss on Blaine."

We cracked up and started asserting ourselves further into comfortable territory. Shay wasn't quite ready to surrender completely, mumbling another something about boys, but came around soon enough to offer her opinion on whose parents were most likely to hook up with each other out of wedlock, if we had ever visited anyplace more dull than our development, if any of us had been anyplace truly beautiful, where we wanted to live when we grew up, what the most grisly way to die would be, and we made plans for a Ranch Ranch reunion ten summers hence, when everyone would be graduating from college more or less, or starting their first careers. Initially we thought of holding it in some restaurant in High School Town, or even the truck stop, but considered how tenuous those businesses were, how likely they were to shut down or turn over, and how unenthusiastic people may be to go to all the trouble of reaching such bleak regions they would maybe rather forget. So we decided on the coastal town I had described to them that I had been to with my parents, since it was more convenient and prettier, while still allowing for a trip to our old childhood wildlife preserve for those inclined. We vowed to adhere to our plan, hypothesizing that doing so would provoke us to do whatever it took to return triumphant, and see The Ranch as something we overcame rather than something that held us back.

The breeze started to cool as the sky made the move from blue to orange, and we figured it was about time to head back before it went from orange to purple. The Strikeout league barbeque would be well underway by now. Nub and I wagered whether our dads would still be at odds, or bro-hugging and saying I-love-you-man. We had nothing to bet but our dignity, as I didn't expect to see my share of the Strikeout winnings, so the loser had to give his Dad a big hug in front of everyone and thank him for the Strikeout league because it taught us so much about life. We added the incentive that if the loser could manage to shed some convincing tears while expressing his gratitude, then the winner would be forced to do likewise with his dad.

I cast my lot for bro hugs, while Nub bet they would still be mad, each of us wagering on our fathers' respective strengths: my Dad's diplomacy and his Dad's competitiveness. Miggy was intrigued enough with learning the outcome to stop by the party before going back home, so he hopped the fence with us and was visibly surprised by the scene when we reached the front of our house: the dozens of cliques of adults and kids milling about the street, the garage doors open of the houses still inhabited, grills blazing in several of the driveways, music from our parents' high school days blaring from some speakers parked in the one of the open garages. All it needed was some booths selling leather goods and ceramic pots to look like a street fair.

"Is it like this every night?" Miggy gaped.

"Pretty much," I told him, then spotted my Dad and Nub's Dad across the street with some other parents, trading tales from their sporting days, re-enacting past events while keeping their beer bottles upright. I looked at them until I heard the signal from Nub that he had seen them, too:

"Dammit."

"Pay up," I told him, and he obliged, clearly not that upset about having to take the stage.

"I'm glad you won," Shay said. "Nub will be much better at this."

Miggy and I chuckled and agreed, and Nub lived up to expectations.

He stepped in front of his Dad and faced him for a melodramatic couple of seconds before clutching him as if he was going to war. His Dad lifted his arms to make way for his son's tackle. He looked stumped as Nub then leaned back to proclaim his love and appreciation. Nub then buried his face in his Dad's chest and started quivering. We assumed it was thanks to his crying act, so Miggy managed to say to me in between his spasms of laughter, "Looks like you're next"

But then it became obvious that Nub was trying to conceal his own laughter.

"Thank God," I said.

"Aw," groaned Shay.

A few of the surrounding adults who for a second thought they were witness to a heartfelt moment playfully turned on Nub, and his Dad gave him a pantomime kick to his backside as he made his way back to us to confirm his payment. So Nub didn't get to see his Dad fall over behind him as the mock kick made him lose his balance and spill his beer all over himself as he hit the ground.

Nub looked confused as he saw our laughter shift into an extra gear, and then was inspired to turn around by the sound of the adults also convulsing into hysterics.

His Dad was lying on the ground laughing along with everyone else, spread eagle on the pavement and covered with beer.

"How is it that you and your Dad both end up on the ground covered in yellow liquid?" I asked.

"At least his dick isn't sticking out," Shay added.

And the four of us hit the driveway and rolled around as though on fire with laughter.

It took us longer than the adults to recover, since they didn't hear Shay's line, and wouldn't have understood it anyway, so by the time we caught our breath and regained awareness, the parents across the street were already composing their re-enactments of the incident, filing away their version for future re-writes. Once more we found ourselves sitting on the ground together. We watched the parents trade imitations for a while, then looked at one another, and seemed so satisfied with how the day had progressed and with being friends.

"I'd better go," Miggy said at last.

"Come on," I said. "Stick around."

He surveyed the block and found nothing to change his mind.

"Thanks, but I need to make sure my grandma doesn't burn the house down."

We said our see-yas and he exited through our side gate to use the fence.

The three of us remained seated, preferring to take everything in rather than join it. We watched the adults gesture and flirt and one-up one another, and watched the kids do the same. It was the same thing every night, and I wondered if it was possible to have fun when all you ever tried to do was have fun.

Something different happened then. One of those four-wheel drive Subaru station wagons pulling a U-Haul trailer turned onto the street and crept through the party. All conversations stopped, and the only people who moved were those who needed to get out of the car's way. A young man in his twenties drove and a woman around the same age rode shotgun. Their waves and tight-mouthed grins seemed to apologize more than greet. They pulled into the driveway of the abandoned house a few doors up from ours, which was one the homes that had never been lived in, that we had assumed was in foreclosure, inevitably due for a sign.

The young couple stayed in the car for a while after they parked. The anticipation built. They must have been just as surprised to see all of us as we were surprised to see them. Someone turned off the music. I imagined them in the car discussing how to make their entrance. And I imagined all of us were reminding ourselves that the proper reception was "Welcome to the neighborhood" rather than "Why in the hell would you move here?"

When they finally emerged from the car, a second blow to our perceptions wiped out any speeches anyone may have prepared. As soon as the woman got out, she opened the backseat door and revealed a baby strapped to a car seat. The halted block party let out a collective gasp, and then started to randomly coo and aw as she unbuckled the baby and it started to cry.

It dawned on us that nobody had ever brought a baby to The Ranch.

"It makes sense, though, now that I think about it," I said as we watched the adults drift toward the mother and child. "This is no place for a baby."

"It's no place for kids and teens, either, but that didn't stop our parents," Nub countered.

"Babies are different," Shay said. "Parents freak out about them more easily. They want to be near family or a hospital when they have a baby around so they can freak out a little less."

"So what's up with these people, then?" Nub asked.

"Maybe they're really laid back," Shay offered.

We watched the man skulk around to the passenger side of the car and shift back and forth on the outskirts of the adoring crowd.

"Or they're really weird," I suggested.

The man caught sight of us kids keeping our distance and gave us a "what's up" nod, first to our trio, then another in general to the kids scattered in various parts of the street. He then attempted to bond with us by gesturing to the hubbub surrounding the woman and the baby and shrugging.

We found out they were his wife and daughter, which was foreseeable enough, but the way we found out was peculiar. When he would come outside to take a walk with the baby in a stroller, he was clearly more comfortable with us kids than he was with the wives who would invite him in for coffee or iced tea so they would have an excuse to hold the baby. Like most of the adults in Rancho Hacienda at that point in the summer, he was always around, but didn't need to take time off to do his hovering. He was a stay-at-home dad and his wife worked as a nurse in High School Town, which is perhaps why they weren't too worried about being isolated with a baby, since she understood the statistical rarity of infants dying, and she knew how to handle a crisis should it come up.

But she didn't seem to be taking into account what a doofus her husband was. The man who was charged most days with looking after their baby girl seemed more interested in sharing tales of his business ventures with a bunch of adolescents than caring for his daughter. His philosophy for building wealth had already failed, but he spent a lot of time blaming uncontrollable circumstances and unscrupulous people for its performance, insisting that it would still be a viable plan when his second act started.

And I didn't have to hide in their bushes at night to hear this; he would share it with us in mid-walk, rolling the stroller back and forth to appease his protesting baby while we shot baskets or hung out in a garage drinking soda waiting for him to shut up. We imagined he spun his yarns for us rather than the adults because he believed we would be more impressed by his schemes and less inclined to understand them, much less call him out on their flaws. If only he knew what I had learned about the aspiring moguls in our neighborhood through their windows, he would probably try to use them for his re-birth. But he preferred the company of people he presumed knew less than he did. He thought he could sculpt his story of fortune gained and lost in such a way as to mold a heroic image of himself in our minds, so when we grew up and went out into the world we could spread word of this misunderstood genius, the one they call Soren.

The stripped down version appeared to be that he leveraged the good living earned by his wife into a miniature real estate empire, and their investment home on The Ranch was the only piece left. It was also the cheapest one, and since her job had mobility, she was able to find work near the one holding they hoped they could afford to keep. Or at least that's what I was able to cobble together from those arbitrary moments that I found myself paying attention to what he was saying.

Soren's arrival did catch the attention of Blaine and his Dad, and drew them out of hibernation, as though they found it necessary to impress the new neighbor who had yet to experience their impressiveness. They didn't necessarily come outside, but instead invited him inside to show him their things: their appliances, their furniture, their sculptures, their hot wife, pictures of their hot daughter, and the hot girlfriend, Lana, who apparently was not invited on the boat.

They took Soren and his wife out on the boat, while Blaine's Mom looked after the baby. I observed all of this without Blaine ever acknowledging me, as he greeted Soren at the door almost every day, or rode past us in the passenger seat of his Dad's car, or loaded up the boat in the driveway.

Soren would tell us how cool Blaine and Steve were. I tried not to laugh every time he used Yuri's American code name. And I tried not to argue with him about their character, for I really did feel sorry for them. Their situation more than any other made me feel good about my nightly reality checking, allowed me to rationalize my snooping as having value, as I imagined I would be a lot more angry and frustrated about being shunned by Blaine had I not understood what motivated it. I still thought they were shitheads; I just didn't dismiss them as shitheads.

Casino Night was the perfect vehicle for them to ingratiate themselves back into the community: a celebration of gambling. (Though I was positive that the irony was lost on them.) It was typically them in so many other ways, too. The invitations were mailed, rather than hand-delivered or extended in person. The large, square envelopes made the hundred-mile trip each way from the regional post office where the mail was sorted and sent back to complete the ten-foot trip from their mailbox to ours. And the contents within were designed to dazzle. The card was a tuxedo coat and bow tie that opened to a tinny version of the James Bond Theme emanating from a small chip inside the fold. The dress code was black tie preferred, but business casual accepted. No actual money would be wagered, but those who built highest upon their initial pile of allotted chips could claim prizes, courtesy of Yuri's company, whatever that was. The prizes themselves sounded familiar, like things I had seen around their house back when I was allowed inside; items touted as rare, valuable, imported, hand-crafted, artisan, but which ultimately struck me as things they were unable to pawn or auction online, and since a yard sale conflicted with the image to which they were clinging, this was a personal narrative-friendly way of unloading them. Their move-out date was clearly coming soon.

The only mild surprises about the event were that it was kid-friendly, since the parties they had previously thrown were adults-only, and that my family received an invitation, in light of kids being allowed and their kid having developed some sort of problem with me. But I reminded myself that Blaine had stopped talking to everyone else, too, other than Lana, and wondered if he would even be there, if he would instead be holed up in his room with her.

Chapter Fourteen

Blaine was there, in a full tuxedo and without Lana. His family members were the only ones adhering to the black tie mandate. The rest of us did the best we could to dress up. We looked like wedding guests, and the hosts looked like the wedding party. The Casino Night employees were in bow ties, too, but wore gaudy vests to insure that no guests would be dressed like the help.

I took a deep breath, approached Blaine, and asked him where Lana was.

"She didn't want to come, since none of the other Barrio kids would be here," he answered, looking around the room for a way out of talking to me any further.

"Soren!" he found his excuse. "Excuse me, Nick."

I watched him glide through the crowd over to Soren, who noticed that I had been left behind by Blaine. Soren said something to him about it, to which Blaine responded by shrugging and waving off any concern. I wasn't interested in calling him on it, certainly not in front of Soren, so I drifted over to one of the gaming tables.

I didn't know how to play any of the games aside from the most basic rules, so I figured I would observe for a while and learn some of the nuances before laying down any of the chips I had been handed by the Casino Night employee at the door.

I never did play. I was too fascinated by watching the people rather than the games; specifically the parents, as the kids haphazardly tossed some chips onto some tables and half-heartedly indulged the theme before rushing into Blaine's media center to play video games on their enormous screen. It had been a while since any of us enjoyed access to it. The parents, meanwhile, wrestled with emotions even more acute than the ones experienced during the ragtag sporting events or the video game contests.

At the Casino Night tables, they had no opponent to focus on, no skills to employ; it was just themselves and their luck, neither of which they had felt very good about for some time. And with misfortune as the sole exterior force they could blame, their reaction to losing was not anger, it was despair. They had cleansed their anger in the streets and the TV rooms. They had thrown equipment and hit pillows and accused other players of cheating. Now all they could do was sit under their own private rain cloud and re-live the day they came home to find the foreclosure cross on their front lawn, and the dreadful trickle of inevitability that carried them to that broken point as they watched one card after another reveal something they didn't want to see, watched the roulette marble bounce and skip dozens of times before settling in some other slot, watched the dice come up with the wrong combination no matter how many times they rolled them. They watched the house win again.

When one of them would beat the house for a few chips, they would nearly weep with joy. They would look upward and hug their spouse. As the night aged, the hugs grew larger with every small victory, with everyone hugging each other when someone beat the odds. Even Blaine's parents joined the group hug when a rare hot streak ignited at one of the tables. Someone was winning. Someone was proving it was still possible.

But then they would get greedy. Again. They would reboot their elevated sense of self and imagine they had discovered some secret, had realized some unique skill that allowed them to succeed where others had failed. And they would fail. Again. The collective hugs would become consoling rather than celebratory. Everyone kept their arms around each other, and they would not let go until it was perfectly clear that the run was over, that they would have to move elsewhere to find something to cheer.

After watching the cycle repeat itself a few times, I grew curious as to how things were going with my generation over in the media room. They had fallen silent since their exit from the gaming floor. The doors were shut, but I still expected to hear some muffled shouts and cheers now and then.

Upon entering I was treated to the cause of the quiet: Soren had turned the first-person zombie shooter game on the screen into a clinic on marksmanship.

"Relax your grip on your weapon," he was instructing Blaine, who was a willing student, and also the only one, apparently, as everyone else in the room was sprawled out half-conscious, as though an actual shooting spree had left Blaine and Soren as the last two standing. "If you can't relax with a plastic firearm, how are you going to do it when you're holding the real deal?" Soren continued to coach. "Hold it like a bird; firm enough to keep it in hand, light enough so you don't kill it."

"There's more fun ways of killing things, eh Soren?" joked Blaine.

But Soren maintained a grave demeanor. "Killing isn't fun, Blaine," he lectured him. "It's only done when necessary."

"Like in a zombie apocalypse." Blaine persisted in trying to keep the session light, blasting away at the undead onscreen.

"Actually these zombies can still be instructive," Soren stood his ground as well. "If someone wants what you have, and they want it bad enough, they'll just keep coming at you. One shot won't do the job."

I looked around the room and exchanged looks with some of my dozing ex-classmates. How could Blaine keep buying into this guy?

"You think people wouldn't kill to live in a house like this?" Soren barked at Blaine like a personal trainer trying to get more sit-ups out of a client. "You think a guy wouldn't risk life and limb for a chance at what's inside? The priceless art? The beautiful women?"

I saw an arm rise from the pile and beckon. It took me a moment to recognize it was attached to Nub. I leaned over so he could speak softly in my ear. "Soren has some real guns and said anyone who listens to him can shoot them," he said. "Sounded cool at first. Then he started talking."

I stifled a laugh and turned my attention back to the lesson.

Now Soren hovered over Blaine's shoulder as though trying to make his voice serve as Blaine's conscience. "Plus it's still an accurate representation of the human body. It's a zombie, but you can still size up a head shot, or a shot to the midsection. And which one is best?"

He turned to the rest of us, expecting an answer, but only Blaine responded.

"Dead center," he called out. "That way you still hit something even if you choke."

Soren noticed me.

"Oh, hey Nick. Didn't see you come in."

I nodded.

"You running the tables out there or what?" he asked.

"Just checking in," I shrugged. "Seeing how much fun everyone's having."

Some brief snorts of laughter rose from the surrounding pile. Soren flashed an agitated smile.

"Always got something to say, don't you, Nick?" Blaine said as he fired away at the undead.

I was so surprised to be addressed by Blaine that, contrary to his accusation, I had nothing at all to say. I sighed and moved toward the door.

"Wow," he said. "No comeback? How refreshing."

I halted my exit. "It's going to be really sad to see you go," I quipped.

Blaine paused the game and turned to face me.

"What makes you think we're going? I don't see a sign on our front lawn."

"You can take a tombstone off a grave, but there's still a body there."

"Are you saying we hid the sign?"

"Easy, zombie hunter. It's just a metaphor."

"And there it is!" Blaine raised his arms. "The condescending, smart-ass remark we can always count on from you."

"What did I ever do to you, Blaine?"

"Don't play innocent, you back-stabber."

The groggy piles of kids slowly started to animate, casually re-positioning themselves to see the action.

"Let me try again," I said. "What...did...I...do?"

"You really want me to say it in front of everyone?"

"I don't know," I extended my arms in exasperation. "I can't have an opinion on something I know nothing about."

Now that everyone was watching, even though they were pretending not to watch, Soren capitalized on the moment to try and look wise.

"This is neither the time nor the place," he put a hand on Blaine's shoulder and extended the other in my direction, as if it had healing powers. "Let's talk about this later. Take a time out. Give ourselves a chance to cool down."

"Us? Ourselves?" I said. "What does this have to do with you?"

"I know you're upset now, Nick," Soren kept up his peacemaker performance. "I get it. And I understand. I've been there..."

"You haven't been shit," I snapped. "All you've done is memorize a bunch of clichés. And Blaine would rather listen to you than me? Fuck both of you."

I barged out of the room and marched toward the front door. There was some congestion there, however, and I didn't want to shove my way through it. I turned to see that the path to the backyard was clear, so I headed in that direction, slid open the glass door, and went outside. There didn't seem to be anyone there, so I let out a long, throaty growl from the pit of my stomach and launched into a diatribe about people saying the same damn things over and over again.

But my rage had enlarged my blind spots, and it turned out there was someone in the yard with me.

"Work hard, play by the rules, and you can be anything you want to be," she said.

I only knew whose mother she was because aside from seeing her at the block parties and a sales pitch for genetically-modified earthworms, I once saw a reflection of her and her husband trying to have sex one night as I sat in a tree that allowed me to see the full length mirror attached to the front of their bedroom closet. He had gotten mad at her for directing him on certain acts that she felt were just missing, and a fight ensued that ended with him watching soft core porn in the living room. She said it again:

"Work hard, play by the rules, and you can be anything you want to be."

She was leaning against the wall to the side of the sliding glass door, her arms crossed, her eyes glassy, looking straight ahead as though her night had not gone well.

"Is that the kind of thing you're talking about?" she finally looked at me. "The kind of thing people say over and over?"

She looked like a mother who would organize a lot of fund raisers and drive her kids wherever they needed to go; but that wasn't possible out here, and she wanted to look sexy tonight, so she squeezed into a dress that must have looked good on her back when she dreamed of a very different future.

"Yes," I said.

"Anything you want to be," she stared back out at the darkness above the wall. "That's the crazy part, isn't it?"

"It is," I said. "Working hard and playing by the rules, okay...but how does that get you to anything you want to be?"

"Well, it keeps you out of jail," she said. "And you can't be anything you want if you're in jail."

I chuckled. She didn't. She kept her attention on the night sky beyond the wall. I considered asking her how her son was doing, as I had never been very close to him, but decided that was not something she wanted to hear at the moment. Instead I offered her my Casino Night chips.

"I never got around to playing," I explained. "It was more interesting to watch."

"Thanks," she said, taking them from me. "This may give me enough to win the Hopi prayer basket."

She smiled at me, gathered herself, and before heading back inside said, "As long as I don't blow it."

Now positively alone, I admitted to myself that I had been wondering the whole time if she was going to make a pass at me, was a little disappointed that she didn't, and was disappointed in myself that I was so subject to teen movie fantasies. Still, though, I asked myself if I would have done anything if she had.

I came to the realization that I would have been too embarrassed by my lack of experience (even though I knew how she liked certain acts performed on her) and embarrassed by her lack of dignity, just as the sliding glass door opened with a whoosh. Soren stepped out onto the patio with an over-compensating smile.

"Contemplating the stars?" he asked.

"No. Not that."

"Your troubles with Blaine?"

"No," I kept the denials coming. "That'll take care of itself. We'll both be outta here soon enough."

"Too bad," he said. "Guys like you should really stick together."

"Guys like us?"

"Natural born leaders."

"I'm not a leader," I said.

"But you're smart," he volleyed. "Naturally smart."

"You like that word. Natural."

"It's the way of the world, Nicky..."

"Nick."

"The people who makes things happen, the leaders, the smart people, those are not learned traits. We're born with those."

"Okay. Thanks. I guess."

"But we can't take those talents for granted," he changed the tone to a more admonishing one. "We have to develop them. Practice them."

"Oh, I get it," it dawned on me. "Sorry I interrupted your class back there, Soren."

"And we can learn some things that help maintain the ideal circumstances to develop those natural talents, keep us safe so we can actually make that difference."

He didn't seem to notice my apology. "I said I was sorry."

"I don't want you to be sorry," he started to sound like he did with Blaine during the video game gun clinic. "Winners don't apologize. If you do what you know is right, then there's no need to say you're sorry. Greatness doesn't compromise."

We stared at each other for several moments. He was very proud of his speech, and I didn't know how to respond to it.

"I should go," I said. "It's getting late."

"It's getting late," he nodded. "You're absolutely right. We're running out of time."

"We?" I was genuinely confused. "You can stay if you want. I was just talking about me."

"I'm not," he said, continuing to grandstand. "I'm talking about all of us who have a responsibility to use our God-given talents for good, before it's too late."

He walked over toward the entrance to the tunnel. It didn't occur to me at first that he knew about it, but as he walked in a straight line toward our homemade birdbath it became clear that he did.

He stood next to our secret gate, the lower half of his body illuminated by the light coming from the house, his upper half in shadow. I could see him point down at our creation, but couldn't see his face when he spoke.

"Every day, every hour, every minute, there are people trying to undo what people like your family have done."

I was furious. "Did Blaine tell you?"

"It's not his fault," he tried to sound comforting. "Lana came through one day when I was here. She knocked on the glass door and I wondered how she had gotten into the backyard with such a big wall in her way."

"Didn't he tell you why we made it?"

"Yes he did. And I explained to him why it was a bad idea."

"So why is it a bad idea, Soren?"

"On principle," he barked. "People who build walls don't deserve to have them undermined."

"We just wanted to hang out with each other."

"You wanted to hang out. They wanted in."

"You're so full of shit."

He walked in my direction, stepping into the light. "Wrong, Nick. Wrong. I'm telling the truth. You're just too young to believe in it yet. And that's good. You should be that way when you're young. You should want to see the best in people. But it's a tough world out there. It's a hard world. And you're reaching an age where you have to start understanding that. Because if you don't, it will eat you alive, and you'll never have a chance to use that brain of yours."

I couldn't even manage to say good night. I just turned around and headed back into the house, to the front door, and out into street. I walked around the neighborhood several times before going home; past the empty houses with their front yards growing wild and their windows as lifeless as they were dark, past the playground we had defiled with its tanbark almost completely drained from its base and its slide covered in skid marks from our bicycles, past the construction site with the edges of its wood frame chipped and splintered from our constant battering and the materials stored inside now completely depleted and scattered in pieces around its perimeter. We had indeed been stupid, been naïve; and I was no exception. I gave Soren credit for that. But what constituted smart was hardly settled in my mind.

Chapter Fifteen

I probably would not have noticed that Soren's gun safety program had made the transition from video guns to real ones had I not decided to pass on the following night's block party. I had decided to stay in my room; it offered the kind of solace that the street scene's forced attempts at forgetting could not provide. I didn't feel like forgetting; I wanted to read quietly about human recklessness and watch movies about our natural tendency to screw up and apply those stories to our circumstances; I wanted to learn from it all, not stuff my face with hot dogs and chips and sneak a beer with friends or try to get high off the secondhand smoke coming from the joints a few parents would light up in their garages.

The bass from the amp in our neighbor's garage lightly rattled my walls as I lied on my bed with my head propped up to read. It sounded like the theme this evening was dance music, as the tempo was fast and repetitive. I tried to escape it by repositioning myself in my parents' room. The club-like beat did fade slightly, but still obscured the sound of gunshots that I eventually picked up on through their window. The sun was still just above the horizon, so I got up to see if I could find the source of the shooting.

From my second-story vantage I saw Soren and Blaine out on the range with some cans lined up along the top of the embankment, firing at them with their backs to The Ranch. Blaine looked as though he was struggling at this point, many of his shots raising the dirt in front of the cans, or hitting nothing at all and whizzing over the cans out into the distance. I wondered how far the bullets went before they landed and bounced to a stop, how close they would get to the hills.

I also wondered what sort of advice Soren was giving Blaine, what coaching platitudes and paranoid slogans he was rattling off. As unlikely as it was that I would be able to hear them, given their distance and the noise coming from the street, I still wanted to find out if I could pick up anything, and went downstairs into the backyard to try. My reality checking through the backyards and windows of The Ranch had sunk from nightly to every few nights to rare, as the returns on my observations had started to diminish. The scenes were becoming repetitive, the patterns familiar. All of the problems were the same; the only thing that changed were the people who avoided them.

But Soren's mentorship of Blaine had the potential to offer something new. I stood on the bottom beam of our fence so just my head peeked over, but aside from the sporadic shooting and the occasional disjointed sound of Soren's voice, I couldn't hear them.

"What are you looking at?" a voice startled me from behind.

I turned to see Shay peering over our side gate at me, just as I was doing over our back fence at the target practice.

"Sorry," she smiled at having made me jump. "I was just checking to see why you weren't out in front tonight."

I gestured for her to come over, remaining silent even though there was no way Blaine and Soren could hear me. I realized this by the time Shay reached me.

"Check it out," I nodded for her to perch next to me and see what I was seeing.

I watched her watch them and figure out what was going on. "Is that Blaine?"

"Yes."

"And that must be Soren's gun."

"It is."

She watched a little while longer. "What's the purpose of this?"

"I've got some ideas," I told her.

"Like...?"

"It's fun."

"Brilliant." She sighed, stepped off the bottom beam, and turned to lean against the fence.

"I've got some others," I said, maintaining my post.

She ignored my offer and pressed on with her main purpose for tracking me down. "It's official. We're leaving."

"Now?" I asked, stepping down to join her. "Tonight?"

"No," she assured me. "Day after tomorrow."

I didn't know what to say. Plenty of people had left already, but this was my first close friend to go.

"I'm going to miss you," I finally said.

"You know I'm going to miss you," she replied in a jokey tone that lasted but a moment before she started to choke up. I hugged her, and then rocked her back and forth as she cried harder. I was shedding some tears too, but remained a bit more composed thanks to the shock I was also experiencing at having stirred this much emotion in someone.

"I love you so much," she said in my ear.

Hearing it so close made me shudder, as I went from shock to shame at not being able to match her intensity. I told her I loved her, too, but could tell that it didn't come across as sincere when I said it.

"Thank you for trying," she said, laughing bravely.

"But I do," I unlocked myself from her embrace and looked into her eyes. "I really do love you."

"I know," she said. "And I know it's different."

We stood quietly for some time, looking down for the most part, occasionally giving each other a small, lost smile.

"I'm ruining this," she said. "I'm sorry."

"No," I countered. "It's me."

"What have you done?" she asked. "You haven't done anything wrong."

I sighed and tried to think of something comforting to say. "Well," I offered, "I blew it with you. That may not be wrong, but it's pretty stupid."

I glanced her way to see if that worked. She was holding her gaze my way. Then she stepped toward me and gave me what I guess was my first kiss, but I was too surprised to experience any other emotions besides surprise. My only memory of it is that it happened. The guilt I felt afterwards remains much more embedded, as it wasn't my intention to lead her on.

"We have two days," she said.

"Shay..."

"I'm not expecting anything. I mean, we're never going to see each other again, anyway."

"That's not true," I jumped at the chance to say something comforting again, and hopefully not screw it up this time.

"It is true," she maintained. "And you know it. We'll keep in touch for a while, maybe, and even if we do, it's going to fade. And that's fine. It should fade. It would be weird if we didn't meet a bunch of new people as we grew up, enough so that there's no room for the old ones. It's healthy..."

She stopped herself and took a deep breath.

"I want you to be my first," she said.

Before I had a chance to be speechless, she qualified her request. "I don't necessarily mean all-the-way sex," she explained. "I just mean...I don't know. Whatever happens."

My guilt came doubling back. I couldn't bear to turn her down, so I stalled.

"I'll find an empty house," I came up with. "One that's unlocked, or has a window left open."

Her smile released a level of joy I had become unfamiliar with since summer had started; it allowed me to forget for a moment that it was in response to a lie, that I had no intention of following through on my house hunt. But that moment passed, and I had to find ways to stall in order to let my primary stall take effect.

"I told my parents I wasn't feeling well," I said. "I should go back inside, not blow my cover."

Shay imitated a drunk parent. "Oh, hey baby, you feelin' better? Well come on out an' party! Whoo! Give your mamma a kiss..."

I laughed, relieved to get back to the kind of interaction we usually had. Then I realized she really did want a kiss. I obliged, but adhered to the mother theme in my approach.

"I'd invite you in," I said. "But we wouldn't want to get caught."

She grinned and kissed me again. I kept it short.

"Save it for later," I said, which seemed to appease her. She hugged me instead, which would have felt great if I didn't also have to start choreographing my tap dance of avoidance that I would be performing over the next two days.

"Love you," she said as she pulled herself away and headed for the gate.

"Love you too," I said, and knew it sounded more sincere this time, because I imagined what I was really saying was "I'm sorry."

Chapter Sixteen

One of the worst parts about living in Rancho Hacienda that I had never realized until my deal with Shay was that there was nowhere to hide if you were trying to avoid someone: no friend's house in another part of town, no town, and none of the things you could pretend to be doing in that town in the places they would be done.

There was only so much time I could spend at Miggy's before he would want to go outside, and I didn't want to tell him why going outside wasn't appealing to me at that juncture. So the first part the day after I pledged to do with Shay whatever it was she expected us to do was spent sprinting from my fence to Miggy's house and back again. The non-committal parts of my talk with Shay, though, on the subject of saying good-bye and trying to part on memorable terms, did make me think of a place I could hide, as uncomfortable as it may be.

I even ran into her on my way there. Or more to the point, she came running out of her house as I tried to walk quickly past.

"Looking for an empty?" she asked.

"I'm working on it. I tried some backyards earlier."

"Need some help?"

"Maybe later. Right now I'm on my way to Blaine's."

"Really?"

"Really."

"You're kidding."

"I just said 'really.'"

"I'm just...shocked."

"Well," I explained, relishing an opportunity to be honest with her, "our going away plans got me thinking about Blaine and me."

"You're hooking up with him too?" she teased. "You slut."

I smiled. "I just feel like we've been through too much, he and I, and I want to see if there's any chance to make nice before we're gone."

She looked at me as though proud, as if I was her son and I just got a diploma, or emerged in my tuxedo on my wedding day. Continuing to think of her in such motherly terms reminded me why I didn't want to be intimate with her, as much as I liked her, as much as I loved her.

"Good luck," she said, and gave me a hug. I assumed she avoided kissing me because we were on the sidewalk surrounded by windows.

I reached Blaine's house and took a few deep breaths before ringing the bell.

Having Blaine answer offered some relief right away, since at least I didn't have to ask one of his parents if he was home and explain why I was there if they went to fetch him and he refused to see me.

"What?" he said.

"Can we talk?" I asked. "No smart-ass remarks, just to try to leave here as friends?"

"I guess."

He walked towards the media room, leaving me to close the door and follow him.

There was a zombie movie playing on the screen.

"So you're really into zombies now," I noted, resisting any cracks about not getting enough zombie action through video games.

"Soren recommended this series," he explained as he sat down on the couch directly in front of the show. "It's pretty cool. It's like a realistic look at who would survive if shit goes down. The zombies are just kind of another obstacle, you know, just there for the people who aren't really thinking about things when they're watching, who just want to be entertained. It's really about what happens if things got real again."

"Again?" I asked as I sat on the side couch that connected to his portion at a right angle.

"Before everything got cushy, back when the strong were allowed to be strong."

It was really hard not to go down a very snide path on the subject, but I genuinely did want to see if I could patch things up, or at least make enough conversation to hide out from Shay for a while. So I avoided a discussion of the end times and focused on our own situation.

"I wasn't playing dumb the other night at the Casino party," I said as Blaine continued to watch some guy fight his way out of a staggering horde of undead by swinging a sledgehammer into their heads. "I really don't know what I did to piss you off so much, and if you could tell me, I'd like to do what I can to make things right before our time is up here."

He paused the show, freezing a screen shot of a zombie's head spewing special effect juice courtesy of the sledgehammer, then turned to me.

"I had an interesting talk with Lana," he said. "And yes," he adopted a smug look, "we talk."

"I wasn't going to say anything."

"But if you were...am I right? Something like that?"

"I don't know. I told you, I'm not here to do that."

"You're not that smart, Nick. See? I can write your snappy lines for you."

"So what was your talk about?"

"Okay, fine. Avoid the subject."

"What subject? You brought up that 'interesting talk' you had with Lana."

"Just admit that your gig isn't being smart, it's being an asshole."

"I'm an asshole," I recited. "There. I said it."

"Like you mean it," he insisted.

"Are you kidding?" I was about to get up and leave.

"She told me what you said about me to her and Dulce on the day the boat arrived; the boat I invited you on, the boat I took you on."

I needed a moment to remember what he was talking about. Getting beat up by Dulce was my first recollection of that day, then came the reason why: she thought I was accusing them of being users because I asked them if they liked Blaine for his bling.

As soon as it came to me, I apologized.

"I'm sorry, man. I really am. I had just found out we were losing our house. I overheard my parents and they weren't going to tell me. I wasn't thinking straight."

"You were feeling jealous," he offered, now appearing very placid and content with having me grovel.

"I guess. Sure. I was definitely angry. Just lashing out."

"Jealousy is weak," he stuck to his thesis.

"I'm not proud of whatever caused it."

"If people weren't jealous, there wouldn't be any crime, people would stop trying to take things from other people."

"Good point."

"Jealous people should focus on getting their own things instead," he proclaimed. I started to hear Soren's influence. "They should use that emotion more productively. And if they don't, they should pay the price."

I wasn't interested in hearing a speech from Soren by proxy, so I tried to keep him out of it.

"Can you forgive me?" I asked.

Blaine seemed irritated that I wasn't getting swept up into the vision. He exhaled and leaned back in the couch.

"I must admit," he said. "I've wondered if what you said is true; if Lana likes me for the wrong reasons."

I was trying to think of something uplifting to say when he filled the pause before I could:

"I mean, she gives great head. And watching her do it is just like...the most beautiful thing I've ever seen. Especially in front of my full-length mirror so I can see it from as many angles as possible."

I'm not sure what my reaction was, but he looked at me to make sure he was getting one before he continued.

"But still...I'd like to think there's something there. Some meaning to it."

I gave up searching myself for a contribution and instead searched him for any indications of his intent. We stared at each other for quite some time. If we had deemed it a staring contest, I would have won, for he cracked first, into a smile.

"Would you like me to go into more detail?" he said.

"No."

"Come on," he leaned closer. "Want me to describe her body to you?"

"No."

"Liar. Deep down, you do."

"Maybe so. But that doesn't make it right."

"How do you know?"

All I could come up with was "Because it feels wrong."

"Bah!" he waved me off. "It feels wrong," he adopted a whiny voice. "I don't feel good about this. Feel, feel, feel." He mouthed a fart noise and went back to a normal voice. "Stop apologizing for what you want. If you want something, go for it; and if you have something, defend it. That's all there is to it, Nick. That's life. You think about things too much. Now get out of your head and let me tell you about Lana's tits."

I never imagined I would want so badly to turn down such an offer. "Forget about me. What about her?"

"Who cares? It's not like I'm going to marry her."

"Can you even hear yourself?"

"It's a great story. You know, one of those doomed romances. Like Romeo and Juliet. You probably know that story, read it or seen a movie of it or something. They were doomed, right?"

"Right."

"So there you go."

"Forgive me if I'm about break my promise about smart-ass remarks, but there is no giving head in Romeo and Juliet."

He laughed. "Of course there is. They just don't show it. That's why my story is better."

I was tired of him putting me back on my heels, so I decided to play to my strengths and make him feel foolish about bringing up the Romeo and Juliet comparison. "You're only doomed because you want it that way. They were forbidden from being together by their families."

"So are we."

"Please," I jumped at the chance to start waving off his points. "Their families hated each other. Your families have never even met."

"They don't have to. Hers is on that side of the wall," he gestured. "And we're on this side."

My ploy had fallen flat. He had yanked us out of the literature category and back into Soren's philosophy of Great Men Can Do Whatever They Want And Not Apologize For It.

"So that means you automatically hate each other?"

He shrugged. "We just want different things. One is on the take, one is on defense."

"Like you're not getting anything out of this?"

"I'm talking big picture. You're thinking too small."

"Small, yeah, well I was talking about your dick."

"There we go!" Blaine slapped his thigh. "One last shot. Good one, Nick."

He reached for the remote and unfroze the screen, allowing the zombie's head to finish exploding. Blaine kicked back on the couch and looked over at me.

"We had a good run," he said.

I nodded. He watched the show and waited for me to leave.

"What happened?" I asked.

"I grew up," he said.

"You met Soren," I shot back.

"He just helped me figure things out sooner." Blaine remained focused on the screen, on the hero blasting away at the human-like targets who were no longer human. "I would have gotten there eventually."

"Yeah," I said more to myself than to him. "I guess you would have."

I got up to let myself out. At the front door I looked over and saw half of Blaine's mother through the frame of the entrance to the kitchen. She was running a sponge over a chopping block. She saw me and smiled, and I assumed the other half of her was smiling too. I waved good-bye and shut the door behind me.

I was actually hoping to see Shay on my way home. I wanted to talk to her about the end of friendships, and how people change, and how distressed I was about the things Blaine said, not about me, but about the world, and how he sees it, and how what rained down most on me was the sickening thought that he was not alone, that I would be encircled by the same ideas everywhere I went for the rest of my life, but usually would not know who was harboring them.

But Shay was nowhere to be found. I walked slowly, giving her a chance to see me from wherever she may have been, and then realized my time in Blaine's house was probably too brief, that she was assuming I was going to be there longer, and she was occupying herself up to a point she figured would be reasonable to check on me.

Then again, nobody else was around, either. I had never seen the neighborhood so empty since our final summer had started. All of the garage doors were closed; I could hear the groaning of my shoes echoing against them. I felt like screaming as loudly as I could, just a scream, no words, just to see what would happen. But I didn't bother. Not because it would be embarrassing, but because it would be depressing. Because all that would happen is that people would look out their windows, maybe a few would stand in their doorways, and once they saw it was just some kid acting out, they would go back to whatever it was they were doing, and forget it ever happened within minutes. Nobody would even approach me at that night's block party and say, "Aren't you the kid who screamed?"

Chapter Seventeen

The block parties had been getting more intense as everyone seemed to be spiraling faster as they drew closer to the drain they were destined to go down.

That evening's spectacle continued the trend. I sat on my front lawn like a Buddha garden ornament trying to tranquilize the thoughts inspired by the time spent earlier in Blaine's lair, thoughts of everyone seeing everyone else as something to conquer: sexually, physically, financially, competitively. Then I imagined they couldn't all be thinking those things; no, quite the contrary, some of them would get off on being the abused. Meanwhile, parent looked at child as the next great hope to make the dreams of victory come true, to stem the losing streak. I even supposed that some hoped their child would become a bigger loser than they were if that's what they needed to feel better about themselves. As for the children's perspective, I imagined it was the same as the grown ups', and that their fantasies of being on top or on bottom applied to either a fellow child or an adult (either their own parents or someone else's).

As the sordid visions mounted as quickly as my failures at keeping them at bay, my posture slumped and expression tightened, and I looked less like a Buddha and more like someone on the floor of a padded room being watched by the orderlies to see if a strait jacket was going to be necessary.

That also seemed to be Shay's interpretation, more or less, as she sat down next to me.

"Things didn't go well with Blaine, I take it."

"Worse than any worse-case scenario I imagined."

"How so?"

"I not only couldn't save our friendship, I now hate mankind."

"You mean humankind," she ribbed.

"You're right," I said, agreeing with her as though it wasn't a joke. "Women and children. Them too."

"What happened?"

"I asked him the same thing."

"And?"

"He said he grew up."

"And growing up means…?"

I took her cue and tried to come up with a summary for what Blaine said. I re-crossed my legs, did my best to get back into Buddha mode, and took my time. I wanted to get it right. I looked around at our neighbors, young and old, for inspiration.

"Everything is a negotiation," I decided. "But not really. One side has already won. They have the upper hand. They just decide if they want to give up anything."

"Like you and me," she said.

I surrendered a smile. "I guess so."

Feeling a part of the fray and not pretending to be above it was liberating. This was exactly what I was hoping for when I sought her after fleeing Blaine's house, and I appreciated her more than ever.

So much so that when she said "I found a house" I didn't recoil. I was actually rather eager to express my gratitude in some way, to give in and relinquish the upper hand.

"That's where you were this afternoon?" I asked.

"You were looking for me?"

"I needed you."

She kissed me and this time I enjoyed it. I decided that this was the one I would record as my first kiss. I didn't care if anyone saw us. I was proud of myself. I didn't need to sneak her under a fence and hide her in my room. This was my friend. This was someone I respected.

We pulled away from each other and while she looked at me, I looked around to see who noticed. Nobody seemed to. I was disappointed. I did see Chris finishing a hot dog and slinking off into his garage and through the door that led to the backyard. I imagined he had a date with Dulce. Unlike Blaine's underground relationship with Lana, about which I felt self-righteous, when it came to Chris and Dulce keeping their rendezvous secret, I felt bad. There may have been something about race or class that pressed upon them, but I had a feeling it was mostly because neither was someone you'd want to bring home to your parents, and they each knew it: about each other, and about themselves. I was now not only proud of my association with Shay, but grateful.

"Which house is it?" I asked.

"The North house."

"Is there a house that's more to the north than the rest?"

"No," she giggled. "The North family. The Norths. Remember them? They left way before school was even done, like in March, before a sign even went up in their front yard. Their daughter was in about fourth grade, I think."

She was even excited about the irrelevant details.

"There may be an animal inside," she said. "Maybe a family of them. There's a big hole in one of the window screens facing the back yard. That's how I got in."

I looked askew at her. She gave me a playful slap on the arm.

"If we make sure one of the rooms is clear and shut the door, it'll be fine. And besides, it's on a quiet street that no one parties on. It's perfect."

She reached out and took my hand. "Don't worry. I won't give you rabies."

We kissed and got up to make our way to the house. A few people finally took notice of us as we walked hand-in-hand.

"About time," said Nub.

"Yeah," Shay replied. "Just when I'm about to leave."

"You're leaving?"

"Tomorrow."

Nub fell silent. His eyes sagged and he reached out for a hug. Shay obliged and they held their embrace for quite a while. I enjoyed watching two friends say good-bye still as friends.

"We'll keep in touch," said Nub as they separated.

"Definitely," Shay agreed.

"Where you guys headed?" he asked.

We hesitated and looked to one another for a manageable response.

"Oh, I get it," Nub waved his arms. "Forget I asked. I'm happy for you two. Have fun. I'm gonna miss you, Shay."

They briefly hugged one more time and we continued to our retreat as Nub gravitated back into that evening's party.

"I'm happy for us, too," Shay said as we turned the corner and veered away from the grill smoke and the drinking and the laughter.

I smiled at her and was going to respond in kind, but seized up with a sudden sense of dread. So I just kept smiling as best I could, which was convincing enough to Shay, as she maintained her contented stride. While she knotted her arm around mine and started to lean on me as we walked, I frantically tried to figure out what was happening to me so that I could find reasons to refute myself and get back to looking forward to being with her.

We turned another corner and found ourselves deeper into deserted territory. The red-lettered signs were even more dense, burnt lawns with white foreclosure crosses stuck in them far outnumbering the well-manicured patches. The occupants of the few homes still occupied were not home, opting for yet another night out on the next block. We could have gotten together right there on one of the front lawns and had just as much privacy as the empty house would provide.

I realized it was privacy that was freaking me out. We weren't on display anymore. I couldn't show off. It was no longer about demonstrating to everyone what a great guy I was compared to Blaine. Now I had to actually be with the girl I was so proud to be with. I had to make her feel as good as she made me feel. And I wasn't sure I was able to do that, or if I even wanted to try.

We came upon the house and she led me through the side gate. I thought that if I just went along with her then everything would be fine. I enjoyed kissing her enough earlier, but was now afraid that had merely been out of gratitude and relief. Well, if I could fake her out with my smile, maybe my kisses would be convincing, too.

She led me to the window with the hole in the screen and she was saying something, had been talking the whole time, but I was too busy trying to calm my fears behind my smokescreen smile. She picked up on my apprehension, and I managed to hear her ask if everything was okay; it may have been the second time she had asked.

"What kind of animal do you think it is?" was the first digression I could think of.

"Raccoon, possum," she speculated. "I think if it was a mountain lion or a bear someone would have noticed by now."

"Maybe a skunk?"

I was now fully back in the moment as I found myself looking right into her eyes, which were loading up some anger.

"Are you wussing out on me?" she said.

"Don't play some kind of manhood card on me, Shay."

"So you are."

"I didn't say that. I said shaming someone into being with you seems like a pretty crappy way to do it."

"Because I said 'wussing out'?"

I sighed and decided to use my agitation as energy to forge ahead.

"Just get in the house," I quipped, gesturing to the battered screen. "I'll show you who's a wuss."

"Ooh, baby," she teased, happy to be back on course.

I followed her in, and we stood in the hollow room. It smelled less like animals had been there and more like people had not: a musty layer of disuse overwhelmed any other scent. There was also a feeling that seemed to haunt it, the spirit of a dream cut short. We wordlessly started to walk through the rest of the house, looking it over as though we were interested buyers, perhaps because acting like a young married couple would enhance the mood, but more likely out of curiosity, and as a respite from the anticipation of what we were about to do; a chance to examine the evidence from a seminal phase of our lives before engaging in the next one, before creating a memory that was going to be inescapable for each of us, either good or bad.

We knew the floor plan, as we had lived in the same maze for the duration of our friendship. So we knew that the last room we were approaching was the master bedroom. And as we entered, we even knew where the bed had been, according to the imprints in the carpet.

"They were a pretty young couple," Shay broke the silence. "They must have had some good sex in here. Maybe they left some toys or whips or something..."

She went to the closet, which was slightly opened, and slid the door all the way to the side. The sound of the tiny wheels rolling along the tracks was suddenly replaced by her screams.

An enormous cat bounded out of the closet. Only it wasn't a cat. It was a raccoon. Its eyes caught the fading natural light and glistened. It stopped in the doorway of the bedroom and glared at us through its mask.

"Go away!" Shay barked. "Shoo!"

But the animal stood in place; not in a threatening manner, but in a way that seemed to dare us to do anything about it. I figured it was my turn to try something. I stomped my foot in its direction. The raccoon flinched slightly, but didn't turn tail.

"What do we do now?" Shay asked.

"Hold on." I went to check the master bathroom and found a spray bottle of cleanser under the sink that the Norths must have used to clean up after themselves during the move. I brought it into the bedroom and brandished it at the raccoon, spraying the bleach-smelling liquid. It retreated slightly, and with a few more squirts, trotted down the hall.

Shay slammed the door behind it and shivered with grunts. It occurred to me that maybe the raccoon stood its ground because there was a family of them left behind in the closet.

"Aw, man," Shay responded to my hypothesis. "Well, would you check please? I already got jumped."

I agreed strictly out of obligation and tiptoed to the closet. Standing at the edge of the opening, I bowed just far enough to look inside. There was barely enough light for me to see it was empty.

"Nothing," I announced. Then a light clicked on and I jumped with adrenalin.

"How can you tell?" said Shay as she manned the light switch by the bedroom door.

"Turn it off!" I snapped.

"Sorry I startled you."

"Someone might see the light in the window!"

"Oh, yeah."

She turned it off.

"That reminds me," she said. "Do you think anyone heard me scream?"

"Nah," I assured her. "Too much noise at the block party. And somebody would have come knocking by now."

"Maybe they couldn't figure out which house it was and they're running up and down the street looking around."

The master bedroom did not have a view of the street. We looked at each other, and at the closed bedroom door.

"Together," she said.

"Together," I agreed, and we braced ourselves at the door as if preparing to storm an enemy bunker.

"Lots of noise," I reminded her. "Just in case it's still out there."

"But we're checking to see if anyone heard me scream. Now we're going to yell?"

"Well," I shrugged, "if anyone did hear you, then this will draw them closer, and we'll know for sure when we look out a window."

"That's why I fell for you," she said. "So smart."

"I'm just good at making up excuses for things. Ready?"

"Ready."

I turned the knob and we went screaming and yelling down the hall with arms waving. As we started to realize the raccoon was not there, we turned our braying and flailing into dance moves and ooh-ooh chanting that kept the beat for us as we grooved around from room to room and laughed at ourselves. We barely managed to remember to check one of the front windows, and the moment after we did, we were all over each other.

We paused after a couple of minutes to move back to the master bedroom, so we wouldn't be under a front window, and we would be in an adult room rather than a kid room. Even though none of the revealing decorations and furnishings remained, we still knew which room was which, and one of the major points I had learned about sex from my months of observations and minutes of experience is that it's as much a mental act as it is a physical one. As if to further prove my conclusion, somewhere during the walk from one room to the other, my doubts took advantage of our break to shadow me again.

I went along with her anyway. I didn't want to hurt her feelings, and I didn't want her to lash out at me as a response to that hurt. So as we lied on the floor, I kept returning her kisses and moved my hands around to places I was comfortable with, like her back and the sides of her thighs, and rubbed those places vigorously to give the impression I was enthusiastic. And when she started moving her hands to places on me that made me wince, I contorted that reaction into a passionate moan and pressed myself against her tightly enough so that her hand would get stuck between us. She finally caught on when she managed to slip past my defenses and feel that I wasn't getting hard.

"What's wrong?" she asked, trying to sound concerned but doing a mediocre job of concealing her irritation.

"Nothing," I replied, doing an even worse job of sounding unconcerned.

"Don't do me any favors," she gave up all pretense and sat up to mope with her chin on her knees.

It was dark now, and I was glad I couldn't see her very well as I spoke. I felt as though I needed to work out some ideas, and doing so out loud would help, in the way writing down thoughts can help make sense of them.

"I started to think of the future," I said. "I don't want to start doing this for the wrong reasons because I'm afraid maybe I'll keep doing it like that. I don't want to convince myself that I'm attracted to someone or convince myself that someone is anything other than good sex."

"And what am I?" she said, still wrapped around herself. "Am I ugly? Or am I a piece of meat?"

"Nobody said anything about being ugly or a piece of meat."

"How else am I supposed to take your comments, Nick?" she unfolded herself and turned to face me by propping herself up on one arm. I couldn't make out any of her features, but the feeling of being stared at was unmistakable.

"Just because someone isn't attracted to someone else doesn't make that person ugly. It's a personal opinion."

"You're right," she dismissed me, turning away and sitting cross-legged. "Forget I asked. Like we don't already know. We've talked about this before, and now your limp dick makes it official."

"Stop it," I raised my voice. "Just stop it. There'll be plenty of guys who are going to think you're hot, all right? Plenty. Forgive me for seeing you as a friend. I wish I didn't, Shay. Believe me. I've thought a lot about it. You're awesome. My girl problems would be solved for the rest of my life if I could fall for you. But did you think I was lying to myself all this time? That all you had to do was jam your tongue into my mouth and I'd see the light?

"I guess I thought you were a typical guy."

"Ah, here we go," I said, settling down into the assumption she was questioning my masculinity. "Forgive me for not wanting to fuck anything that moves."

Only it wasn't an insult. I realized that when I noticed she was crying softly.

"Oh, God," I said. "I'm so sorry, Shay."

Her head was down and her heaving back was curved in my direction as she tried to brace herself against her tears.

"Shay..."

I was waiting for her to tell me off.

"Shay..."

I thought if I said it often enough, she would finally turn and unleash a great big Fuck You right in my face.

"Shay..."

I wanted her to. I wanted her to blow my hair back with anger.

But she didn't. She just kept weeping. So I shut up and sat behind her.

We sat there for quite a while. By the time she recovered it was pitch dark except for a dim glow cast through the window by a streetlight on the next block beyond the vacated backyards. In addition to the weak light, the next block also provided the faint sounds of the latest party now in full swing. Shay took a deep breath that distinguished itself as the one she was using to finally pull herself together.

"I don't care if it's a lie," she said. "I just want to feel good."

I thought about what she said for a few moments. Then I moved closer to her and kneeled behind her, rubbing her back and her shoulders. She reached back to confirm that I was free from hesitation, that I was a typical guy after all. She made quite sure.

We didn't actually have sex. We ground through a fully-clothed dry run, which may have been technically safe, but proved to be physically painful in its own way afterwards. My lips throbbed like a skinned knee, I could tell I was going to have a collection of rashes around my torso, and it felt as though I pulled every muscle in my crotch.

We didn't say much as we walked back to the noisy block where everyone went to forget their mistakes. We held hands, and asked each other if we were okay a couple of times. Our answers sounded identical, in that the only feeling informing them was exhaustion. I barely wondered if I had satisfied her. I was too busy being disappointed in myself. Whatever it said about me that I couldn't go through with anything until I had been assured of power, control, and no obligations, it made me no better than what I had seen through the windows over several weeks of midnights.

We stood on the perimeter of Shay's last block party at The Ranch. I saw her Mom and Dad twisted into a drunken, clumsy make-out session being cheered on by a small crowd of likewise drunken parents. I glanced over to see if she saw them, too. She did, and caught me looking at her.

"Are you going to say good-bye to me tomorrow?" she asked.

"Of course," I said, and meant it.

"I only want you to do it if you really want to do it," she said, without a hint of irony.

I couldn't help but laugh. She caught on and laughed as well.

"Do you want to hang out some more?" I asked. "Join the party?"

She exhaled. "I already said good-bye to Nub, and it was really nice. Running into him again would be awkward."

"That's a good excuse," I complimented her. "Take it from an expert."

"Everybody here is an expert."

She gave me a fatigued grin, let go of my hand, and walked away.

I waited for her to turn and look back one more time, but she didn't. She walked straight to her house and went inside. So now she was feeling ashamed? Her options all along had been either anger or shame? Anger if I didn't go through with it, and shame if I did? I really knew how to make a girl feel good.

Nub and most of the remaining kids were several doors down the street, staking out some pavement beyond the party boundaries to play Kick the Can. I was too worn out to play, probably not even capable of running in my condition, so I hopped the fence to see if I could spend some time at Miggy's and decide if I wanted to talk about what happened with Shay. If Lourdes was there, she could provide some sound insight if I could muster the nerve to talk about it with her.

But there was something like a block party going on in The Barrio, too. Peppery smoke was rising from the backyards, Banda music blared from a car parked on one of the dirt paths separating the ramshackle homes, and dozens of fluorescent camping lanterns perched and hung throughout the site. My first impulse was to smile at the improbability of something good coming from our parents' lost summer, that the faint clamor of a never-ending party from over the wall, and perhaps the first-hand accounts from Miggy and the boys, had motivated more frequent celebrations of community on this side of the divide.

As I stood and watched, however, I realized that I was not interested in stepping out from behind the darkened outskirts and into their light. It struck me as presumptuous after all the weeks of Ranch Ranch parties that were not explicitly off-limits, but certainly not welcoming. And it would have been uncomfortable, anyway. I heard the language I couldn't speak, the laughter I couldn't access, and felt as though I should stay on my side. The shared experience was purely on the surface. We all liked to eat, to laugh, to listen to music, to forget, but how we did all of the above was so different. I spotted Lourdes flirting platonically with a couple of older men, one of whom called his wife over to tease her about something Lourdes said. The wife waved her husband off and shook her head, and they all got a kick out of whatever was happening. I couldn't identify Miggy. He could have been anywhere, since each house seemed to be open to everyone else, and about half the fun and all the work seemed to be going on indoors. I couldn't spot any of the other guys either, including JD and Chuy, so I figured they were all together and up to something in one of the homes. I missed going to school with them. I missed having the neutral ground on which to meet.

I continued my observations for a while. As much as I wasn't compelled to crash their party, neither was I interested in ours. I watched all the beer being consumed with smiles and laughter, saw Lourdes take a swig from her sparring partner's bottle, which incited approving howls from the circle of which she was the center of attention, and I came up with an idea: as long as I had already experimented with intimacy that night, I may as well make it an adulthood doubleheader and see what alcohol was about.

The ice chests in the garages that lined our block parties were never monitored; most of them had beer and soda mixed together in the same bin. I climbed back over the fence and found that tonight was no exception. I didn't even have to leave our own garage to find a few cans of beer floating around in some ice water amongst the box-store brand colas. It was a brew I had often heard the parents making fun of for how watery it was, which was perhaps why there was still some left in the cooler, and which was fine by me, since I figured I should start with something as close to water as possible. I snuck them over the fence and found a spot on the ground between the two parties. I could see theirs and hear ours.

I wasn't used to drinking something bitter; everything I had drunk throughout childhood, aside from water, had been sweet. The closest comparison I could make to the taste of beer was the club soda I once had when Dad took me to an insurance convention and we went to an expensive restaurant and, not wanting to look juvenile by ordering a Coke, I was faked out by the word "soda" in the title. The club soda had also tasted like carbonated sea water, but since beer was supposed to create some sort of giddy feeling, I stuck with it and drank quickly enough to conduct my experiment, but not so fast that I felt bloated with belches awaiting their turn.

My initial reactions had little to do with lightness or euphoria. I felt ponderous and very focused on my surroundings, albeit in small doses and on very specific items; the bass line of the music from over my shoulder at The Ranch was a source of close scrutiny for a short while, then a small narrow window glowing from just below the roof line of a house in The Barrio in front of me caught my unremitting attention as I wondered what or who was casting the shadow that flowed through it every so often; I tried to see if the shadow adhered to a pattern, if the beats or seconds between its movements could be measured. I tried to connect the bass beat of the music to the restless shadow. I tried to forget what happened earlier that evening, which I had assumed the beer would help me do, since forgetting struck me as a key reason why our parents were drinking so much, but I found the alcohol made the memories that much sharper, the recollections more vivid.

I still had one more full can remaining when I decided to stop the experiment and summarize my findings, lying back and looking up at the stars for inspiration. That's one thing I always appreciated about The Ranch's distance from civilization: you could see every possible star visible to the naked eye. I found it interesting that people seemed to rely on sex and booze to help them forget their troubles, or ease their loneliness, when from what I could tell based on my brush with each, all circumstances were amplified instead. Maybe the effects varied from person to person. Regardless, I decided that both were better suited for good times rather than bad, since they seemed to enhance whatever peak or valley was providing the backdrop for the screwing and drinking being done.

I laughed into the sky, up to the stars, at fancying myself such an undiscovered genius. Oh, if only the world knew. If only someone who could spread the word were lying there with me, and could edit my thoughts to make them more coherent to those in need of what I had to say. But I was alone in the dark, on the other side of my fence and beyond the circle of light cast by The Barrio. I sat up and looked around, imagining that this is how animals see our world, the same perspective of the raccoon we had driven from the master bedroom of the North house.

I stood and started making up my own animal spirit dance, lunging and prancing with a high-pitched wavering moan. I thought of how much more impressive it would be with bells jangling from my wrists and ankles, and a deep drum beat, and a magnificent outfit of feathers and animal heads, and about two dozen other people doing it with me.

"So this is why people formed tribes," I said in between wails. "To make their spirit dances kick ass."

Then I laughed at myself again, at my wit and my stupidity, and added, "So this is why people drink."

I raised the intensity of my dancing; I shoved some gravel into the two empty beer cans and shook them rhythmically in lieu of a tribe, I howled louder, spun around faster, and stomped my feet harder, as though prodding any underground spirits to swallow this whole development, to return this patch of earth to a time before Rancho Hacienda ever happened. I whirled myself into a frenzy until I fell down and into hysterics.

Then I settled into a sleep I wasn't sure should be called passing out or napping, as it didn't last very long. The parties were still going on at The Barrio and The Ranch. Each was more subdued, though; attendance dwindled on the dirt paths of Miggy's neighborhood, and the music had been turned down in mine. I got up and dusted myself off and rubbed my scalp, sending mini dirt clods and pebbles flying from it. The remaining full can of beer caught enough light to catch my eye. I picked it up and out of curiosity threw it as high into the sky as I could to see if it would explode when it came back down. It did slightly, a small hissing dribble coming from the top, but not enough to be satisfying. So I threw it again, enjoying the feeling of doing the kind of thing we all did before the invasion of the parents. This time it spewed a fountain of beer that waved back and forth as the can rolled to and fro from the pressure being released.

When the show was over, I sprung back over our fence and went up to my room for a fitful sleep, alternating between anxiety at having to face Shay in the morning, and sadness at having to say good-bye to her.

Chapter Eighteen

I almost missed her. My fretting finally exhausted me and led to a deep sleep as the sun was rising. I awoke to the sound of Mom gently tapping on my door and loudly talking through it.

"Nick?" she said. "There's a girl named Shay out front. You were supposed to say good-bye?"

Cursing to myself and hollering back a "yes, just a minute," I put on some shorts and a t-shirt and burst through the door with the sudden focus of someone responding to a fire alarm or an emergency phone call.

"Do I know Shay?" Mom asked as I passed her in the upstairs hall.

"Not if you have to ask," I said as I rushed downstairs.

Shay stood in the doorway and cut a peaceful presence against my apologetic whirlwind.

"I'm so sorry," I pleaded. "I hardly slept last night."

She started to speak and I was compelled to explain what I meant.

"But not because of what happened," I interrupted her momentum, then lowered my voice: "I had a few beers from my parents' cooler later on."

"And that had nothing to do with us?" she smirked. "It was just a coincidence?"

I exhaled. She let me try to think of something to say for a few moments before rescuing me.

"Just keep in touch," she said. "Okay? It's not hard in this day and age."

I nodded, enjoying the dynamic of keeping my mouth shut. Besides, I could tell I had really bad morning breath. I kept the theme going by reaching out for a hug. She obliged, and we clung to one another for quite some time. I enjoyed feeling her breathing, and her heart beat, and her breasts. I realized it was because I didn't have to worry about them anymore, and that our tryst had made it much easier to say good-bye to her.

"Sorry if I screwed up what we had," she choked up as we parted.

"Don't be sorry," I said in all sincerity. "I'm grateful for everything."

She leaned in and rested her forehead on mine, looking down at my chest as she traced shapes on it with her finger. One of them may have been a heart.

I started to get impatient, but didn't want to be mean. I waited for her to do what she needed to do. Finally she stood up straight and looked at me with tears in her eyes. I was shocked at how little it affected me.

"Bye," she barely managed to say.

"Bye," I tried to look and sound more sad than I was.

She started to cry, but I was confident it had nothing to do with my reaction. As if to confirm my self-assessment, she came at me for one more hug and whispered "I love you."

I thought of returning the same whisper, but was not confident that I could deliver a line about love convincingly. I remembered from the night before how afraid she was of being regarded as ugly. So I told her she was beautiful. She didn't look at me as she pushed away and trotted down our driveway, so I was left to wonder if it worked.

I stood in the doorway long after she was no longer in view, searching myself for some sort of emotion. Her parents' car drove by with her in the backseat. We caught a glimpse of each other and waved, and I thought that I must have looked quite despondent standing there, which would help her trust in what I said. Then it occurred to me that it wasn't her I was trying to inspire, it was myself. I really wanted to have a reaction, but couldn't conjure one up; I reached for something and found emptiness far greater than all of our evacuated homes put together. I clung to the possibility that it may just be a hangover, but imagined that would feel temporary, like something that could be cured. This felt permanent, like something that could only be managed.

I shut the door and walked past my parents, who were sitting in the kitchen, who had also cried in front of me while I stood dispassionately by the sign that had pierced their story. I went to my room and spent more time in bed, most of it staring at the ceiling.

I wondered if this is what it meant to be a man.

My self-imposed confinement went on for a few more hours. I had no intention of breaking it until I heard a large vehicle rolling into our neighborhood in low gear. I assumed it was a moving truck come to make a pick-up at Shay's. I peeked out my window to see if the sight provided any last-minute sensations, but saw that it was a different sort of vehicle entirely.

It looked like one of those shuttle buses that drive around airport loading zones and bring people to hotels or rental car lots. Only this one was decorated with a real estate company logo. As it passed by our house, I could hear a faint voice over a microphone from within the bus, saying something about buying multiple lots and the interest rates available. It continued slowly down the street and stopped in front of a cluster of foreclosed homes. A group of smartly-dressed people filed off the bus, while from out of the houses still occupied drifted a smattering of parents dressed for a day of waiting around for that night's party.

The parents looked at the bus and at each other, and started moving in its direction. The people fresh off the real estate shuttle didn't notice the Ranch Ranch residents. The real estate agent had their attention as he led them into one of the houses, plus their view of the approaching posse was obscured by the bus. Not that they had anything to be concerned about; I took the parents as curious spectators, and left the window to try and think of what to do next, having exhausted any possibilities that staring at the ceiling offered.

I noticed some reflections flashing in various parts of my window, and went back to look through it. More parents were arriving from other corners of the development, passing by our house on their way to the space being surveyed by the real estate tour group. I re-positioned myself where I could see the bus and gauge just how big the horde was becoming. It was fairly sizable, looking like a group of people waiting outside a courthouse for the verdict in a show trial.

The realtor and his clients must have also watched the mob grow through the windows of the vacant house they had been sizing up, as they came out at a cautious pace, as if bracing themselves. Some of the parents started yelling at them. I couldn't make out what they were saying, so I ran down and outside to get closer.

"Scavengers!"

"Blood suckers!"

"Vultures!"

Variations on a theme of taking advantage of others' misfortune were being lobbed at the tour, whom the realtor shepherded back into the bus. The shouts were scattered; single words for the most part, no slogans that had developed into chants. The realtor smiled sheepishly and got back on as well.

The bus started up and made a U-turn. The gang of parents had continued to swell, with more of us sons and daughters joining them. We followed the bus as it crept back down the street, and a slogan emerged:

"We're still here!"

Most everyone adopted the chant and repeated it full throat, over and over, as we marched behind the bus. I assumed it would exit through the gate, but it turned into the block where the North house sat, the most bank-owned block at Rancho Hacienda. The windows were tinted so I couldn't see any of the tour group's faces, but the realtor was obviously determined to see this through. He had sprung for gas and promotion, so he was not going to waste the trip.

That's the way he carried himself as he walked down the stairs of the bus after it parked in front of an entire row of houses hung with foreclosure signs. He applied his resolve to help him conceal his nerves as our group continued to chant "We're still here!" None of his clients followed him outside. By order or default, he was doing this alone. He gestured for quiet, and finally got it.

"We are not disturbing any current occupants," he said. "We respect your privacy."

"Those are our friends' houses!" hollered a voice from the back of the mob.

The realtor took a deep breath. "Not anymore."

The boos were loud and sustained, eventually giving way to pockets of "We're still here!" The two mixed together, boos providing background for the main chorus. The agent made another mild attempt at asking for quiet and realized it was futile.

Help arrived from inside the bus. A red-faced man dressed for an office party stormed the bottom step, keeping him just above the realtor, and started berating the crowd. It was difficult to hear him at first, but the swarm quieted down if for no other reason than curiosity.

"It's not our fault you people can't manage your money!" was the first complete sentence I could hear out of him. "Take some responsibility! Live within your means! Get a job, for Christ's sake! What are you all doing here in the middle of the week at this time of day, anyway?"

The boos returned and the realtor tried to guide his client back up the stairs. The tour member complied, but screamed in some last shots as he ascended:

"And you call *us* vultures?! *We're* the parasites?! You people are pulling the rest of the country down with you! People like us are here to save it!"

His last comment as he disappeared with the realtor into the shuttle was "Grow up!"

The horde gave up on slogans and analogies and simply started to curse at the tinted windows. The agent appeared again on the steps, but could tell there was no more room for coherent thoughts. He turned and said something to the driver, then the doors exhaled and shut. The Ranch gang was furious at being ignored by someone they didn't want to listen to. They charged the bus and started banging on the windows with their fists and karate-kicking the sides. The engine started and rather than disperse, our parents spread themselves around all sides of the bus and lifted their anger higher, hoisting it up and back to a time before people walked upright. They were just screaming now, no words were formed. Their bodies shook and their fists flew. The rest of the kids and I shrunk to the outside of the circle and looked at each other, vexed by the terrible impression that childhood never ends. I darted to an area in front of the bus to see if I could figure out what was going on inside through the windshield, which was its only un-tinted window. The driver looked merely irritated, as though stuck in traffic, which lent some perspective I found comforting.

I relaxed a bit and started to connect with some friends and told them this would pass. They seemed prepared to believe me, but then a couple of gunshots made everyone jump and scream; then a couple more sent everyone ducking.

All was quiet. I looked out from under my arms in the direction of the shots, and there was Soren, handgun still raised in the air, holding the pose to make sure as many people as possible saw him. Once he estimated the moment was about to pass, he silently walked to the bus and knocked on the door, which I had to hand it to him was a smart move, as I thought for sure he was going to say something stupid. He held his hands up and the gun upside down in a gesture of peace. The door opened and he went inside, then disembarked a minute later. The bus pulled into gear and Soren directed it with his gun. The stunned crowd cleared a path, and civilization returned as we watched the real estate shuttle drive away.

Chapter Nineteen

As we rehashed events throughout the rest of that afternoon, my friends and I weren't sure what was more frightening about our parents: the way they turned into animals when attacking the bus, or that they still thought Soren was cool.

My folks were as baffling as any of the rest. We ate dinner together that evening, "in case we forget to eat at the barbeque," according to Dad, who was feeling really jolly about everything, and I tried to stay quiet as they went on about Soren, figuring they would stop eventually. But they proceeded to credit him with "saving us from ourselves" and "re-establishing law and order" and "reminding us of a higher power."

"Oh, please," I couldn't take it anymore. "He loved having an excuse to shoot his gun. That's all."

They seemed surprised that a boy my age wasn't enamored of a lone gunman.

"You don't know what we were capable of," Dad said.

"I was there," I reminded him.

"So you saw," he pleaded his case.

"Yeah, you were in danger of breaking a hand or a foot from banging them on the side of the bus."

Mom tried to diffuse an argument while still hyping Soren. "It's not us I'm relieved about," she said. "I'm glad he stopped us before we got our hands on anyone in that bus."

"Thank God someone kept their cool," Dad seconded her.

"The bus driver seemed pretty cool," I muttered.

"What do you mean?" Dad asked.

"He didn't seem to feel like he was in any danger."

"How do you know?"

"I could see his face," I explained. "He was annoyed. And so was everyone else in the bus, I'll bet. They weren't scared. They weren't thinking 'Oh my God, somebody save us.' They were thinking 'I wish these idiots would shut up and get out of the way so we can get out of this dump.'"

They glared at me like a couple of kids who had just been admonished.

"What?" I said. "Can't I have an opinion on the situation?"

"Sure," Dad answered, still sounding child-like. "It's wrong, but you're welcome to it."

Mom slid in again. "I just don't think you understand the gravity of what happened today, Nick."

"Yeah, what would a teenage boy know about rage?" I scoffed.

"Exactly," Dad pounced on the chance to make a point. "Now imagine that rage in a whole group of adults."

"It would have passed," I sighed. I could tell I was sounding more condescending and on the verge of losing their attention, but couldn't stop myself.

"Maybe not before we did some serious damage," Mom said. "To ourselves or others."

"Maybe, maybe, maybe," I held up my arms and let them drop onto the table. "Soren's got you charmed, all right. Yeah, maybe you would have, and maybe someone will break into our house tonight and rape us all, and maybe zombies will storm our gate."

"Nobody wants bad things to happen," Mom said. "But they do."

"Of course they do," I fired back. "But bad things shouldn't get you off."

And that was it. We were done for the evening. I didn't feel that bad for saying it, though, because it gave them a chance to act like parents again. They grounded me for the night, insisting that I stay in my room and was not allowed at the block party. I did my best to act like it was punishment while gladly complying. I had few friends remaining at this point, anyway, which was something I meditated on as I otherwise enjoyed being cloistered for the night.

My dwindling number of friends and growing appreciation of solitude pointed me back in time. I was becoming the same person I was before we moved here. It was as if I had been granted a couple years' worth of experimenting with being a more excessive and wild sort, and now the phase was coming to a close. It hadn't really been me this whole time, just a response to a situation. The default setting remained.

I alternated between sitting at my desk watching online episodes of an anime series I wanted to catch up on, and lying on my bed reading *Animal Farm*, another book I pretended to read in school but only now decided to explore. I didn't notice how late it had become until I saw some headlights weaving through the blinds in my window. I found it odd that anyone would be driving through the block party. The last time that happened it heralded the arrival of Soren and his family, so I got up to see what was going on.

I was surprised to find the party long since ended, the garages closed and the street drained of people, providing a clean getaway for the vehicle I was trying to make out. It looked like the latest lease deal driven by Blaine's Dad, but I wasn't sure until I saw his Mom's SUV following several seconds behind. And right behind her was a trailer she was towing filled with items covered in a tarp.

They were sneaking away.

More of my Ranch period was passing by my window and pushing me closer to whatever the next period was going to be.

They left the boat in the driveway. Some men came for it a few days later. Nub and I asked them where they were taking it. "Back to the dealership," they said. Soon after that a truck came for the furniture left behind. We asked the movers where that was going. "Auction," they said. And finally the foreclosure sign went up.

Soren served as their unofficial spokesman, and even he didn't know where they went. All he knew is that it had to be someplace where it would be easier for Blaine's Dad to do business; that he needed a state, or a country, that provided him with more freedom. And Soren hoped that he would find it. He claimed that Steve (who evidently never told Soren his real name was Yuri) had a lot to offer, and any system that stifled someone as gifted as him was a broken one.

He also claimed that the foreclosure was a mistake by the bank, the result of miscommunication, or missing paperwork; the story tended to change whenever I overheard him talking about it. I started to wonder if Soren had even spoken to them before they left, if he even knew they were going to leave, or if he had just decided to appoint himself as their apologist after the fact.

Because of the alleged mortgage snafu, he had agreed to keep an eye on their house for them. This usually amounted to Soren circling the property every morning with a momentous expression as he looked it up and down, though he occasionally made a show of going inside with the key Blaine had given him during his apprenticeship, being sure to jingle the other keys on his loop as he did. I was certain that Blaine had simply forgotten to get it back from him, and that Soren made no effort to give it back so that he could use it as a prop to prove what faith people had in him.

One such morning he passed by our front yard after making his rounds as I emptied out some coolers from the previous night in front of our garage while Mom and Dad nursed hangovers up in their room. Soren had given up trying to recruit me, but was still pleasant enough, perhaps as a hedge. He nodded in my direction as he stepped over the trails of water that trickled down our driveway and into the gutter from the melted ice I was draining.

"I'm surprised you don't wear a shoulder holster and a gun when you do that," I tried to keep it light. He stopped and faced me.

"I may have to start," he said, oblivious to my attempt.

"I know you like guns and all," I sighed. "But you can still joke about them. The gun gods won't think any less of you."

"Maybe you need to get more serious," he said.

"Oh, why? Because I need to face reality?" I was hoping to get him moving again. "Come on. Who usually ends up being the crazy person, Soren? The one who jokes around too much, or the one who takes things way too seriously?"

But he stood there and tried to look like a disapproving adult. "Please don't think of something to say," I asked him.

"I don't have to say anything, Nick. I can show you something."

"Really?" I was genuinely intrigued.

"Really." He gestured for me to join him.

I couldn't help but pause at the idea of going anywhere with Soren. But I figured at the very least it would provide an opportunity to call him out on more ridiculousness.

"Lead the way," I said.

I assumed he was going to retrace his footsteps to Blaine's house, but before we got there, he crossed the street and headed for Shay's. He glanced over his shoulder to make sure I was still following, and pushed through the side gate into the backyard. He led me to the sliding glass door and waited there as if expecting a crowd to gather before starting his presentation.

"I discovered this unlocked after the family moved out," he announced, sliding the door open and close to prove his point.

"I thought you were just keeping an eye on Blaine's old house."

"When Blaine and his father asked me to watch over their property, it occurred to me I should watch over the whole development."

"The banks will be very grateful."

"Some of us are still hoping to sell our property," he shot back. "And with so many residents leaving, and a non-existent police presence, it would be very easy for things to get out of control. Have you heard of the Broken Windows Theory?"

"No,"

"Criminal Justice authorities have conducted studies that show when a neighborhood appears to be looked after and in order, crimes are less likely to be committed. But if a neighborhood looks shoddy, like nobody cares, then crime goes up."

I felt as though I should raise my hand before speaking. "Interesting. But who would be committing crimes in an empty house? There's nothing to steal."

"Fair question. But you need to think beyond theft. Consider vandalism, or trespassing."

And with that he opened the door and beckoned me to follow him.

I pondered whether Shay had left the door unlocked on purpose; if she thought perhaps I would want to search for traces of her after she had gone. I hoped that whatever Soren was going to show me, it wasn't something personal of hers intended for me. Not that I was pining for her or hoping for such a tribute, but she was still a friend, and I didn't want anything between us violated by Soren.

We went upstairs and my nerves were firing on all ends as he led me to Shay's bedroom door. I wondered if he had seen the two of us together and was taunting me. I tried to cover my jitters with the calmest expression I could manage.

He opened the door and my mask almost cracked when I saw a sleeping bag and a half-melted candle on the floor, as I thought it may have been a shrine in honor of our farewell dry hump. But before I could betray my own privacy, I threw together an assessment of the situation: the candle was embossed with the logo of a popular teen vampire series, and the sleeping bag was a faded Disney princess model. Shay's room was serving as a love shack for Chris and Dulce. I went from my heart in my throat to a laugh in my belly. If Shay really had left the door open deliberately, it wasn't so those two could take their school bus groping to a higher level.

Soren had a very different perception of the layout. "What's so funny about trespassing?" he snapped.

"Nothing," I settled down. "It's wrong. I know. But if you knew who these people were…"

"And you do?" he said.

"Yes."

"How do you know?"

"The dude is really into vampires. He's more into vampires than you're into zombies. He even looks like one. Well, a really dorky one. You must have seen him by now: Long, stringy hair? Dark trench coat? Bad skin?"

Soren kept his focus on his version and tried to make it right. "Souvenirs from that series are everywhere. And if he loves it so much, why burn the candle? Why not keep it in good condition? And what about the sleeping bag?"

I looked down at it and felt a tremendous amount of empathy for Dulce through this ragged childhood relic, imprinted with beautiful cartoon princesses that she could never hope to emulate.

"It belongs to his girlfriend," I said.

"What is he, a pedophile?"

I started laughing again, thinking Soren had finally allowed himself to joke about one of his dogged pursuits. But no, he was serious. My laugh gave ground to a sigh.

"He's not a pedophile," I clarified. "He's a lot of other things, but not that."

"So what's with the sleeping bag?"

"She's poor," I explained. "They don't just throw something out when they outgrow it, or give it to the Goodwill. She probably got it from the Goodwill."

"They?" Soren emphasized.

"She's from over the wall."

"Ha!" he exulted. "Just as I thought."

"What exactly did you think?"

"Squatters," he said. "From over the wall, like you said. Or under it, as the case may be. I should really fill in that tunnel."

"Oh, for God's sake," I groaned. "They're not squatters. He's from this side."

"But she's not."

"They just want a place to screw around."

"What's wrong with their own homes?"

"Their parents probably don't approve."

"And why would that be?" Soren asked in a provocatively smug tone.

If I was older or bigger I may have punched him. "I know what you're getting at, and it's not like that. Didn't you hear my description of Chris? Haven't you seen him? He's the good-looking one of the two. And their personalities are even uglier. They're both hideous, Soren. The Mexican one, and the white one. Either one would horrify any parent."

"As a parent, I'm horrified alright."

"And you haven't even met them," I went for the light touch.

"I'm not talking about them specifically," he once again rejected my latest effort. "I'm talking about this," he gestured toward the sleeping bag. "What they're doing."

"Well, hopefully they're being careful. You're so good at gun safety lectures, maybe you can give them a talk on safe sex."

"The squatting," he growled. "The invasion."

"We're back to that?" I couldn't believe it. "Did you hear anything I said?"

"Why are they in this neighborhood?"

"Because half the houses are empty."

"Nice houses," he said. "Way nicer than anything on the other side of the wall."

"They...are...not...living...here...Soren,"   I   annunciated. "They...are...fucking."

"They're not living here yet," he maintained. "This is just the first step. Blaine's girlfriend, now this one. How long before families start following their kids? This may not be my house, but it's my neighborhood, my daughter's neighborhood, and I'll be damned if I'm going to let it turn into the outskirts of Tijuana. If I want to raise my child in squalor, I'll move there. But don't bring it to me."

I was too frustrated to even register frustration. I felt resigned. I had tried to make him see my point of view, but it was beyond my capacity. I was about to say good-bye, but that would be extending him more courtesy than he deserved. So I just left. He insisted on getting a last word in:

"Think about it," I heard him say as I descended the stairs.

I walked back to my house but didn't feel like stopping. I wanted to keep walking. I took several laps around The Ranch, tapping the red and white signs hanging from the crosses as I passed them by, as though giving them high fives, leaving them swinging in my wake. I still felt like walking, so I walked out the front gate, pausing at the camera to stare into it. I stared at whomever was on the other end for quite some time. I fell into a trance. Instead of being compelled to walk, all I wanted to do was stare into that camera, expressionless. I wondered what was happening on the other end; if someone was monitoring it live, or if they just reviewed recordings later. If someone was live, I imagined him calling people over to "Check out this kid;" if it was a recording, I imagined him later that day bringing the recording over to someone to "Check out this kid." I started to speculate that maybe there was no one on the other end, that the camera was a decoy, like an empty police car on the side of the highway to trick people into slowing down. Once that thought took root, I started walking again.

I walked past The Barrio, as I didn't yet feel like talking to anyone. I walked across the quiet intersection, and through the skinny forest to the fence surrounding the factory. I still didn't know what it did, what it made. I didn't know anything. Even when I knew what people did, I didn't know why they did it.

I reached out to see if the electric fence was turned on. It was. I jerked my hand away. Then I touched it again, to see if I could keep it up longer. I started grabbing it with one hand, then two hands. I wanted to see how much of my flesh I could press against the throbbing metal and for how long. With both hands clutching the diamond-shaped patterns of chain link, I rattled it to see if that allowed me to withstand more of the pain. Then I tried bellowing while I clutched it. Then simultaneously rattling and bellowing. Every method I tried, every attempt to extend my time, resulted in about the same length, and it was short. I kicked it and felt no shock through the rubber sole of my shoe. So I kicked it several more times. I kicked it so hard and so often that I started to pant. I thought someone may come out of the building and start to yell at me to stop. But no one did.

"Hey!" I shouted at the building. "Hey! Anybody in there?"

My voice echoed off its walls and scattered across the mottled pavement. When my echo faded away, I could hear the hum of machinery.

"Hey!"

I shouted several more times, but never heard anything other than my own voice bouncing back at me, and the sound of machines I could not see.

Chapter Twenty

"Nick, right?"

"Yes."

"I thought so. Good to see you! Come on in! I'll get Chris."

His Mom was much more pleasant than he was. Certainly more attractive. She led me into the living room.

"Can I offer you anything? Something to drink?"

"No, thank you. I'm fine."

"You sure?"

"Yes, thank you."

"Okay. Great. Well, have a seat. I'll go get him."

She seemed really happy that someone was calling on her son. She had been a regular, rather sunny presence at the block parties, while the Dad had continued to work throughout the summer send-off, often staying wherever his job was located for days at a time. There was still no foreclosure sign in their front yard.

Chris wasn't the least bit happy to see me, which was understandable. I wasn't sure if I should first apologize for all the crap we had given him, or launch right into the main reason for my visit. Either way, I felt we should go outside before speaking, as I did not believe her for a second when his Mom said, "I'll leave you two alone."

When I suggested we head out, he bristled.

"I'm the middle of something up in my room," he said.

"Just for a few minutes," I tried to say casually while looking at him in a manner that would communicate the importance.

He wasn't biting, though; or he wasn't understanding my body and facial language.

Sure enough, his Mom piped in from the next room. "Oh, go on, Chris. It's a nice day. Go outside in the daylight for once this summer."

Chris sighed and complied. As soon as he closed the front door behind us, he asked me "What?" But I insisted we keep walking down the street past a few more front yards before I divulged my purpose.

"Soren found your love nest," I told him.

"What are you talking about?" he tried to play dumb, but was too dumb to do it well.

"In Shay's house," I said. "The sleeping bag, the candle."

"So what?"

"So what...that he found it? Or that there's a sleeping bag with princesses on it and a candle with vampires on it in Shay's house?"

"That he found it," Chris confessed. "Why did he show you?"

"He thinks there's some sort of Mexican invasion happening, and that your stuff proves it."

"Seriously?"

"That's why he was prowling around Shay's house in the first place. He's patrolling the neighborhood trying to find excuses to shoot someone."

"Come on..."

"I know, right?"

"Is he high?"

"Kind of. Just not on drugs. Actual drugs."

"What do you mean?"

"Never mind. Could you talk to him?"

"About what?"

"Tell him the situation. Let him know that Dulce just wants to fool around with you, she's not bringing her family over."

"Her family hates me."

"You met them?"

"No. We just figured they would hate me. And mine would hate her."

I almost laughed, since I had assumed as much; but he was so sincere in his assessment, and so saddened by it. I not only caught myself, but had an abrupt change in perspective. I felt a rush of empathy for him similar to the one I experienced for Dulce when I had taken a good look down at her sleeping bag on the floor of Shay's deserted house.

"Maybe her parents would surprise you," I offered. "Or maybe yours would."

He shook his head. "Look at us."

"Yeah, look at you. You found each other." I never imagined I would one day find myself imploring either of them to see the beauty of their relationship. "I'll bet they'd be happy about that."

"You've met my Mom. Seen my Dad. They want me to grow out of this phase. They think I'm going to turn into something I'm not and meet some woman who doesn't exist."

"At least you've got time to work on them," I reminded him. "It looks like you're staying in your house."

"They are," he said. "I'm not. I'm going to art school this fall."

Now I was thrown off balance even more. I didn't even know he had graduated this year, much less that he had any discernible talents.

"Congratulations," I recited as the news continued to sink in.

"Thanks. But now I'm not sure I want to go."

"Why?"

"Because of Dulce."

"What?"

I sounded so astonished that I was afraid I would lose his confidence. I tried to backtrack.

"I mean, it's such a great opportunity, and you can visit her on the weekends, or on holidays."

"My parents don't want me to come back. They want to visit me in the city. They want to see how much better my life is becoming."

"Well, that's nice. I guess."

"How can my life get better without Dulce in it?"

My rush of empathy slowed to a drip. The revelations about his school and his prospects prevented me from rooting as hard for their relationship. I decided to get back to the business at hand.

"I've never been in love, Chris, so I don't know what to tell you about that. But this thing with Soren...please. Talk to him."

"So now you're my parent, too?" he snorted.

"You said it yourself, you haven't got much time left with her. Just make sure it's because you're leaving for art school, and not because you're getting yourself killed. Or her. Think about Dulce."

"Oh, please."

"You don't know him."

"And you do?"

"Yes. He had Blaine under his wing, or under his spell. Under something. And he's always wanted me there, too. I don't know why."

"Because you're so cool, Nick," he wisecracked.

Whatever chance we had at coming to some sort of bon voyage reconciliation was passing, it seemed, and now all I could do was implore him from a distance.

"Could you just talk to him?"

"No."

"You're going to risk your lives because you don't like me?"

"You're jealous and you're full of shit," he said.

"I'm sorry, Chris," I tried to make my exasperation sound like remorse. "I'm sorry we've been so mean to you, that I've been so mean to you. I think it's really great that you got into art school, and really crappy that I didn't even know you were an artist. I wish I could make it up to you somehow. I'm trying now, by telling you about Soren and how badly he wants to use his guns, and how he might use them on you and Dulce, but if there's something else I can do to get you to listen to me, I'd like to know. What can I do?"

He stared at me for a while.

"Just leave me alone," he finally said. "You had your chance."

I may not have convinced him to take my advice, but I appeared to provide him with satisfaction at having gained the upper hand for once during his time on The Ranch. He smirked and walked back home with a fulfilled stride.

My past was exacting some retribution, and not solely by virtue of Chris refusing to listen to me. That wasn't even the main reason, as far as I was concerned. What bothered me the most was learning that he was someone worth knowing. All that time I imagined him in his room smoking weed, getting drunk, when what he had really been doing was thinking about things and creating things. I had overlooked a kindred spirit thanks to my buzz over finally being the member of a flock. Chris probably didn't even know where or how to get weed, and would have been too scared to buy alcohol from the willing cashier at the freeway ramp mini mart. It was just a way to try to get some attention. A terrible way, to be sure, but was it always up to the other person to present themselves to my liking? Shouldn't I be able to brush off a bad first impression and dig for any hidden value?

I wondered if there were any others amongst the remaining kids, particularly the cast-offs, with whom I should get in touch, and maybe keep in touch, before it was too late. I had never before anticipated a block party more than the one coming up that evening.

My plans were waylaid before the first burger hit the grill, however, by Nub's announcement that he was moving the next day.

"And you're just telling me now?" I barked.

"I've tried to tell you, but when I stop by your house you're out wandering around somewhere, and you hardly ever come to the parties these days."

I took a deep breath. Not only was I lousy at finding the right friends, I wasn't very good at being a friend when I did find one. We stood there in front of his garage, unsure of what to say to one another. I looked around at the preparations going on for that night's gathering.

"Fourth of July is just a couple days away," I said. "You're not staying for that?"

"We have to be in the new place Mom found before the end of the month, and Dad gets a big fat bonus for working on the holiday," Nub shrugged. "He says we need it to help cover the rental deposit and the moving costs."

"Damn," I sighed. "Down to the Nub..."

He groaned and reached for a little bit of laughter.

"I've been saving that for when you left," I admitted. "It didn't come out like I thought it would."

"It wasn't that bad."

"Sorry we kept calling you that: Nub."

"I deserved it. That was really stupid, peeing on that fence."

"I can't imagine how painful that must have been."

"Just wanted to make everyone laugh. Be a part of the group."

"Join the club."

"Same thing."

"I know. I meant *join the club* as in, I'm in that same club of wanting to be part of a group, and doing really stupid things to get into it."

"Oh, yeah. I see what you're saying."

"I should have put it a different way."

"Doesn't matter. We figured it out."

"Yeah. We got there."

We both surveyed the block as it drew closer to assuming its nighttime identity.

"Well," Nub narrated what we were watching, "maybe we should celebrate all the stupid things we've done by doing something really stupid tonight."

"Like what?"

"My Dad bought a couple cases of bottle rockets it looks like we won't be using on the Fourth."

All my intentions of approaching these last days on Ranch Ranch with maturity and reflection vanished. Nub was no less excited to do something stupid. We managed to maintain our grip on enough sense to realize we couldn't blow through two cases of incendiary devices on the sage-speckled open range over the fence. That was our arena last year and we started a brush fire that all of us were able to extinguish thanks to our concerted foot-stomping. Our numbers were far less this year, what with all the evictions, so as much as we would have liked to see Rancho Hacienda burn to the ground, we thought better of it and I mentioned the deserted block where Shay had found the empty house for our last night together.

We emptied the bottle rockets into a canvas equipment bag and told the few parents who greeted us as we lumbered along that we were heading over to the empty block to play strikeout. This was somewhat true, as there were a couple of aluminum bats in the bag that we intended to use, along with some clear snowboarding goggles, but there were no balls in the bag. We softly imparted our plan to the neighborhood kids still left behind as we passed them by, then the small bunch of us loitered on the abandoned street until our folks cranked up their music.

I batted first, and had a hard time making contact with such a small, fast target. Nub did his part by having pretty good aim as the pitcher. He didn't actually use a bottle or section of pipe; he just gripped the end of the stick and let it fly from his fingertips when the lit fuse made contact with the rocket. Finally I measured the pace of the rocket and the location Nub was spotting consistently and hit a few. There was nothing to field, though, as the tip of the rocket would burst into glowing scraps of paper, which put the potential fielders on the ground in peals of laughter, anyway. I offered to switch places with Nub, but he was enjoying firing the rockets and offered to pitch to everyone. As the other kids donned the goggles and took their hacks, I ran to get some additional props to try out: an old seven iron Dad kept in his closet to swing at burglars, a cheap lightweight frying pan, one of those big plastic fat bats designed for little kids that still leaned in our backyard from the days when we had a neighbor whose dog would get into our yard and Mom would bonk him with it, and a ping pong paddle stripped of its rubber facing.

The golf club was the hardest to make contact with, but fun because Nub would lay the rocket on the ground to light it and it would scoot along the pavement toward the point of impact. When we did manage to hit it, we could actually get the glowing leftovers airborne, since it was a seven iron and had some loft, so everyone could try to catch the battered remnants as they fluttered earthbound. The frying pan made a satisfying clang when the rocket would hit it, which would then echo for a couple of seconds. Likewise the fat bat provided a fun thump at the end of the rocket's hissing trail as it would bump the hollow plastic barrel. The ping pong paddle sucked.

Occasionally a rocket would explode before reaching the swinger, which would make him jump and everyone else laugh. Every time.

I ran to get Miggy, ran right through the front gate and flipped a double bird to the camera. Miggy invited JD and Chuy to come along, and as we walked back through the gate I pretended to do a poor job of hiding them behind me as we passed in front of the lens.

It was our Lord of the Flies days re-visited, a reunion that celebrated our freedom and our stupidity. And it only got better when Soren entered our ring.

I was in the what we referred to as "the outfield" waiting my turn to swing something when he appeared, so I was closest to him and first to notice.

"Oh no!" I shouted. "It's the cops!"

"You're lucky I'm not a cop," Soren said in his best steely voice.

"They'd never let you be one," I laughed, emboldened by how much fun we were having. "Wait! That's it!" I pressed on. "You're one of those guys who got rejected by a bunch of police academies, aren't you?"

"I wouldn't have anything to do with any police department," he said.

"Oh my God," I ignored his response. "Why didn't I see it sooner? It's so obvious."

It was dark, and the street lights cast a lot of shadows, so I couldn't see his face all that well. But his body language spoke of tension.

"You wanna play?" Miggy asked Soren.

"What, and lose an eye?" he answered.

"We've got goggles," Chuy said, lowering the frying pan and pulling the goggles off his head to offer them up.

"And lose a finger?" Soren stuck to his theme.

"Don't bother," I waved them off. "You guys haven't met Soren. Maybe you can't tell in the dark, but he's not a kid."

"He just likes to hang out with them," Nub chimed in.

"And lecture them," I added. "Hey, Soren, tell us about firework safety. Please!?"

"How about I just tell you about a kid I once knew who got burned on over eighty percent of his body while playing with fireworks."

"I call bullshit!" Nub yelled.

"I call to arms!" I raised my fist in the air and ran to where Nub stood with the bag of bottle rockets. "To arms, men!"

I grabbed one and snatched Nub's lighter, aiming the rocket at Soren. It whizzed out of my hand in his direction, not coming that close to hitting him, but making him flinch as it blew up a few feet behind him. The other guys seemed a bit stunned.

"Maybe I should talk to your parents," Soren said.

"Maybe I should tell these guys how you feel about Mexicans," I said.

"Home safety and protecting your property and your family has nothing to do with race," he bit back in a wavering voice.

I swiped another rocket and lit the fuse while I extended my arm in his direction. He stood his ground as the fuse grew shorter and finally ignited. It went over his head and exploded just as he ducked. "Go home, fraud!" I yelled. "Go coach a soccer team if you want to yell at young boys."

I took another one and pointed it at him as I flicked the lighter. We again squared off while the fuse burned its way into the barrel. I went for the legs this time. He jumped to the side but just high enough for the desired effect.

"Dance, bitch!" I screamed, no longer feeling cheeky about our exchange. I was instead filled with an exhilarating hatred for him. I reached for another bottle rocket, but Nub blocked my way.

"That's enough, Nick," he said in a tone nestled between stern and lax that any parent would be wise to perfect.

I scanned the rest of our playmates, their motionless half-lit figures making the block look like a sculpture garden at night. Soren was frozen as well. He looked in my direction and I looked in his, neither of us able to see the other's expression in the hazy glow of the streetlights. I thought for sure Soren would insist on grabbing the last word before exiting, but he just turned and walked away after giving me what I assumed he imagined was his most intimidating stare. Not long afterwards, the boys from The Ranch who had followed me and Nub to the vacant block nodded their good-byes and headed back towards the noise of the block party.

The silent aftermath that continued to immerse the rest of us was broken by JD blurting out a "Whoa!" We all looked to discover the source of his reaction. A patch of one of the dried front lawns was smoking, a grass fire trying to take root. JD started tramping on it, and we rushed over to join him. He had pretty much squelched it by the time we added our footfalls.

Now that we had saved The Ranch from a fiery end, the guys wanted to know what my deal was with Soren, particularly the boys from The Barrio.

"I've never seen you like that," Miggy remarked.

"It's hard to explain," I hemmed. "It's just...the guy is living in a fantasy."

"And firing bottle rockets at him is supposed to snap him out of it?" Chuy chuckled.

"You're right," Nub said, responding to my initial point. "He's living in a fantasy. He's a dork. So get over him."

"I think he's gonna get someone hurt," I maintained. "Or killed. He's so determined to be a hero."

"Come on," Miggy downplayed my prediction. "He doesn't seem that crazy."

"You don't have to be crazy," I said. "Just desperate."

"He's in your head," Nub strengthened the chorus of opposition. "Don't let him do that. He's winning."

"I'm not in a contest with him," I defended myself. "I just think if we were, like, in another time, another place, he would be part of a lynch mob or something, and he would say he was doing it to protect his family. Always with the family. I swear, some people just have a family so that any stupid shit they do they can say they were doing it for their family."

"Now you're sounding crazy," Miggy said.

"If you had heard what I heard him say about the people in your neighborhood, Miggy, you wouldn't be sticking up for him."

"I'm not sticking up for him," Miggy snapped back. "I didn't say he wasn't a prick, I just said he didn't seem crazy. And I don't like seeing you let some prick get you all worked up. You're better than that."

I exhaled and started to wonder if they had a point: if I was projecting way too much onto Soren; if I was the bigger psycho between the two of us rather than the bigger person. My most revealing interactions with him had been one-on-one; no one else had been there to second my opinions. And all of us were so deeply in our natural state just moments before, so in line with the way things were before The Summer of The Parent; if I couldn't convince them to join me in chasing off Soren with bottle rockets at that point, I could be way off in my assessment of him, and of myself. I considered the thing which disturbed me the most about him: his certainty; how the possibility of being wrong never occurred to him. I didn't care what it was grounded in, whether it was his failures or his childhood or some hidden birthmark. What I did care about was whether it was rubbing off on me. Was I being too sure about him? Becoming that which I despised? But then maybe that was the greatest weapon of the unflappably unquestioning person: their unwavering belief forced others to bend to their will, to overthink their own positions out of a begrudging admiration or jealousy over possessing a head so clear of doubt, a certitude about everything that most can't adopt about even one thing.

"It's nice that you're looking out for everyone," Miggy shifted his tenor, sympathetic to the loaded pause I was unable to break.

And as much as I appreciated his delivery, the words stung. *Looking out for everyone* was one of Soren's themes. It's what he imagined he was doing. Now my best friend was crediting me with the same impulse. At least he meant well.

Miggy meant well, that is.

Soren did not. Soren would look back on his life as a failure if he got through it without shooting someone.

As for me, I wasn't sure. I liked to think I meant well. I could even make a case for looking out for everyone. But I was afraid that what I really wanted was to be better than Soren, and for everyone to notice.

"We'd better get going," Miggy said, as my ongoing silence must have convinced him there was nothing more he could say.

"I'm sorry I ruined the game," was the only thing I could think of to say that would come out the way I wanted it.

"The game was great," he said.

"Awesome," JD agreed.

"Soren ruined it," Chuy said. "Not you."

"He was going to break it up somehow," Nub added. "And besides, this was mostly your idea. I just supplied the bottle rockets."

"Thank you," I said to the group, nodding as I did, and nodding for several moments afterwards in rhythm to a beat that was composed to keep tears from surfacing in my eyes.

It worked until Nub broke the news to them that he was leaving tomorrow. Each then took turns giving him a handshake blended with a one-armed hug, and instead of preventing tears from falling, my nodding shook them loose. I made sure I was outside the beams cast by the streetlights, hiding in the dark, though I had a feeling the dampness may have caught some reflection, so I wiped my face by lifting the collar of my shirt over it when nobody was looking.

As we parted ways with the three of them at the gate and Nub and I walked back to yet another party, I asked him if he needed help loading anything tomorrow, or with any last-minute packing. He didn't, so I made him promise that he wouldn't leave without saying good-bye, and that saying good-bye involved me standing by his car as he climbed in, and waving to him as the car pulled away.

"I need a normal good-bye," I explained. "Just one normal good-bye."

Chapter Twenty One

I did everything I was supposed to do; everything I had planned on to get my wish for normal, but it left me wanting. Nub's car turned the corner and disappeared from view and a notion plunged into my emptiness that good-byes help prepare us for death, each one a small rehearsal.

Entertaining such a thought made me miss our days of mindlessness and rowdiness even more than I had during the peak of our reunion with it the night before; the part before Soren had shown up and turned our roar into a stutter. I never had so many friends before, much less ones who could get me out of my head, and now I was losing them in a steady procession, each departure sending me further back into solitude and the over-examined life it fostered.

I looked around the hushed block, all the doors shut, the inhabitants sleeping late or dozing in front of the television or doing something virtual on their computer, and I wondered why they bothered putting away the party supplies every night, since the grills and coolers and speakers would be wheeled right out again. I suspected the practice lent some dignity to their lost summer. Nobody was going to drive through our neighborhood and see artifacts from a party that people were too lazy to clean up after. It was just us. And it was heartening to think that our parents had not totally forfeited the impulse for maintenance and routine. Even if they were just paranoid that the banks would come after them over any damage done to the houses, that still implied a level of responsibility.

The Fourth of July was the next day, and in light of all the concern being demonstrated over appearances, I imagined the date held more significance for a lot of the remaining residents above and beyond its traditional meaning, that they were holding out for one last blowout before bailing, saving their last party for when everyone else for thousands of miles was partying, too, and doing so out of pride, not to bury their shame. Then they would rejoin the workforce and move to a place where they could pay someone rent at the end of each month as proof they belonged there, for while the clean street and driveways could verify their civility to themselves, "upkeep" was not a very inspiring purpose. They needed to feel useful again.

My parents did not contribute any evidence in support of my premise. They were quite the contrarians, actually, at least when it came to the part about moving. They had been discussing when they would go back to work, but appeared content to live free of rent (and mortgage) for as long as possible. If the Fourth was to be the last party for some, it wouldn't be for Mom and Dad, even if that meant drinking alone together on the weekends for the duration of our stay.

While there was something rather maudlin about their determination, be it steeped in cheapness or stubbornness, there was also good news buried inside their pact: each day the Sheriff's Department didn't show up to enforce an eviction notice brought me one day closer to High School Town with Miggy. And once the school year started, it wouldn't matter when they moved, as I could make my case that transferring schools would be one more trauma they would be inflicting on me, one more than I could handle.

Realizing the high value of the guilt I had access to, and that my last remaining friend was my best one, helped me punch through the gloom that hung in the air left behind by Nub's car.

I walked through the front gate to pay Miggy a visit, turning our lark from last night into tradition. No more scaling fences and burrowing through tunnels. I passed by the camera, deliberately paying it no heed, but couldn't resist leaning back and blowing it a kiss for old time's sake.

The Barrio was just as quiet as The Ranch, but for a different reason: the adults were at work. However much their recent spate of partying was imitative of the adults on our side of the wall, they were still limited on the number of days they could do so.

The relentless wind that powered through the valley always had a more cinematic effect on The Barrio when it stood dormant; the dust on its paths swirled in miniature twisters, the loose ends on the homes creaked and whined, and its many holes provided a chance for the gusts to whistle through them. The tightness and smooth surfaces of The Ranch offered little opportunity for the wind to create any drama; all it could do was irritate.

I knocked on Miggy's door and Lourdes answered. The day was getting better by the moment. She smiled and I barely heard her say, "Hey, Nick. It's been a while."

Seeing her didn't make me nervous, though. It inspired me. "Could you tell Miggy '2442'?"

"Um..." she waited for an explanation.

"It's the code to our front gate."

"Well look at you, gunning for a Nobel Peace Prize."

"Yeah. The one for Physics is too hard. So you've got the day off, huh?"

"Every Wednesday."

"Damn. Seriously?"

She looked confused. "Yes."

"If I'd known that, I'd have been here every Wednesday."

"Putting on some moves, too," she laughed. "What's gotten into you?"

"Time, Lourdes," it felt great to talk to her again. "There's not much time left. There never is, but I've been forced to learn that at a very young age."

"Miggy!" she called into the house. "Would you come take this weirdo off my hands?"

She held the door open and I walked inside just as Miggy entered the main room from the hall.

"Caught me," he said. "I was gonna pretend I wasn't home."

I noticed their grandmother wasn't in her chair or in the kitchen and asked where she was.

"The cats ate her," Miggy said.

"Miggy..." Lourdes wearily protested.

"Didn't even notice for a while," he continued. "We figured she was under the pile of cat hair."

And on it went for the rest of the afternoon. Their grandmother was spending a few weeks with one of her other sons who lived a few valleys away, so we had the house to ourselves. When we reached a lull in our goofiness, I professed my gratitude at having them as friends, and my excitement over my parents' freeloading since it appeared to be delivering us to High School Town. We then seriously considered whom we might focus on as potential landlords. Lourdes reminded us of how best to appeal to them before breaking out the yearbook. I appreciated how much more willing she was to provide not just advice but specific marks this time around. Her interest in helping us find a place had me hoping, as unlikely as it was, that we could room in the same house with her, but when she mentioned that she had a deal worked out with one of her friends on student council, she said nothing about including us in the living arrangements.

I invited them to the Fourth of July party the following night. I was embarrassed that the wall had become so much more insurmountable since our parents took to the streets. I thought maybe The Barrio would be having a party, too, but it was during the week, and schedules on this side were not so much affected by holidays as they were by how much work needed to be done. Lourdes was working during the day and was going to stay in town, but Miggy agreed to come over.

Due to intermittent dance contests and wrestling matches and snack breaks, our strategizing and philosophizing did not stay in one place for long. Some sessions were conducted outside in their yard, others inside the house, either sprawled in the main room or standing around the kitchen, and we had music playing the whole time, so we didn't hear the gun shots. We just heard the screaming; screams that sounded as though they were coming from a little girl.

We went outside to see what was going on and saw Dulce running away from the The Ranch. I was surprised to discover her as the source of the screams. The sounds coming out of her reminded me of the princess sleeping bag I had seen in Shay's empty house.

Dulce saw us and veered in our direction.

"Somebody tried to shoot me!" she cried as she reached us. "Please let me in!"

Lourdes led her inside as Dulce continued to gasp. "Nobody's home at my house. Is there anyone behind me?"

Miggy ducked outside and came right back in. "Nobody," he reported.

"Someone tried to shoot you?" Lourdes sat her down on the couch in the main room and rubbed her back.

"I was climbing a fence to go see Chris," she started to calm down, still breathing heavily. "One of the empty houses. The one I go through to get to the other house we use."

"Use for what?" asked Lourdes, who then quickly figured it out before Dulce could answer. "Never mind," she shook off her previous question. "So what happened next?"

"I was almost over the fence," Dulce sniffed. "I was like balancing on the top, and I heard a shot, like a firecracker. It scared me, and I fell into the yard of the house. Then I heard another shot and the grass near me, like, exploded. The grass is all tall and dry from nobody living there, and the shot knocked a bunch of it over. I figured out what was happening and got real scared. I couldn't move. Another shot blew over some more grass, and I didn't know what to do..." she started to re-live the moment, it seemed, and looked terrified. "I thought if I go over the fence, then I'll be right up there like a sitting duck, but I wanted to get back home, so I just did it. I climbed the fence as fast as I could and ran back here, and right when I started running a shot kicked up the dirt to the side of me and I started screaming, so I don't know if there were any other shots."

Now that she was finished screaming, running, and telling the story, she started crying.

Lourdes hugged her and asked Miggy to call the Sheriff's Department.

"Tell them to go to Soren's house," I said. "I'll give you the address once you've got them on the phone."

"You sure?" Miggy asked as he was about to pick up the phone.

"Who else would it be?" I replied.

"I know the guy's a tool," Miggy said. "But you need more proof than that."

I glanced at Dulce hunched over on the couch with Lourdes patting her on the back and looking as though her arm was getting tired.

"He showed me the room that Dulce and Chris have been using," I said, watching as Dulce stopped rocking back and forth and sat upright. "It's like his inspiration for thinking that your neighbors around here are trying to take over Rancho Hacienda."

"What the fuck?" Dulce barked in my direction.

"Glad to see you're feeling better," I quipped.

"Didn't you tell him the truth?" she said.

"I tried. But he's got a raging hate boner for The Barrio and it makes him see what he wants to see. I tried talking to Chris, too, to warn him. But he wouldn't listen to me, either."

"Thanks to his own raging boner," Miggy added.

He and I then waggled imaginary erections at each other in a mock fight, complete with clashing-sword sound effects.

"You think this is funny?" Dulce hollered. "That pendejo tried to shoot me!"

"Would one of you idiots just call the police," Lourdes scolded us, but I could tell she was trying not to laugh.

Miggy picked up where he left off and dialed 911. I could tell that Dulce was glaring at us while I waited to provide Miggy the address when needed. Once I did so, I got up the nerve to look back at her. Her eyes were indeed trained on us, but she was unable to fight off the tears that were undermining her usual hard stare. I tried to contribute some verbal comfort to go along with the physical that Lourdes was providing.

"I'm sorry about what happened, Dulce," I said. "I tried to explain the situation to him, the guy who was shooting at you. I really did."

"How did you know it was our spot?" she asked me, sounding embarrassed.

"Who else would it be?" I shrugged.

"Maybe some of those freaky parents of yours over there. Don't tell me none of them aren't sneaking around on each other."

"With princess sleeping bags and vampire candles?"

She wanted to get mad at me, but surrendered to a little bit of laughter instead.

Miggy hung up the phone and announced that a deputy was on his way.

"In how many days?" Lourdes joked.

"They said in about a half an hour," Miggy answered. "There's some dude staking out meth labs by that pimento farm on the way to High School Town."

"They told you that?" Lourdes asked.

"No, but what else would they be doing around that dump?"

Dulce tried to remain the center of attention. "Do you think he was really trying to shoot me?" she blurted out in my direction.

"If he was, I don't think he would have missed," I said. "He loves spending time with his guns, so I imagine he's a pretty good shot. He was just trying to scare you."

"Why didn't Chris say anything?" she said out loud, to no one in particular. Lourdes, Miggy, and I exchanged looks to gauge whether it was necessary for one of us to answer. I was about to say something, figuring it was my responsibility since I was the one who had spoken with Chris, but Dulce forged on before I could give it a shot.

"Pussy," she said, and we all winced. "That's all he wants from me. He wants it so bad he makes me run through the fucking border patrol while he sits back and waits on it. Waits for my pu—"

I interrupted her before she could say it again.

"That's really not the case," I said a little too loudly. "I'm pretty certain he just didn't want to alarm you. He loves you."

She looked at me sharply. "Did he tell you that?"

"Well..." I wasn't sure what to make of her reaction. "Yes."

She clutched her head and let the back of the couch catch her.

Miggy and Lourdes weren't sure what to make of her response, either. "Hasn't he told you?" Lourdes asked.

"Yes," Dulce said as she stared up at the ceiling. "All the time. Guys have the biggest mouths."

"He didn't tell me anything else," I assured her.

"It's between us," she railed. "It's private. What we have is special."

"You're acting like talking about love is the same as talking about sex," Miggy said.

"If he can't keep his mouth shut about one, how can he keep his mouth shut about the other?" she growled.

"Sorry, I just don't see it," Miggy pressed on. "I don't see what's so bad about Chris telling someone he loves you."

"Because people will laugh," Dulce said, a slight crack in her voice.

Miggy heard the struggle and fell silent. We all did.

"Because no one will believe him."

"We do," Lourdes offered. "We believe him."

Dulce snorted and put up her defenses again, though she spoke quietly when she addressed me.

"What was your reaction when he said he loved me?"

I really wished she hadn't asked me that. I hesitated and she capitalized on the pause.

"Of course," she said.

"Well, I didn't laugh," I defended myself.

"But you didn't believe him."

"I don't believe anyone who says they're in love when they're in ninth grade."

Lourdes appreciated that line. She provided an agreeable grunt and Dulce looked at her as though betrayed. Then she trained her pained expression on me again.

"I'll bet you didn't flinch even for a second when Blaine said he loved Lana."

I took a moment to relish the chance to tarnish Blaine before responding. "Blaine never told me he loved Lana."

"Seriously?" Dulce was stunned.

"All he wanted to do was tell me all the things they did, and I didn't want to hear it."

She looked at me with hatred that I assumed was intended for Blaine.

"You were right about him," she said.

"I never said anything that bad about him to you," I reminded her. "Only that he was popular because he was rich. Or pretending to be."

"Yeah, well he was pretending to get it on with Lana, too. They didn't do nothing, except for him begging all the time, telling her he loved her and then trying to unzip her pants."

Now I was the one who was stunned.

"He told it to you all upside down," she continued. "All there was to tell was how many times he said he loved her, not how many times they got down."

I shouldn't have been surprised. Nonetheless I was reeling a bit. I was more disappointed in myself than I was upset with Blaine; disappointed I took him for his word, quite possibly because the thought of Lana doing something to someone, even if it was Blaine, was a turn-on. And refusing to hear the stories only made me a hypocrite; I could compromise my thoughts of Lana while assuming a righteous stance. I wanted an excuse to talk to Lana. Maybe Dulce had it wrong.

"Speaking of Lana," I said. "Do you want one of us to go get her?"

"We don't talk right now," Dulce shook her head. "She turned everything around and said I was wrong to do what I do with Chris, just because she didn't want to do much with Blaine. Acted like she was all religious and was waiting till she got married."

"Maybe she is," I said.

"She's just scared," Dulce countered.

"She's smart," Lourdes added.

"And I'm dumb?" Dulce was now thoroughly disenchanted with her one-time comforter from but a few minutes ago.

"No," Lourdes explained. "It sounds like Chris treats you nice. Not like Blaine."

"That's what I told her," Dulce lightly slapped Lourdes' arm, as though they were old friends once again. "But she goes and get all superior on me."

"Her feelings were hurt," Miggy chimed in.

"I didn't say nothing to her," Dulce shot back. "She started it."

"By Blaine," Miggy clarified.

"And he's good at it," I added. "Very good at hurting people's feelings."

Everyone looked at me. They seemed to be waiting for an explanation. But I had none. I could tell them what happened between us, but that's all. And I didn't want to. I wanted to put him behind me for now, as far behind as possible, for I had a feeling he would go far in life, and I didn't want to think that was the way the world worked. If I couldn't lie to others very well to make it in that world, I could at least lie to myself to make my place in it bearable.

I changed the subject by asking Dulce if she wanted me to get Chris instead, or wanted to call him. She was still hesitant to cross into Ranch Ranch territory, so Lourdes and Miggy told her she could use the phone.

We didn't want to hear the story again, so we turned on the television while Dulce bowed in the corner of their kitchen and replayed the events for Chris and seduced every bit of guilt and sympathy from him that she could. Neither Miggy nor Lourdes asked me any follow-up questions about Blaine; they either realized I didn't want to elaborate, found Blaine's crappiness obvious enough, or didn't care. So we sat there and depended on the television to keep us from asking each other anymore questions for which we had no answers.

Dulce eventually came out of the kitchen. She seemed to be thrusting her heels into the floor with each step, and it felt as though the thin foundation of the house may not hold. She fell into a vacant spot on the couch and joined us in our inertia.

"Everything okay?" Lourdes finally asked.

"Yeah," she answered.

"Is he coming over?" Lourdes asked.

"Nah."

"Are you going over there?"

"Nah."

Lourdes, Miggy, and I exchanged looks as she stared at the screen. I spoke up.

"Why don't I go over and see if the deputy's been there. Make sure Soren's been warned. Then maybe you can go over."

"Okay," she said.

I reminded Miggy about tomorrow night, told Lourdes how great it was to see her again, and said to Dulce I was sorry for what happened. I lingered and tried to coax her out of the house with me, swinging my arms as I stood there and bouncing on my heels, but she didn't budge.

"Got anything to eat?" she asked Lourdes and Miggy.

And with that I set off across what I hoped had been re-classified as a de-militarized zone.

My curiosity as to whether Soren would shoot at me too, should I climb a fence in the wrong direction, almost made me forget my vow to always use the front gate. I veered right in the alley and headed for the street that our gate shared with The Barrio. Upon reaching it, I noticed in the distance across the fallow fields that a Sheriff's Department patrol car was driving toward the freeway. I turned left and walked beside the high, whitewashed cement wall, and past the faded sign we had battered so thoroughly while waiting for the bus, the sign that advertised the "Final Phase".

Nothing appeared out of the ordinary as the gates parted for me and shushed closed after I passed through them. There was no evidence of an event that had left people lurking in their front yards gossiping. Perhaps it was still too early in the day, and no one had heard the shots above the volume of their electronics, or had seen the patrol car since they weren't in the habit of looking out windows that rarely revealed anything new on the other side. Maybe the wind had blown the sounds away from the neighborhood and into the valley, carried the gunshots into the hills.

Soren was outside, though. He seemed to be waiting for me. He stood in front of his house, several doors down, looking in my direction. I avoided looking at him and went inside. Mom was monitoring the microwave oven as something slowly spun around inside it.

"Will you be joining us for dinner?" she asked me.

"No barbeque tonight?" I answered with a question of my own.

"Everyone thought it would be a good idea to take a night off and get ready for the big bash tomorrow."

"All right, then. Dinner it is. Thanks."

We were about to take our leave of each other until dinner, it seemed, but then she added: "Soren was just here looking for you."

I wasn't surprised. "Yeah, I saw him out front."

"What did he want?"

"I don't know, I didn't talk to him."

"I still don't get it," she shook her head. "He's not that much older than you, but has a family and some life experience. I would think he'd be a great role model. Someone to hang around."

"Did you notice anything odd before he came over?" I asked her.

"No."

"Sounds? Unfamiliar cars in the street?"

"No. Why?"

The doorbell rang.

"Never mind," I said. "I'll get it."

I answered the door.

Soren greeted me with, "Were you over the wall?"

I greeted him with, "You're lucky you're not in jail right now."

"What was the reaction over there?" he asked.

"Shock. Panic."

"Did you call the Sheriff's office?"

"My friend did."

He smiled and gestured toward his house. "Let me show you something."

I sized up the situation for a moment, then leaned back into the house. "How soon till dinner, Mom?"

"Half an hour, maybe," her voice carried in from the kitchen.

"I'm going over to Soren's. Be right back."

"That's great," she said, and clearly meant it.

I had never been to Soren's house before, and never looked through any of his windows, either. His arrival had not only coincided with the diminishing returns on my voyeuristic reality checking, but once it became clear that he was spending some of his nights desperately searching for signs of the apocalypse, I did not want to inadvertently cross paths with him in a dark backyard, at least not without a bulletproof vest on.

He put a finger to his lips as we entered and whispered that his daughter had fallen asleep on the walk they had taken around the block after his previous visit to my house. She was slumped in the car seat that he had detached from the stroller and set on the coffee table in the living room, her head tilted to one side with her lips puckered into a sleepy pout. She certainly was cute. As I grinned at her he murmured that his wife was pulling a shift at the hospital. Upon mentioning her it occurred to me that his wife was clearly in charge of the décor of the house. It was filled with furniture that was designed to appeal to a wife's sense of nest-building without making the husband feel completely neutered. Framed photographs of the three of them were perched on every tabletop and hung on every wall, each frame unique, and each photo pretty much the same: beaming husband and wife on each side of a baffled baby. They reminded me of the pictures my family used to have in our old house, which we had stopped taking when I started to look like a kid who spent a lot of time in his room, and which we did not unpack after moving in to our new house.

Even the entertainment room was pretty standard-issue young couple. He led me there after we had looked at the baby for what seemed to me about thirty seconds too long. The room was decked with more pictures of themselves and their daughter and a couple of those old-fashioned looking French theatre posters framed on each side of the equipment center. I had expected Confederate flags and Nazi paraphernalia, at least a heavy metal band poster or two, and chastised myself for thinking in stereotypes.

He took his phone out of his back pocket and connected it to the television.

"I want to make sure you can get a good look," he said a bit more loudly, now that we had some room between us and the baby. "I took the bug screen off the window in our bedroom upstairs so I can lean out and get more of a panoramic view," he narrated as he tapped and slid his fingers around the front of his phone.

A video of the stark valley behind the fence line popped onto the screen in front of us, obviously shot from the window he had just described. He panned across the expanse, past the train tracks, past the remains of our bike race course, past the mounds over which we had jumped and off of which Blaine and Soren had shot cans. He held the camera phone as steadily as he could, reaching the point where it faced the fence line, slowly aiming it back and forth along the border.

"Do you do this often?" I asked as we watched the product of his surveillance.

"No. I usually just set the camera on the windowsill and review it later," he said, keeping his focus on the screen. "I got lucky with this one."

The perspective swung back in the direction of The Barrio, and he seemed to find a visual cue he had been waiting for to begin some prepared commentary:

"Even if it was just a couple of kids using that room, like you claim, kids like the ones who were in our neighborhood shooting bottle rockets with you last night..."

"I've known those guys since we moved here..."

"....that's how it starts," he talked over me, adhering to his speech. "Like I said. First it's the kids, then the adults."

In addition to rehearsing his spiel, he had apparently also timed it, for right at that moment Dulce came into view. She was walking toward the fence of a vacated yard, overgrown with weeds just as she described. I was so flabbergasted that he had taken video of the incident that I almost failed to process what he had just said.

"Adults?" I countered.

"Yes," he said, thinking nothing of it. But a moment later he looked over at me suspiciously. "That's not a grown woman?"

"That's the girl who uses the room with her boyfriend. I told you about her."

He turned his attention back to the video. We watched Dulce struggle to scale the fence, clutching the top of it while her feet slid on the boards as though running in place.

"I thought you were exaggerating," he said.

"Nope."

His disbelief drew him closer to the screen.

"So the boyfriend..." he started to speculate but wasn't sure how to complete the sentence.

"You might like him. I think I mentioned before that he's into vampires. He could be your new gun buddy."

"Vampire fans aren't like that," he said, snapping out of his haze of realization. "They're more artsy."

I was about to question his claim, but realized Chris did adhere to that stereotype. We watched Dulce finally discover a method. She hurled one leg up to the top of the fence, and mustered up the other one after letting it dangle for several seconds. According to the description Dulce had given us at Miggy's house, we were about to reach the part when shots were fired. I started to wonder if he had captured that as well, just as the screen went blank.

"I'm not so sure my wife would work that hard to make time with me," he grinned. "Maybe when we were first dating."

"You didn't film the shooting?"

"I needed both hands to hold my weapon steady. I got enough on video, anyway."

"Enough of what?"

"Proof."

"Proof?"

"Of trespassing."

"That's not your house."

"Doesn't matter. The deputy said I was within my rights. I showed him the video."

"Shooting someone trespassing on someone else's property is okay?"

"I'm a Good Samaritan. They named a law after people like me."

I needed a moment to gather my thoughts.

"I don't believe it," I finally said.

"Call the Sheriff's Department. Again. I'll give you the deputy's name."

"That's not what I meant," I explained. "I'm saying, okay, it's your right. But does that make it right?"

"It's a violation of property. And who knows what they might do once they're in."

"Yes. Who knows. Better kill them just in case."

"I had no intention of killing her. And the deputy understood that. I just wanted to scare her."

"But you could have."

"Not a chance. I'm a good shot."

"I mean it was an option. You could have if you wanted to."

He shrugged. "Not worth it. The trial would cost a fortune."

My disbelief imploded into a speechless glare. Soren could not help but notice my reaction.

"I'm just trying to be rational," he said. "People get so emotional about these kinds of things."

I stammered down a couple of paths before finding one I thought might work. "Would any judge be allowed to keep their job if they sentenced someone to death for stealing something from their neighbor's yard?"

"You keep mentioning death and killing," he replied. "I would never shoot to kill without first assessing the threat. No responsible gun owner would."

"You couldn't even assess the age of the person you just shot at."

"That's different."

"And a lot easier, I would think."

"It doesn't matter. Like I said, I'm a good shot. I can wing someone if I have to. Shoot to injure."

"Life is not an action movie, Soren!" I was yelling now.

"But I'm an action guy," he said, maintaining a level of calm that I imagined was another way to convince himself that he was the reasonable one in our debate.

Waking the baby with my bellow didn't help my cause, either. He seemed appreciative rather than upset that I had startled her and made her cry.

"See what happens?" he said.

Then he left to go hide behind his daughter again. He made a verbal show out of cooing to her in the next room.

I stared at the floor for a short while before exiting, neither of us exchanging a word.

Mom asked me how things went over at Soren's and I told her exactly how things went. She didn't say anything in return, but I saw her thinking, and tried to remember the last time I saw her doing that. She silently finished preparing dinner and asked me to tell Dad what happened when he came down to join us. I did so and then he started thinking. They looked at each other and thought some more.

This was more fun than the day we went to the coast. I started eating and watched them.

"Should we talk to him?" Mom decided to ask Dad.

"I don't know," he said. "I mean, I'm glad he's keeping an eye on the neighborhood, but I suppose it might be a good idea to let him know we're keeping an eye on him."

"It does seem like he's maybe getting a bit...over-zealous." Mom agreed.

This was wonderful. They were openly questioning a previously-held position in my presence. I felt so mature. And not the kind of maturity I had to fake when they broke down in front of me, or had to swallow as I listened to them through their door and learned they didn't always think very highly of me. This time it was mutual. We were equal parts of a conversation. I challenged their point of view and they took it seriously. Dad even joked that perhaps Soren wasn't the only one who had been going overboard in his pursuits, and Mom and I chuckled knowingly.

Self-deprecating humor to boot! I was falling in love with them all over again. Their realization that they didn't have to know everything to earn my devotion had finally caught up with my discovery of their limitations. The pressure was off. Our dinner that evening was like one long exhale. We didn't eat and talk so much as we breathed. I asked them what some of the funniest stories of the summer were so far, and they told me tales of themselves and other parents making drunken asses of themselves, shared secrets of which parents had fallen into one-night stands with each other, none of which I had seen through any windows because they tended to take place during the parties before I would commence peeping, and even if I had witnessed one, I probably wouldn't have known since I didn't have a strong sense of who was married to whom.

When Mom and Dad asked me what kinds of mischief us kids had been making during our parentless phase that led up to the parent-ridden summer climax, I did not disclose the voyeurism, but spared nothing when it came to our group activities. (Which I rationalized was what they had asked for. I alone had engaged in the spying, and they had asked about the misadventures of us kids as a group. Hence, I was still indulging our newfound honesty.)

We then argued good-naturedly over who was the bigger group of idiots, the children or the parents. I naturally claimed it was them because they should know better by their age. They countered with no claims of superiority, and instead reasoned it should be a draw because the idiocy that starts in childhood never really goes away, it just goes through periods of dormancy.

I couldn't recall ever feeling quite so satisfied as my head touched down on my pillow that night. As if my brain required at least one concern to keep itself anchored, however, I noted that we had all refrained from openly attaching any morals to the stories we shared, even though they were clearly as much confessional as they were entertainment. At least that's how I heard them. That's how I remember them. Maybe they were just funny stories. Maybe all we had to atone for was whether we told them well, whether we got a laugh, and any message imparted was created by the listener.

Chapter Twenty Two

Dad seemed a lot more intent on pushing a purpose to the front of his stories after a few beers the following night, on Independence Day. His renderings were not as crisp, the humor was less self-effacing and more self-loathing, and any laughter he induced was nervous. He and I sat with a few other fathers in folding chairs manning the grill in front of our house, lined up as though we were watching a youth soccer game or a concert in the park. Each father had packs of firecrackers that they would unwrap and fidget with, untwisting the wicks from the jumbled helix in the center as they talked and drank and stoked the briquettes. One dad had a lighter and would occasionally light a firecracker he had unraveled and toss it under someone's chair, who would of course kick up his feet and cuss while everyone else howled. The latest victim would then join in the laughter, too, because he had no choice. But like the summer itself, the gag dragged on too long until finally the dad next to mine threatened to break an empty beer bottle across the forehead of the firecracker-thrower if he did it one more time.

Dad tried to break the tension, but his attempt only added to it.

"When does changing the knob on a bedroom door, or inflating a bicycle tire, stop being this amazing thing only your Dad can do, and start becoming the kind of thing any schlub with the right tool can do?" he posited woozily.

If only the other dads could have seen him the night before, at the top of his game.

"Fourth grade?" one of them arbitrarily chose a number.

"Longer ago than I can remember," said another.

"Let's ask someone who's young enough to remember," said Dad, looking over at me.

The sequel to last night's blockbuster conversation was falling terribly short of the original.

"Oh, I don't know," I hedged.

"Man, if you can't remember at your age, it must've happened about, what, age three?" said the dad who had threatened the firecracker-thrower.

"Maybe it never did," my Dad said, still looking my way.

"You still think he's Superman?" firecracker dad asked me with a chuckle.

"I'm saying maybe he never thought of me like that," Dad said, only now taking his eyes off me and staring out into the street.

"Feel free to talk about me like I'm not here," I offered as lightly as I could.

"It's just habit," said one of the dads, I don't know whom, as I tried too hard to join in the uncomfortable laughter that tried too hard to convince Dad that the dig was worth laughing over.

"Don't sweat it, man," the firecracker-thrower said, switching over to words in appealing to Dad, who continued to stare out at the street. "We've all been guilty of it this summer."

"This year," added another.

"The past two years," came another voice. I wasn't seeing anyone at that point. I looked at the ground while trying to gauge the state of my Dad out the corner of my eye.

"There must have been a time," Dad said, turning to face me again. "You were in awe of me once, right?"

I returned his look.

He continued. "Not anymore, obviously. But you'll grant me that. There was a time."

"Of course there was," I told him.

"I guess I'm the one who should be able to remember," he said.

"It's not like you can read minds," I suggested.

"Actually it's pretty easy to read a kid's mind," he said. "Especially your own kid. But you need to pay attention."

The other fathers started to announce that the grill seemed ready and checked to see who needed another beer. I glanced over at Dad, who had taken to gazing at the street again.

"You need to pay attention," he repeated.

He was saying it to himself, as our sitting companions had by then vacated their chairs and amped up their search for something to do besides contemplate.

But I heard him, and I wondered if that was deliberate, that he was seeking a compliment from me, an ostensibly unsolicited compliment, rather than a direct response to anything he had said.

The best I could imagine saying was something like "don't worry about it we all screw up sometimes life goes on," but kept it to myself since I assumed that wasn't what he had in mind. We were the only two still sitting in the lineup, though, and I got a little panicky over the silence, feeling more obligated to fill it with each passing second.

Dad didn't seem to mind the lull, but he was the one who broke it.

"Thank you," he said.

I was relieved. And confused. "For what?"

"For turning out okay."

"Oh. Sure. No problem."

Just as I began to wonder why Dad used the word 'okay', I jumped in my chair as Miggy clamped his hands on my shoulders from behind.

"Dude," I swung my arm around and he avoided my backhand. "Why didn't you go through the front gate?"

"Not used to it," he said. "I didn't even think of it until I landed in your yard. I was afraid for a second that I tweaked my ankle jumping off your fence and then finally remembered, 'Oh yeah, Nick gave me the gate code.'"

Dad had not flinched while Miggy had startled me, but the references to fences and gates had him looking our way.

"You remember my friend Miggy."

Miggy came around and shook his hand.

"Of course," Dad said loudly, overcompensating for his beer buzz. "Happy Fourth."

"Happy Fourth of July to you, too, sir."

"You gonna help us blow up some stuff tonight?" Dad groaned as he rose from his chair and unraveled his limbs.

"Sounds fun," Miggy played along.

"We're all about fun here," Dad inserted at the end of his next grunt. "All about fun."

He looked over at us and grinned, fully recovered from his bout with the folding chair and standing comfortably upright. "I'd better see if your mother needs help. God bless America," he nodded as he started inside, his ability to walk steadily not having caught up with his ability to stand.

Once he was through the back door of the garage and in the kitchen, Miggy looked over at me.

"Have you asked them about high school yet?" he asked.

"No."

"Is your Mom as wobbly as your Dad?"

"Probably pretty close. She's got a bottle of wine going while she's making the side dishes."

"Then you should ask them tonight."

"They're hammered every night. Well, almost."

"But it's a holiday, and I'm here. They'll feel generous and feel pressure at the same time. Come on," he gestured into the garage. "Let's do it now."

"What? No."

"Before you think about it too much."

He had me there.

"Fine," I grudgingly agreed.

"Woo hoo!" Miggy gave me an exaggerated cheer and overly hysterical grin as he held up his hand for a high five. I brushed past him and mumbled that he was a wanker, which cracked him up as he followed me inside.

Dad was sitting on the counter in the corner where the cupboards met, drinking his latest beer, while Mom was pretending she hadn't just been situated between his legs making out with him and that the pot of beans on the stove really did need to be checked.

I explained our plan to them as Miggy hovered in my blind spot. I knew he was looking at them with a pleasant determination since they were having trouble keeping eye contact with him, doing so only on occasion and focusing primarily on me.

"Well," Dad started, then looked at Mom to make sure he hadn't blocked her from initiating the response. She didn't appear to know what to think, so he proceeded.

"It's not exactly Harvard Prep."

"Nobody is saying it is," I reminded him.

Mom jumped in. "I think your Dad's point is that it seems like a lot of work just to go to a public high school, and no offense, not a very good one, I hear."

"It's okay," I said.

"It's what you make of it," Miggy backed me up. "My sister is going to be a senior, and she and her friends take advantage of it and do some really cool things, form clubs and stuff, and they're feeling real good about their college applications."

"And if you do make the effort," I joined in the defense, "it looks great to be from a poor area and show that you're determined to get out. Colleges and businesses, they love that stuff."

"Makes them feel good about themselves," Miggy added.

Mom and Dad looked at each other in a manner that suggested we had pleasantly surprised them, if not convinced them.

"What about us?" Mom said. "We'd miss you."

"We've already lost a lot of time with you over the past couple years," Dad said.

Now they had caught me by surprise. I figured they would question the logistics of it, but not from an emotional standpoint.

"What's the main job of a parent?" Miggy cut in before I could come up with anything.

Far from being taken aback by Miggy's forthrightness, they seemed impressed, which I imagined could only help our case. They carefully considered his question, and I waited on their reply with keen interest.

"To love their kids," Mom went the standard route.

"But why? What is that supposed to help the kids accomplish?" Miggy pressed.

"To be happy," Dad said.

I silently started to root for one of them to say something interesting.

"What does that mean?" Miggy asked him. "What makes a person happy?"

"Love," Mom maintained.

"Besides that," I snapped, then backed off when I heard myself. "When a person feels love then it's easier for them to do things that make them happy. What are those things?"

"Sounds like a math problem," Dad grumbled.

We were losing them.

"A job," Mom caught on, "a partner, hobbies, pastimes."

"Things they need to find on their own," Miggy kept the pursuit on track.

We all glanced at one another at various times over the next several seconds. I felt like we had won it with that final surge, but was looking for validation.

Dad slid off the counter and drew everyone's attention.

"Since we seem to have the self-reliance part down," he said, "let me ask about the love."

I hesitated. "What about it?"

"Well…" Dad also hesitated in his reply. "Do you feel it?"

He said it as something of a joke, but was clearly a bit nervous once it started to hang there.

"Yes," I assured him. Then I looked at Mom. "Yes."

"Then say it," Dad said, wandering playfully toward me, in full joke mode now. "Say 'I love you', dammit."

"I love you," I smiled, staving off his jabs to my midsection with my forearms. "Was I supposed to say 'dammit' too?"

"You'd better visit us," he poked some more; I felt like I was about five years old again.

"Okay," I giggled.

"Every weekend," he kept it up.

"Okay."

"And write us every night."

"I will."

"Letters," he said. "No texting. If you're going to boarding school, we're doing things the old-fashioned way."

I was just laughing now, enjoying the feeling of freedom and security.

"Your mother will be devastated if she doesn't find a letter in the mailbox every day."

"Absolutely devastated," Mom echoed him.

Dad stopped prodding me and clutched me in a hug. He exhaled deeply into my shoulder and down my back. I could feel him relax. I could tell he was relieved.

He told me to go hug Mom as though he was a coach who was sending me from the bench into the game. After doing what I was told, we separated and I thanked them both. Neither responded verbally; they just performed variations on a shrug and smiled.

"Do you think they'll remember the deal by tomorrow?" I muttered to Miggy as we made our way through the garage.

"They're not that drunk," he said.

"You were brilliant in there," I told him. "If I'm ever in trouble, I want you as my lawyer, even if you're not a lawyer."

We reached the front yard and Miggy stopped us. "Dude..." he held my gaze for a few moments. "We're in!"

We embraced and smacked each other on the back repeatedly while we did so.

"I feel like I got into Stanford or something," I said as we switched to locking our hands in an arm-wrestling shake.

"That's the next stop," Miggy beamed.

"Man, I can't settle down," I said as we unhitched our hands and I bounced around.

"Should we sneak a beer or something?" Miggy chuckled.

"Nah, I tried that once. Didn't work out too well."

"You did?"

"Yes."

"Without me?"

"Sorry."

"When?"

I paused and pondered whether I wanted to reveal the true circumstances of my beer night. But after what we had just accomplished, I decided that I owed him all the honesty I could manage. So I told him about getting together with Shay.

"And it made you want to drink?"

I suggested we snag a couple of the empty folding chairs. We positioned them out of range of the grilling station and I told him, without getting too graphic, about the fits and starts that Shay and I went through on the night we tried to force passion, and how difficult it is to tell who is more frustrated when devotion runs only one way: the unconvinced or the unpersuasive.

"I thought when guys shared stories of hooking up with girls, it was supposed to be fun," Miggy speculated.

"Well it was originally a story about why I got drunk for the first time," I reminded him.

"True," he said, and I noticed he was being a bit fidgety.

"I'm sorry if it bothered you that much," I said. "I don't want you to be all down on love or anything."

"No," he relaxed a bit and smiled. "It's not that. You're just being so honest, and I'm thinking maybe I owe you a little something too."

"Oh yeah?" I was intrigued.

Miggy thought for a moment. "Yeah," he decided.

He positioned himself in the chair as though some sort of natural disaster might occur once his secret was revealed.

"I've seen Lana Torres naked," he said. "Many times. Many times more than Blaine, apparently."

"What?" I lurched forward. "How?"

"Through her window."

I lurched backward. A few more repetitions of my lurching and people would think I was having a seizure. I looked up at the orange and purple streaks left in the sky by the disappearing sun. All those hours, all those nights peeking through windows, all those scraped forearms and bruised shins, and all I got was an unflinching exposure of the present and a harrowing peek into the future. Miggy meanwhile had glimpsed timelessness.

I started to laugh.

And when Miggy asked me why, I told him about my own adventures in voyeurism.

Unlike my heaving back and forth, his reaction involved rapt stillness; he held every word with disbelief and delight. What unified our responses and our confessions was the tremendous sense of relief. We had both assumed that our exploits would be discovered rather than offered, and of course regarded as deviant. Instead they were shared, and as we moved past the initial exhilaration of unburdening ourselves, our actions started to seem natural, like admitting to masturbating.

"We should conduct a joint operation," Miggy suggested. "Celebrate the Fourth and our future takeover of the high school by doing some reality checking together. That's what you call it, right? 'Reality checking'?"

"Everybody's going to be outside tonight," I reminded him. "Unless you wait till, like, two in the morning."

"Maybe not," he said mischievously.

"Oh?"

"I saw Dulce using the tunnel earlier," he announced.

"Does she fit in the tunnel?"

"That's cold."

"I'm serious."

"Apparently she does."

"Damn, those people are horny."

"Let's get 'em."

"Why would you want to see that?"

"Not to spy. To scare them."

The prospect had me halfheartedly stifling a laugh.

"We'd have to find them first," I threw out an excuse just as feebly.

"That's part of the fun," he argued. "And we're good at it."

"Well, good at sneaking around. I don't know about finding anything."

"Speak for yourself. I found what I was looking for."

"But you know where Lana lives."

"Shut up and let's do this."

And off we went.

We started with the North house. I warned him about the possibility of raccoons before we crawled through the battered screen. Upon landing we heard no signs of life, and upon skulking through the house and pausing breathlessly beside every doorway before ducking our head in, confirmed that it was empty.

We tried Shay's old house. The sleeping bag and candle weren't even there, much less Chris and Dulce.

We then cased the house with the yard into which Dulce had tumbled and dodged bullets, but found it locked and lacking any soft spots. As we let ourselves out of the side gate, I surmised that if this house was available they would have used it by now, since they were already using the yard for access. The connection between yard and house seemed to inspire us at the same time.

"You don't suppose..." Miggy said.

We headed over to Blaine's old house and ducked around the back when it seemed no one up the street at the barbeque was looking our way. Most were eating or drinking while the others were starting to line up a fireworks display in the middle of the pavement and tossing around firecrackers as something of a warm-up act, so it was easy to be inconspicuous.

The yard was drying out and stripped of its statues. The grass was not as tall as the longer-abandoned properties but starting to become shaggy. The entrance to the tunnel was no longer upholstered by our makeshift birdbath. Only the piece of drywall remained, with some frayed holes left over from where the decoy had been attached.

"They took the birdbath?" Miggy noted.

"If they sold it online I think we deserve a cut," I said.

We turned to survey the house and saw a faint light flickering in Kelsey's old room.

"Naturally," I chuckled, thinking of the glimpse of heaven I used to imagine that window held.

Miggy backhanded me in the shoulder and put a finger to his lips.

I nodded and we walked over to check for openings, starting with the sliding door. It slid.

"I can't believe it," I whispered. "This house is Soren's pet. He must have left it open by accident."

We sidled through the opening we had already created, not wanting to crack it any further and risk any more noise. We adhered to our vow of silence as we made our way through the living room and entry hall. The emptiness created louder echoes we were careful to avoid. The stairs were especially tricky, as every step seemed ready to whimper. We decided to take each step together, figuring the possibility of a louder creak was preferable to a double dose of a softer one. Plus the sound of firecrackers outside provided some cover.

When we reached the top of the stairs and felt we could relax a little, we started to hear the noises. Our looks of recognition were accompanied by gentle moans, grunts, and deep panting. Miggy mouthed a disgusted-looking "Oh my God" at me, but of course we forged quietly on. We got down on all fours just before reaching the opened doorway with the single candle's worth of light shining through it, as the heated noises maintained a steady pitch. We sat down next to each other and leaned back against the wall beside the frame, continuing to exchange expressions of horror which doubled as efforts to stifle our laughter.

Then we heard Dulce stop moaning and speak through her heavy breathing.

"I love you, baby. I love you so much."

And our expressions paused.

"I love you too, Dulce," Chris responded just as breathlessly.

Miggy and I stopped looking at one another. Dulce and Chris kept proclaiming their love, sounding as though they were having a contest to see who could be more intense and heartfelt in offering themselves up to the other.

When we finally exchanged looks again, I could tell Miggy was feeling the same way I was: like a total creep. I suggested with a head tilt that we should leave and he agreed.

I led the way down the stairs, and around the midsection of the flight, Miggy leaned forward and murmured, "Did you ever think you'd see the day when you'd be jealous of Chris or Dulce?"

I leaned back to respond and lost my footing, so instead of the witty riposte I had intended, I yelped briefly and overcorrected in regaining my balance, slamming my hand onto the bannister and causing it to vibrate like a tuning fork.

We tore down the rest of the stairway, and as we sprinted across the ground floor we started to laugh.

"You couldn't wait till we were outside to ask me that?" I managed to say through my laughter-in-motion.

"You couldn't talk and walk at the same time?" he gasped back.

He beat me to the sliding door and threw it open as wide as he could, but its track was heavy with grit and left little room to pass. We barged through the modest space together and landed in a pileup outside the door. He emerged first and opened up a slight lead once more as we headed for the hole in the ground.

I heard some firecrackers pop and felt a sting in my back. Within a few steps my whole body cramped up and I collapsed to the ground. There was just enough light left to see Miggy submerge into the earth and pull the cover behind him, oblivious to whatever just happened and imagining with glee that I would be hounded by Dulce, with Chris looking on as a very satisfied witness.

But it was becoming clear to me that things were heading in a far worse direction. I could not catch my breath. I reached back to feel what had stung me and my fingertips dipped into a slick of blood.

I stared at my hand and remembered every other time in my life I had seen my own blood on my fingers, from the fresh piece of printer paper that slid through the tip of my pinky in the first grade when I had no idea paper could do such a thing, to the blood test when I was jabbed by a needle held in the beautiful slender hands of the young woman who worked in the lab.

I heard Soren's voice. I heard him announcing the date and time and address. I tilted my head back and saw him upside down from my vantage point, broadcasting these items into his camera phone as he ran toward me. And after more of my life sped past me, after I recalled bursts of other moments when I had been running, had been laughing, had struggled to catch my breath, had watched friends leave me, I realized what Soren had done.

He reached me and hovered over me and only then realized how wrong he was. I could tell it was more than just the mistaken identity that had not gone according to script; one of those non-fatal shots he had bragged about was now killing me. He was so shocked that it took him a while to remember to stop recording.

"This wasn't supposed to happen," he said, and a surge of images in which I saw so many other people say the same thing splashed over me. It reminded me of the notion that everything and everyone is connected; but looking up at Soren, I hoped this wasn't true. I found myself unconcerned with whether there was a heaven, but wishing very hard for a hell that would serve as his destination when he found himself in my situation someday: staring life in the eye while saying good-bye to it. And as my separation drew near, I decided it would be best not to leave soaked in bitter thoughts, and turned my attention away from him.

I rolled my head in the opposite direction and saw Miggy peering out from under the piece of drywall, eyes wide open, his tears catching the glow of the fading sun. I used my eyes to implore him to stay put, and as he lowered himself quietly back down, I smiled at him as best I could.

I didn't know what was to come, but what had come before was rendered in stunning sharpness. I looked at the dying grass and noticed every spore on the tips that were trying to blossom now that they weren't being cut down; they bowed in the breeze and gestured towards a birch tree that had tripled in size since I first entered this yard, its branches now filled with thousands of little leaves whose wiggling in the wind made them look like schools of tiny green fish circling the white trunk. Each leaf seemed to look back at me, life on earth returning my gaze, as my breathing became my countdown. I searched the grass and the leaves for patterns, for purpose, but instead of finding an answer, ended up asking the same question over and over again: "Where does it all go?"

I caught sight of some smoke rising in the distance from the factory whose product remained a mystery, the smoke floating higher into the sky until it disappeared. I may have felt a train thunder past, heard the blaring of its horn, but wasn't sure anymore what was happening and what was recollection, what were dreams, and if my life had even occurred. I hoped that if it had been real and there was some other place expecting me, that I could grow a little taller there, and leave something behind other than sadness over a short obituary.

Epilogue

Soren's panicked mug was replaced by the faces of all the people I loved, of Mom and Dad and Miggy and Lourdes, and I felt myself being lifted into the air, floating over the valley and into a bright light and a warm feeling of being saved. I awoke to find my enemy had been vanquished, and that I would be waited on constantly, my every need attended to while I indulged my interests in books and film. I seemed to have made the great discovery that no living human can claim to have found.

But I couldn't return to the wild side of me I had found on The Ranch; I couldn't run, run as fast as I could, run away from someone about to tag me, move my legs into an even faster gear and feel my knees pump higher as my feet barely touch the ground and carry my body away from the outstretched hand behind me and toward the open spaces ahead. I couldn't ride my bike so hard as to wonder if I would be able to control it if I had to turn or brake even slightly. I couldn't throw myself into the bushes, or slide headfirst along the grass or better yet, through the mud after a heavy rain. I couldn't run.

I couldn't do these things because it wasn't actually heaven, or any name given to an afterlife.

Miggy collected his bearings and proceeded through the other end of the tunnel and ran for help. The hospital sent a helicopter as my loved ones waited with me. Soren's wife used her nursing connections to arrange for full-time help that was paid for by a gun rights lobby that wanted to prove they weren't all like Soren. They even paid for my education as well, so great was their determination and deep were their pockets. I suspect that had I not survived, their money would have gone to Soren's defense team and I would have been posthumously vilified and held responsible for my own death during the course of his trial, but nonetheless I'm grateful. I've been left with few illusions about anything.

Even the thrill of watching Soren get divorced and sentenced was tempered. And not because I'm paralyzed. No. Like everything important, it's invisible; it's because no matter how many hang gliders I'm strapped to by well-intentioned people or surfboards I'm spread on as they guide me over some two-foot waves at low tide or inspiring interviews I dutifully provide or dates I go on that inevitably include a moment in which I am told how courageous I am, nothing is as liberating as when we owned what our parents only thought they owned, and nothing so lucid near death as my sense that paradise has nothing to do with lying around unchallenged.

But the call of the conventional is strong; it cradles, pampers, and obscures any glimpse of something different. So I allow everything to blend into an amorphous feeling of pleasantness; the promise of Rancho Hacienda at last fulfilled only after we left, and the valley slowly starts to reclaim the land that once had no price.

Also by Sean Boling

The Current Mr. Orr
Devin's Best Afterlife
Once in Two Lifetimes
Revenge and Wellness in the Sweet Hereafter

Standalone
Cut Flowers
Abraham the Anchor Baby Terrorist
Pigs and Other Living Things
The Summer of Our Foreclosure
Satellite Campus
A Charter to That Other Place
The Latest Version of My Love Story
Show Them What They Won
The Name Field
Should
Moral Adjacent
Over Here We Have

About the Author

Sean lives with his family in Templeton, California. He teaches English at Cuesta College.